And then [...] moned him. [...] running towards her. She was shaking. Her whole body quivered from the inside out. Hot blood rushed and she imagined she could feel it—actually feel it—surging from one place to another in her veins. From one place to another. She swallowed but the lump growing at the back of her throat only got bigger. Her vision blurred.

He had her by the arm. He wasn't saying anything. His eyes were just locked with hers. His breath was coming so fast that hers became more labored. She struggled to let the air in and out deep and steady but it came out sputtered and erratic. Tears streamed from her eyes, mixing with the burning haze around her. She couldn't focus. His broad hand wrapped all the way around her upper arm and she could feel him squeezing. He wouldn't release her, not from his grip and not from his eyes. And he still stood there silently. He didn't even know he was hurting her.

—∾—

Inside Out

Grayson Cole

Genesis Press, Inc.

INDIGO LOVE SPECTRUM

An imprint of Genesis Press, Inc.
Publishing Company

Genesis Press, Inc.
P.O. Box 101
Columbus, MS 39703

Copyright © 2011 Grayson Cole

ISBN-13: 978-1-58571-437-7
ISBN-10: 1-58571-437-2
Manufactured in the United States of America

First Edition

Visit us at www.genesis-press.com
or call at 1-888-Indigo-1-4-0

Dedication

To my Mother. Yes, Ma'am. It all comes back to you.

Chapter 1

The beginning of summer, two weeks after graduation from the world's most tedious MBA program, saw Tracey McAlpine moving back home with her parents, whether she wanted to or not.

That Saturday, she ambled toward the main entrance of the Galleria trying to keep up with her mother, who was going on and on about God knows what. A few words registered: "...even though the house isn't going anywhere. The more I think about it, the more it sounds like a good idea. Maybe we should get a storage unit near home. That way, if you decide not to come back here, then all the stuff will... I saw that look. Well, no, I guess we don't need a storage unit. Besides, it's only an hour anyway. We can get it any time. And your dad said he would check on the place on the weekends..." And so on and so forth, never stopping to realize that Tracey was going to catch fire. And she *was* going to catch fire. Even filtered by clouds and magnolias, Alabama sun burns.

Besides, everybody knew Southern heat and her condition did not go hand in hand. It was so hot and so sticky, and she was breathing so hard that particular day that catching fire seemed inevitable. Her hands tried to ease the pain in her lower back by pressing her hands there. Sweating like a pig by the time they got inside the mall, she stopped to wipe one hand repeatedly across her brow. Relief from the heat remained elusive even in the cool building. She was definitely going to catch fire. She wondered if that was what made her want to cry. Or was it her mother's incessant chatting? Or was it those new female hormones that had changed her body so much?

Man, she hated him right then.

"Tracey, are you listening to me?"

"Yep."

"*Yep?*"

"Yes, ma'am, I'm listening to you."

"Then what did I say?"

"So when exactly can Daddy make it?"

"Oh," her mother breathed, digressing nicely, "he said he'd get out of his meeting late tonight. He'll probably drive up with the truck tomorrow to pick up your things." Tracey nodded, pleased with her diversion. Her mother was talking again, moving on to the subject of going to church the next morning.

It didn't matter how many times she told her mother that she did not feel like going to church, Mrs. Carolyn McAlpine wasn't having it. Tracey would be in church in the morning regardless of what she said. Her mother could always accomplish this feat by issuing an executive order, but hated doing that. She thought of herself as a benevolent dictator… which is why Tracey wasn't surprised when she declared that her daughter wasn't going to be a heathen and they were definitely going to church.

Her mother probably figured she was so far gone, it merited extreme action. There was no distraction that could prevent her from enforcing this decision. As she went on, Tracey paused to catch her breath, another mistake in a string of many.

"Tracey, honey, are you okay?" Her mother wrinkled her honey-colored brow as she spoke.

Tracey's mother was 1940s movie star gorgeous. Like Lena Horne or Dorothy Dandridge. Classically pretty with big, warm brown eyes, a straight nose, and generous lips, she turned more heads at twice Tracey's age than Tracey did. Her clothes were always perfect, along with her makeup and her hair, too. Though tall like Tracey, she had a slender figure that gave her sort of a sparrow-boned look. "High-school skinny," Tracey had heard one of her friends call her. She had smooth café-au-lait skin that glistened. It was skin without a single mark or scar to prove she had ever been a child. When Tracey was little she'd wanted to be light like her, but was instead dark like her daddy. Tracey loved the way her mother's perpetually straight hair shifted in the wind and then moved softly back into place. It fell heavily between her shoulders like that of her Cherokee grandmother. Tracey had real honest to goodness black hair. Perming barely tamed its autonomy.

On that sweltering day, her mother was wearing a salmon-colored pantsuit and looking the picture of comfort as she swished next to Tracey like royalty. Tracey felt even worse than she normally did walking next to her. She was a big, lumbering, unkempt thing trying to stay cool in a place with too many people and too many scents. On top of that, she was catching fire, burning up, and probably going to be sick.

Her mother repeated her question.

"Yeah, Mama, I'm fine."

"You probably need to rest for a little while." She started to press her hand to Tracey's forehead as if her grown daughter were still a child. Tracey couldn't let her. She would be calling an ambulance in a heartbeat. So she stepped back. Her mother scowled at her. "Well, just be a baby, why don't you! Good Lord! Listen, I'm going to run into Barron's to pick up the things we need for the house. You need to sit while I do that and rest. How come you didn't tell me you were feeling bad? Never mind," she said and began to rifle through her purse. She pulled out a perfectly folded bill. "Here."

"Mama, I don't need your money," Tracey responded, keeping to a ritual that had spanned her whole college career. Out of grad school and plunging headfirst into a part of womanhood Tracey wasn't halfway ready for, she was trying desperately to show her independence.

Her mother extended the bill toward her despite Tracey's argument. "Why don't you go to the food court and get yourself something to drink and eat? The liquids will help cool you off, and you know Dr. Singh wants you to eat more regularly. You need to sit down for a minute anyway. I'll meet you in the food court in twenty minutes, tops. Okay?" Tracey nodded, not because she was in agreement but because she was trying to back off from her mother as she pressed her slender fingers to Tracey's forehead again. "You feel warm," she murmured.

"I'm fine, Mama."

Her brow remained furrowed.

"I'm sure after I sit down I'll be fine."

Her mother chewed her lower lip, but in the end accepted Tracey's words. "Here," she said, attacking her daughter with the money again.

"Fine." Tracey took the cash because her mother gave her no choice. Usually she would have debated until her mother got disgusted and stalked off, but that day she wasn't up to it.

These days her mother was always looking at her as if she were trying to figure out where she went wrong. Maybe Tracey could have taken it better if her mother were angry with her. Instead, she got a pain in her chest when she could tell her mother was turning her disappointment inward. It was as if…as if her mother looked devastated and hurt in a way she had never seen. And when she looked that way Tracey could only do whatever it was she wanted and hope the expression went away.

Besides, this gave Tracey a chance to be alone and indulge in her favorite pastime. Feeling sorry for herself had been her signature practice over the past few months. She had become a pro. At home, she would turn off all the lights and let the fan blow instead of the air conditioner, which froze her regularly. Since the fan didn't do much for the already stifling June heat, she wallowed in sticky hotness daily, sitting, as best she could, on the floor in her tiny bathroom. Its window opened beneath the shade of a great big oak that frequently sheltered a soft and fragrant breeze. Tracey would ease down, and because she couldn't sit with her legs drawn up to her chest anymore, she spread them in front of her: one foot next to the shower, the other by the door jamb. She would rest her hands and forearms on her stomach because that was the most comfortable place to put them. Sometimes, she would move her hands down over her belly. Even in the dark she could see its outline plumped up on her thighs.

Too bad it was getting too difficult to get back up. No matter, she was already expanding her morose horizons. She felt sorry for herself whenever she could. Even there in the mall she was perfecting this science.

It doesn't get any worse than this, she told herself over and over again as she took her mother's advice and went in search of the food court.

As she waddled down the main arcade, she felt alarming discomfort pulling and punching her face into a grimace. Her hands reflexively went down to her stomach as she stood still trying to catch her breath.

"Tracey?" *Damn, how did she manage to catch the slightest pause even from fifty feet away?* Her mother was next to her before Tracey knew it. "Tracey, are you sure Dr. Singh said it's okay for you to be out? I wish I'd gone to that last appointment with you. I know I shouldn't have listened to you. I know I should have gone. And I have you out here like this. I—"

Right then, Tracey's head decided it wanted to spin. She felt tingling beneath her tongue and saliva pooling in her mouth. She needed to swallow, but that hurt. "I would have…come out…anyway." She could hear her own voice drifting away. She tried to make the words stream together, the way they did when everything was fine. But she didn't guess everything was fine. No, she was drifting, blissfully drifting, away from the heat, away from her mother.

In a vision, she saw Garrett. She whispered his name. She told him that she still loved him.

Her mother shook her. She put a hand to her head. Flames rippled over her skin like rapids.

"Baby, are you all right?" Her mother's voice was shaky and urgent. She held on to Tracey, trying to anchor her.

"I'm fine," Tracey answered and, with a herculean effort, smiled. She patted at her face with a napkin she got from God knows where, then shuddered as heat pumped through her again.

"Tracey… Good Lord, you're burning up!" The sound of her mother's voice barely registered.

And then she saw him again, as if she'd summoned him. He was coming towards her. He was running towards her. She was shaking. Her whole body quivered from the inside out. Hot blood rushed and she imagined she could feel it—actually feel it—surging from one place to another through her veins. From one place to another. She swallowed, but the lump growing at the back of her throat only got bigger. Her vision blurred.

He had her by the arm. He wasn't saying anything. His eyes were just locked with hers. His breath was coming so fast that hers became more labored. She struggled to let the air in and out deep and steady, but it came out sputtering and erratic. Tears streamed from her eyes, mixing with the burning haze around her. She couldn't focus. His broad hand wrapped all the way around her upper arm and she could feel him squeezing. He squeezed so hard that her arm was throbbing painfully, making her cry even more. He wouldn't release her, not from his grip and not from his eyes. And he still stood there silently. He didn't even know he was hurting her.

Tracey felt her mother wedge her body angrily between the two of them, but it was too late. Fire consumed her. She was about to die. She knew it. Then Tracey was falling, but there were arms catching her. She knew them. She called to him. "Garrett, I'm so sorry. I'm sorry! I'm so sorry." The ground beneath her was still giving way. Moisture was bending all the images before her eyes; heat was making them swirl. Then pain took her into its heart and everything went black.

Chapter 2

Tracey had spent the majority of her day at the Carlisle Center. Volunteering at the community center was typically high-energy, but that day had been particularly busy because it was the first in-service of the school year and every parent on earth had decided to choose that day to work, or go out of town, or do something that meant dropping their kids off there. She'd raced home to change into the worn clothes she chose to wear when she worked there. Days of coming home with either too many questions about the designer clothes she wore *or* having those outfits covered in finger paint had taught her the importance of dressing down. A half hour after leaving, she slumped exhausted in the first floor hallway of the old law building, praying she would make it through this one more appointment to discuss her thesis. Then she could go home and curl up on the sofa for an hour or two.

Leaning there against the wall, she saw a white guy come out of the bathroom down the hall but didn't pay him much mind. That is, until he sauntered up to her and said, "The sink is overflowing in the men's bathroom down the hall. And there aren't any paper towels or anything."

She studied him closely. For a fraction of a second she had the impulse to touch his face. *Crazy*, she thought—something to do with those great yellow hazel eyes, lion eyes.

"I'm sorry?" she asked, ignoring her response to his eyes, genuinely confused. His eyes focused on something behind her right shoulder. Tracey turned and looked. She was leaning next to a door that read CUSTODIAN. Although she *had* just come from the center, and looked something like a vagrant in her paint-covered old overalls and ratty gray windbreaker, Tracey nevertheless took offense at his assumption. Maybe she didn't look like an MBA student, but she did look like *a* student. Tracey took a whole lot of offense. She hardly ever stood up for herself in those days. She couldn't get words out fast enough when angry or indignant or upset, but whatever look she gave him was immediately effective.

"Oh," he sputtered. "My bad."

Before Tracey could say anything, she saw Dr. Alexander Burke, her Employee Rights professor and a longstanding family friend, a few feet away.

"Mr. Atkins." Dr. Burke inclined his head. The guy nodded in returned greeting. "I'm sorry, but I need to borrow Miss McAlpine for a moment." He took her arm and led her towards the conference room door across the hall.

Before either of them could open it, the door swung open and a short, fat, red-cheeked man stood there smiling. "Tracey McAlpine, come on in!" He said it as if she were on a game show with him, the happy host. Tracey brushed past "Mr. Atkins" and walked into the room without looking back and began, "Pardon my appearance, gentlemen. I've been volunteering today." For the next half-hour, she talked with the short, fat man, Dr. Ericson, Director of Graduate Student Services, and Dr. Burke, Tracey's faculty advisor, about taking courses in the law school despite being in the MBA program.

Dr. Burke was an attractive, young-looking man, probably not even forty yet. Rumor had it he'd graduated at the top of his law class, practiced for some absurdly short period of time, and then turned right around to teach for some exorbitant amount of money. Rumor also had it that the law school was willing to pay anything to get a "non-threatening" black on staff. After seeing his lavish house and the mild-mannered man himself in action, she figured it was altogether likely. Still, the university leaders obviously hadn't known how seriously he was going to take his position. Dr. Burke turned out to be one of the more respected law professors in the college. His ebony complexion, strong physique, and eloquence commanded attention in class and out. Needless to say, he was the man her father secretly wanted her to marry someday. It was true. Probably not Burke specifically—the age difference would be an issue for her father—but someone like him. This was a source of contention between her father and her. Tracey respected him, but she wasn't interested in Alexander *or* anyone like him.

Near the end of the session, Burke decided to tell her how much he expected from her, especially given who her father was. That was something he never should have said in that meeting. Exasperated, Tracey couldn't pay attention to him after that.

This left her plenty of time to think about the little exchange in the hall and to be indignant. Her mother claimed Tracey thrived on being indignant, that Tracey was dramatic. Her mother took too many personality quizzes, the kind that fit a person into some four-letter group of neurotics just like himself or herself. Over the years Tracey had noticed them getting more specific and irritating her, like those people who dedicate their lives to seeing how far out they can calculate pi. Anyway, she had the perfect opportunity to avenge her hurt ego—or to be dramatic—when she was released from the meeting and able to step outside. As soon as Tracey looked up, there was Mr. Atkins, standing there in the same spot she had occupied. She thought of asking him if he had settled his plumbing problem. Instead, she continued down the hall. Then she turned back. She couldn't help herself. "Excuse me. There seems to be a plumbing issue in one of the bathrooms down the hall. Could you have someone check it out?"

He leaned away from the wall and started to say something. Tracey attempted to go along her merry way but felt a large hand close around her upper arm. She turned.

"Excuse me, miss." He let the words slip slowly from his lips as he elongated the "miss" in a way that elevated the word. "I'm sorry—"

Secretly, Tracey could not get enough of Southern accents. They weren't what one heard on TV. In real life they were beautiful when they were pure. The right ones poured over the listener like warm honey. This guy had one of those, which meant one thing. He was really, really, really white.

"I don't like people getting the wrong impression of me," he drawled. "I'm sorry. It was an honest mistake. I'm sure I would have said the same to anyone standin' there."

"I'm not," she retorted. He rolled his eyes and stuck his hands in his jeans pockets. "Listen," Tracey said, deciding she truly didn't have the energy to continue this. "I really haven't the time or the energy to spend trying to assuage your great white guilt about something I've already forgotten. Get over it. In fact, get over yourself." She gave herself an internal pat on the back and walked away.

Chapter 3

True to her word to Garrett Atkins, Tracey let go of her anger about the incident with him. However, she found it increasingly difficult to forget about *him*. After that first encounter, the guy was ubiquitous! Everywhere she went, every time she looked up, there the hell he was. Late one night, she found herself at the ANM, the university's late-night general store. A person could get anything there, from CDs to jeans to kegs to a fast cheeseburger from the tiny café in the back. In truth, every student that ever pulled an all-nighter had found his or her way to that place.

Tracey didn't need to stay up and study, but one of her frequent bouts of insomnia had led her there. It was a useful condition when, as an undergrad, she carried an eighteen-hour load, worked part-time, and finals rolled around. But not being able to sleep was frustrating when the semester had just started and her workload hadn't ramped up yet. Her body felt tired, but she was awake for no good reason, as usual, in the middle of the night. She had come down to the ANM for nothing really, just an insomniac browsing.

She decided to rent movies. When she went to check out, the girl behind the counter smiled and took Tracey's movies. Petite with narrow shoulders, perky breasts, frosted pink lips, arched, barely existent eyebrows, and upswept blonde hair, she looked young, but she probably wasn't more than two or three years younger than Tracey.

"May I see your student ID?" she asked.

Unfortunately, Tracey hadn't planned on renting movies and had left her purse in the car. She only had cash in her pocket.

"Oh, I'm sorry. I left my ID in my car. Can I leave this with you? I'll be right back."

She nodded and took the movies in her thin and French-manicured hands.

When Tracey heard the voice behind her, she nearly jumped out of her skin.

Garrett Atkins said to the salesclerk, "Don't worry about that, Jenna, I know her. Her name's Tracey McAlpine."

The girl's smile broadened to the point of splitting and she pushed out her chest even more. Without Tracey's permission, she started to enter her name into the computer while talking to Tracey's newfound nemesis. "So Rett, whatcha been up to? I haven't seen you around lately."

Rett, a fitting nickname.

"Not much, Jenna. School, you know. But I hear you're working on homecoming queen for this year already." He leaned lazily on the counter beside Tracey, his warm body turned towards hers. His face, however, was on the girl.

"Well, I *am* in the running," she crooned in mock embarrassment.

"Well *I* know who to vote for." He winked, then smiled at her. He offered up a sexy, hot, and still somehow sweet expression. The girl forgot all about taking Tracey's money. She just giggled and handed her the movies. Tracey could have just walked out and she never would have said a word. Tracey could have vomited, but usually tried not to do that in public. She took the money out of her pocket, nine dollars even, and left it on the counter. She started to walk off. The clerk still didn't turn to her. Lucky for Tracey, she knew when to return the movies. But as soon as she stepped away from the counter, Rett's attention lighted on her. He said some sort of goodbye to Jenna and followed Tracey out of the store.

"Don't I get a thank you?" He leaned his hip against her car. She paused before slipping into the seat.

"First, get off my car. Second, no, you don't. I could have come out here and gotten my ID. It wasn't necessary for you to throw your, how shall I put it, masculine clout around on my behalf."

He smiled at that, almost laughed. And it was almost the same smile he'd given the obvious law school groupie. But somehow this smile wasn't nearly as cocky as the other. It was like he really meant it… or maybe Tracey was as simple-minded as the blonde.

"You know, I'm still waiting for the water to pass under that bridge," he said, chuckling.

Tracey rolled her eyes. "Well, keep waiting," she retorted and dropped into her seat. She was *definitely* getting better at saying her peace. She closed the door without rolling the window down and turned the key. Garrett and she engaged in a sophomoric stare-down for a few seconds before he got off the car and Tracey pulled out of the parking space. She drove all the way home without the radio. She killed her engine, got out with her movies, locked her doors, walked to her porch, opened her front door, walked in, then kicked the door closed behind her, hard. That was probably going to leave a mark. Then she locked it, grumbling.

The very next morning, Tracey walked into the law school lounge to get a cup of coffee and there he was with four of his friends. Apparently one of them had put money in the snack machine but got nothing out. The bag of chips was caught in the metal spiral that rarely wanted to give up its goodies. Intelligent men that they were, rather than walk around to the office to get the money back, they'd decided to try to tip the machine to make the booty fall to the bottom. Tracey ignored them and got her coffee. She hid laughter behind her cup as she continued to be entertained by the display of confounded testosterone. They shook the machine, still not freeing the bag of sour cream and onion potato chips.

Then all at once they got a brilliant idea. A marvelously brilliant idea, or so they thought. Rett positioned himself beneath the machine as the others leaned it against his back. Tracey believed, though she couldn't be certain, that the intent was to hold it up, turn it upside down and shake it until the snack treasure came free. By that time other students had trailed in—all of them women—and the laughter was out of control. Though the other spectators let out unchecked gales of laughter, Tracey tried to control herself. She really did. But she finally couldn't hold it in anymore and, like rapids over a waterfall, the giggles gushed out.

Garrett looked up at her and something happened. She felt something. A spark, a current, a fleeting *something.* He must have felt something too because he let go of the machine. He looked like a guy who'd been caught drinking milk out of the carton by his mother. Then the look turned downright seductive. Tracey was stunned. However, letting go of his part of the mechanical burden wasn't exactly a good idea. A louder-than-loud smash signified the hulking machine's crash to the floor. For a moment, all five of them just stood there, shocked, Tracey imagined. Intriguing hazel eyes found her once more. They spoke to her almost as if she were an accomplice.

"Bright," she intoned dryly. "Very bright." And he laughed. He actually laughed. Then he took off running with the other guys, as if they were children. As if none of them were law students in that very building. As if no one knew who they were. As if school didn't take care of good ol' boys like them anyway.

After that, she saw him everywhere. She saw him with girls hanging on his every word, saw him at the law library, saw him playing football out on the lawn in those worn navy blue shorts. She saw him getting his way all the time, which disturbed her to no end. Because he represented something to her. Maybe it was unfair, but he did. Rett Atkins embodied all that was wrong with the world to her somehow.

Not only that, it was as if he were haunting her. She knew he was not, but still, at those times, she would catch herself staring at him, and he almost always caught her, too. He would look back at her with a crooked smile and squeezed brow that formed his face into a question mark. Or he would just give her his full attention and grin at her. Somehow, every single time she saw that smile, she felt electricity run across her skin. Something was happening. Tracey just didn't know what. She saw him in slow motion, with soft music playing in the background, and that just wasn't right.

Chapter 4

During that period in Tracey's life, she spent most of her time in the small two-bedroom house that had once belonged to her father's mother. She loved her house. It had gone unused for years until Tracey moved out of the dormitory in the second semester of her sophomore year. Dorm life had nearly done her in. Though she wished different, Tracey just wasn't that social. She had always loved her grandma's house, and it was only a couple of miles from campus. There were old, old trees wrapped up in each other in the front yard, and in the dark they almost hid the whole house from the street. Tracey had spent hours in those trees when she was little, cradled in their smooth, concealing branches. As an adult, this house had become her oasis. It became *their* oasis.

The scent of freshly brewed coffee constantly permeated her home. Tracey was positively addicted to it. Before long, Garrett was, too. The first time he came to her was about two weeks after the incident at the law school. It was odd, because he had been on her mind. She couldn't figure out why someone of his lily white shade and popularity-poll-winning smile cared enough to wait half an hour just to apologize to her.

Why someone who didn't seem to have one irregularity about him other than stunning eyes kept looking at her like…like… She didn't know how he was looking at her. This night, as had become alarmingly frequent of late, she was struggling to reconcile these two seemingly different parts of his personality when he showed up at her door.

The night before, Thursday night at the law library, Tracey had been studying with her Employment Rights study group, which happened to be three other black students. She liked her group a lot and they seemed to like her, although she was not sure if they ever really got to know her. Incredibly self-conscious back then, she worried that she would say the wrong thing or make a wrong reference or not *get* a reference they made. So she spent most of her time staying quiet.

She was having trouble focusing that night until she heard the wayward comment: "I don't know why y'all so worried about this course. Dr. Burke has a jones for Tracey anyway. It's gon' be straight up A's across the board for y'all this whole semester."

"Tory," Tracey yelped at the slim, light-skinned fellow. She didn't even know he knew *she* knew Dr. Burke. She narrowed her eyes at Shanda, whom Tracey had met when they were undergrads. Shanda immediately averted her gaze.

"Ahhh, I hit on something then," Tory announced. "On the real, Tracey, what's nekkid between you and old dude."

"Nothing is 'nekkid,'" Tracey replied, rolling her eyes. "For one thing he's an associate of my dad's, and, for another, he's my faculty advisor."

And just at that moment, she looked up. And there was Rett Atkins standing over at the circulation desk writing something on a legal pad. Tracey would never forget what he was wearing: the smile that killed her. She could see his perfect white teeth, his soft lips. Damn, he had lips! Pretty, full, dark pink lips.

When he finally turned his attention away from the pad she watched him direct the smile at the girl behind the counter. She fairly oozed I-want-to-do-you-real-bad at him, letting her hand trail over the soft curl of her dyed red hair. Ridiculous. This guy was ridiculous.

He turned then, throwing his book bag over his shoulder and glancing Tracey's way. She looked off, attempting to immerse herself in the conversation with her peers.

Unfortunately, Shanda drew all of their group's attention to the one place Tracey didn't want it. "Him." She motioned to Garrett who was, by then, standing at one of the catalog computer terminals. "His name's Rett Atkins. He's number three right now, isn't he, Tory?"

"Thank you for bringing it up, Shan." Tory ranked nearer to *seventy*-three.

"I'll personally be lucky to be number three hundred having y'all for a study group," Sabrina complained as she started to pack up her books. She would be studying corporate law that next fall.

"Aww, girl, you know you love it," Tory declared, throwing an arm around her shoulder.

"Whatever," she answered, rolling her eyes. "I'm out, y'all. I gotta go try and enjoy what's left of this Thursday night."

"Me, too," Shanda yawned, grabbing her books, "You coming, Tory? You know you ain't got no car."

"You always talking about somebody ain't got no car. But let me ask you this…who wrecked my car?" Tory grumbled, snatching up his books. "You coming, too, Tracey?"

"No, I think I'll stay for a minute." She just couldn't seem to get up.

"Well, see you later," they called and Tracey watched them walk out of the library.

"Okay, y'all!"

Involuntarily, Tracey surveyed the room, looking for what she knew she shouldn't be looking for. She didn't see Garrett. She stood and stretched and rubbed her eyes. Even after being there for five and a half hours, for some reason she still felt wired. After going to the snack bar to get a drink, she walked out into the cool, breezy night.

A silver moon shone brightly, like all the light she felt inside her. Clouds gray and puffed clung to their cottony brothers and sisters, separated only by that lovely moonlight. Tracey took a breath. She took another, feeling the cool go down her throat into the depths of her stomach. It was about time for the weather to cool off. But she wasn't cool. Inside, she was burning up. Her skin was creeping and tingling all over her body. She closed her eyes and breathed some more. She couldn't stand still. She saw his face in her mind. This was useless.

When she got back to her spot in the library, she decided to go on home. Packing up her books, Tracey realized that two were missing. She looked in her book bag, on the table, under the table, but couldn't find them. She pressed a hand to her eyes and took a deep breath. She was not going to panic, nor was she going to exhaust herself even more. It had been a long night. Either Shanda or Sabrina or Tory had picked up her books by mistake and all she needed to do was call them. She took more deep breaths and took out her cell phone. No one answered.

After leaving messages, Tracey stopped by the front desk to provide her name and number in case the books turned up, then went home.

She called each of them again when she got home. No one had her books or remembered seeing her with them. But she knew she had taken them to the library with her and she knew they had been on the table. She tried to relax.

Chapter 5

"Another shot of Jäger, my friend?" Clay asked as the bartender set another glass of the stuff in front of Rett.

"You just keep 'em comin', boy. I'm gon' show you how to take 'em down like a champ," Rett answered with a grin. He drummed the bar top momentously, then swept up the drink and let it slip quickly down his throat. He held back his grimace like a man.

"Where we goin' next?" Clay asked, knocking back his own.

"Aww, man." Rett slapped him on the back and wiped his mouth with the back of his hand. He hated the taste of Jäger. "I'm going to Kim's. I'll see you back at the apartment later."

"Aw-right," Clay acknowledged, then waggled his eyebrows at a pretty redhead at the end of the bar… at least until a very pretty blonde with pretty hazel eyes eclipsed his view and winked at him.

When his expression changed, Rett tracked his gaze to the blonde at whom he scowled. "Don't make me kick your ass, Clay."

Clay licked his lips and turned to order another drink.

Rett left after greeting the blonde with a half-hug and a kiss just to annoy her. In his car, he looked over at the books on his passenger seat and took a deep, fortifying breath. Then, he punched directions into the nav system.

—⁘—

Late Friday night, Tracey was up and home, as she usually was, drinking spiked coffee and listening to jazz. Maybe it sounded pretentious, but it's what she liked to do. Listening to jazz had been Tracey's favorite pastime ever since her father brought home a reel-to-reel when she was about seven. The coffee came later when he bought her a coffee maker and, when her mother wasn't looking, gave her a bottle of coffee liqueur he'd brought from the islands.

Just when Charlie Parker was about to get into his "Mood," Tracey heard a knock at her door and got up to answer it. She moved slowly, wondering who would come this late. She peeked through the peephole in the door and her immediate reaction was, *There's a white boy at my door*. She rubbed her eyes, but there he stood: Garrett Atkins. She opened the door.

"Hey," he piped, wearing a little boy grin.

"Oh, no, not you!" It was out before she could stop it.

"What do you mean, *not me?*" He chuckled. His voice was slower and deeper than usual. More accented than usual. It put a tickle on the back of her neck. She tried to think about all those movies with the dirty old white man trying to get at some fresh-out-of-church naïve, nubile, young black girl walking down the side of a rural road. It had been done in so many ways in so many movies. Sometimes they got them, sometimes they didn't. But the scenes she could remember weren't working. He wasn't leering at her. He was, however, giving her a tickle.

"What are you doing here?" she asked, agitated.

"Well, it's actually a two-part mission," he started, knocking another smile her way. Another tickle.

She crossed her arms in front of her chest, refusing to fall for it. Those smiles were his weapon.

"Listen, I'm sorry I'm here so late," he said in a rush. "God, I'm sorry. But I couldn't stop thinking you were mad about what happened that first day at the law school. I mean, I see you around every day and every day I think you think I'm a… I'm a—"

"Racist?" Tracey questioned with a quirk of her eyebrow. It was the first time she had heard or seen the slightest hint of vulnerability in this man. She decided to take advantage of it. "It's good that you're worried about that. You should worry. You should feel guilty, too. But it's still no reason for you to come here at this time of night to make reparations. You can leave my forty acres and my mule at the door. I'll get them in the morning." She didn't know if it meant she was somehow getting comfortable with him or not, but Tracey was getting good with the zingers.

She went on. "And may I ask you a question? Do you normally track people down like some sort of stalker just to apologize? I mean, that's just not normal. And you could be in some serious danger coming into this neighborhood at night." Tracey looked beyond him out into the darkness and could see that he had pulled his shiny black SUV all the way up into her drive behind the trees. No one would see it from the street.

"I don't do this all the time." There was the arrogance again. Still, he stood there. At that point, she noticed the books tucked under his arm. He untucked them so she could see them better. "The second part of this mission." His gaze darted around her into her living room. "You mind if I come in?"

"Why?"

"I don't know." He leaned his head against the doorframe and pawed at his eyes with broad hands. Then he pulled his head away from the frame and put his elbow where it had been. He laid his head in the palm of his hand. His elbows slipped on the wood and he teetered. She grabbed for her books before they plummeted to the floor.

Realizing why his accent was so much thicker than usual, Tracey asked, "Are you drunk?"

"Not half as much as I wanna be."

"You're looking pretty drunk to me right now. You're smelling pretty drunk, too." She stood there staring at him for a long while, wondering what to do.

"Listen, I'll get outta here. I probably shouldna come anyway."

There was that sensitivity again. Tracey honestly didn't know what to make of it.

"No, no." She didn't know him that well, but in his condition, he didn't evoke much fear. Besides, he shouldn't be out driving. All very rational. Uh-huh. "No, you shouldn't drive like that. Come in." She moved back into the house and turned the music off. It didn't feel right with it on and him there.

"How'd you find me?"

He didn't sit, just stared at his surroundings.

Walking over to the sofa to look at the prints hanging above it, he replied, "Your address is in your books."

Tracey accepted that answer for about three seconds. "It is not."

"Damn, I should have checked before I said that, huh?" He chuckled. "And not even a thank you for bringing them back."

"Thank you. Now tell me how you found me."

"Easy. I knew your name already. I just had Marsha in the front office look you up for me this morning. I told her we'd gotten our notebooks mixed up and I had to find you 'cause there was a big test coming up. I've been ridin' around for about an hour trying to find your house. Even with the GPS, I passed it like three different times. You really ought to get someone to chop those trees down out there."

"Listen, Detective CSI, I happen to like those trees. Why didn't you just get her to call me or call me yourself so we could arrange for me to pick them up?"

He shrugged.

"That's your answer?"

He shrugged again with another lopsided grin.

"It's late." Her voice didn't hold half the resilience it had earlier. "It would be irresponsible for me to let you drive like that." Tracey closed the door behind him and offered him something to drink. Reflex, pure reflex. That's what one did when one had a guest. Did she really have a guest?

He wanted something alcoholic. After explaining to him that that defeated the purpose of letting him in, she agreed. She gave in because he kept walking around her living room, picking up everything, looking at everything, touching everything. He picked up the heavy wooden fetish her father had brought back for her from the Ivory Coast. He ran his hands over the hips and lips of the roughly fashioned fertility talisman. He turned it in his palm, then set it down on its little pedestal once more, so softly that she never heard it touch. Tracey gave in to Garrett because whenever he spoke to her or she to him, he would watch her face and pay more attention than she was accustomed to.

He studied her as he had that talisman. She gave in to him because she barely had a choice.

Out of milk for white Russians, Tracey started a pot of decaf for an Irish coffee. "Be happy I'm not a cheapskate; otherwise you'd be drinking water."

He smiled. Another tickle. Dammit, she hated it when he did that. She got up and moved into the kitchen. When she came back, he was sitting where she had been sitting, in her favorite spot, her favorite chair, and didn't look as if he was going to move. She didn't say anything, needing a little more time to size up the situation. Plus, she didn't want to be rude.

Tracey handed him the glass, and he tasted cautiously. "This is good. Thanks."

"So happy you like it." They were quiet for a moment. "Okay, I don't mean to sound rude or anything, but why did you ask Marsha for my address and not my phone number?"

He responded—or didn't—by telling her he liked her furniture because it was weird. He seemed amazed when she told him she'd helped her mother make most of it. She pointed out the dark tan leather armchair he had usurped from her, one of her mother's signature designs.

"This is amazing."

"My mother is trained in interior design, but for about the past ten, fifteen years, she's been involved with industrial design as well."

"Awesome," he said. Tracey hated that word. "How'd you get into law?"

"Well, I'm not 'into law' exactly. I'm in the MBA program. I'm hoping to specialize in the legal aspects of operations management. You know, like labor unions, HR policy, etc. It's kind of dry, but I like it. Besides, my father is a corporate law consultant. I guess I took after him."

Garrett was quiet.

Tracey tried to fill the silence. "You know, I hear that people struggling under the white man's burden sometimes feel the need to give confession."

He looked rather perplexed, and Tracey started to laugh.

"That was a joke," she said. He relaxed again and stared down into his mug. "What is it?" she implored. "You want to talk about it? And while you talk about it, would you also please explain why you stalked me. You still haven't."

"Nah, I don't guess so."

But he didn't say anything more. She sat on the couch contemplating how long he would be there and if he was ever going to talk about what was bothering him or tell her why he'd gotten her address. His appearance on her doorstep was probably the oddest thing that had happened to her in her entire college career.

Something occurred to her, and she looked him full in the face. As was becoming usual, his yellow and brown and green eyes met hers dead on. Tracey could feel hers widen, then narrow. "Where'd you find my books, Garrett?"

"Huh?" His surprise and guilt were as evident as Santa Claus's appetite for frequent dining.

"You stole my books, Garrett?" It was barely a question.

"I gave 'em back, didn't I?" he returned with a wolf-ish grin.

"And that makes it okay?"

He shrugged.

"And you're number three—"

"Soon to be number one," he interrupted.

"Good lord! Why did you do this?"

"You remember that day about two weeks ago in the student lounge? You know, when my ingenious friends and I decided to vandalize the Quiki Snack Machine?" His gaze moved from hers briefly, a glance at his mug and back. She nodded. "Well, you may not believe this, but I heard you laugh—"

"Of course I believe it. Everyone heard me laugh. And here's a shocker: I wasn't the only one laughing, either."

"Aw-right, aw-right. But that's not what you won't believe. You won't believe that I never heard a laugh like that before."

35

"There is not a single thing peculiar about my laugh," Tracey said, not at all pleased.

"Oh, but there is," he insisted cryptically. Then he winked at her.

"Anyway," she demurred, "I still don't understand what you're doing here, what you're doing with me." That was a funny choice of words, and they both knew it. Tracey rushed ahead. "Isn't it homecoming weekend or something? Shouldn't you be doing something to show your school spirit?"

"Shouldn't you?"

"It's not my style," Tracey answered, shrugging her shoulders.

"But you figure it's mine?"

She didn't answer that.

"Well, yesss," he drawled. "I was out with some friends on the strip tonight. I was doin' the same old thing I always do on the weekend—homecomin's not for two more weeks, by the way. Anyhow, sometime tonight, I got bored and left."

Tracey pinned him with a stare. "And came here."

He licked his lips. "And came here."

"Why?"

"It bothers me, the way you look at me. It bothers the hell outta me. And I don't know why, but I like you."

"You don't know me."

He dipped his head in the most awkward and entrancing way, almost like a bird running its wing over its head. "You're right. So let me fix that. Where you from?"

"Huh?"

"Where are you from?" He cocked his head to the side.

"Here, why?"

"The accent or the no-accent. You don't talk like you're from down here."

"If you mean I don't talk like you, that's true. I've never had that strong of a Southern accent, and neither do my parents." No need to tell him about Mama's family and how status-conscious they'd been for more than a century. Speech lessons had come so early Tracey didn't remember a time before she had them.

He hesitated. "I like the way you talk."

"Thank you. I like the way you talk."

He studied the wall. Tracey thought maybe she'd embarrassed him. "I been drivin' around since I left the bar, bored out of my mind."

"You shouldn't drink and drive."

"I know, but… I know."

What she felt looking at him, all good looks and charm, and also conflict and sadness, was an instant, deep, and undeniable connection to him. Tracey needed a diversion. "I should tell you I've had extensive contact with alcoholics, and I know that sometimes when one has had too much to drink, it leads to a kind of philosophical degeneration. What I mean is, being drunk leads one to believe he or she is being deeply philosophical sometimes, whereas one is really only being drunk."

"Thank you for understandin'," he quipped. *"Extensive* contact with alcoholics?"

Tracey started laughing and he did, too. "By the way, I was not being hostile. I was being offended."

"I never meant to offend you," he told her with a quick sobriety that bore believing.

"I understand that."

"Good," he chirped. "But I'm pretty sure you've been tryin' to offend me. Man, I can't say *anything* to you."

"I don't think I've been particularly nasty to you, but if I have, I'm sorry." They were silent for a moment, then—Tracey didn't know what got into her—she asked, "Why didn't you go find your girlfriend?" His lion eyes flared for a moment. "I mean, you said you couldn't talk to your family or friends, but I'm sure you have a girlfriend, if not a wife." *Smooth, Tracey, very smooth.*

All he said was "Yeah." Then he shook his head and looked down into his lapis-colored coffee mug. Finally, he slid down further into her chair and offered, "I need some perspective."

"That's what shrinks are for," she muttered before she could stop herself.

"See what I'm sayin'." He raised a wry eyebrow.

Tracey opened her mouth to naysay him, only to shut it again. She was only digging a deeper hole, which seemed to delight him. She didn't want him delighted. "Then why pick me to be your sympathetic ear? Okay! Okay! I'm sorry. I'm listening! One hundred percent focused on you." He clasped his hands over his heart and fluttered his eyelashes. She laughed and he beamed a smile back. She said to him, "You know, you've really got a beautiful smile." His cheeks were flushed as he thanked her. "Don't thank me, it's true. So, what exactly do you need perspective on?"

"Do I just spill it? Just tell you what's been on my mind here lately?"

"I'm not a professional, but I think that's how it's done. Yeah."

"Just like that, huh?"

Tracey nodded.

He took a sip of his coffee. "It's my girlfriend," he started. "Okay, if you were a girl in college—" She raised her brow and began to stir her coffee. "I mean, would you quit school right now to start havin' babies?" Her answer was no.

They spent that night getting drunk and getting sober and getting drunk again. He told her everything from the huge amount of student loans he was amassing to pay for law school to how his girlfriend wanted to drop out, get married, and start breeding as soon as possible. *Babies.* The word made her shudder. Tracey wanted to ask how he'd gotten mixed up with her. But she already knew. The marriage virus had hit many, many girls from her old dorm. Instead of saying as much, she made some crude, drunken reference to "poppin' out puppies." She liked him, and she didn't want to spoil the tenuous comfort between them, but she didn't want to get involved with his life, either.

It was about an entire pot of coffee and half a bottle of single malt past four a.m. when Tracey recalled that she had to get up early in the morning. She said as much to Garrett. He yawned and stood up, stretching his arms way up above his head. He wore short sleeves and she could see the shape of his biceps, the rounding of his forearms beneath his elbows, that little muscle that miraculously appears on the sides of a man's upper arms. His shoulders were broad, his waist and hips narrow. There was definitely something wrong with the way she was looking at him, but she just couldn't stop. He told her he would see her later. Tracey didn't know if he meant around school or back at her house. She didn't ask.

A couple of hours later her head was pounding and dark circles ringed her eyes, but her body still felt better than it should. She drank a huge glass of orange juice and then got into the shower after bringing three of her bushy, macho ferns into the bathroom with her. Tracey lined them up on the floor beside the shower and turned on the water. Wild green arms folded over and over each other, swelling and rising. Babyish plants, they loved the heat and humidity and the care she lavished on them. They flourished in her little house. When she got out of the shower, Tracey checked the time, got dressed, then headed out to the Carlisle Center. She was meeting her new friend, Monica, a counselor at the facility, for lunch when she finished her teen pregnancy counseling session.

Chapter 6

"Where do you want to go?"

"I feel like Thai." Walking out of the building, Moni took a cursory look around the parking lot. All clear. She pulled out a cigarette and lit it. "I'll drive 'cuz I don't want to get smoke in your car."

"I didn't know you smoked."

"That's because no one sees me smoke around here." Monica pulled her short self up into the seat of the burgundy SUV. She always felt as if she were climbing a tree when she got in the thing. "You like Thai?"

"Yeah," Tracey answered. "Love it, but nobody ever wants to eat it with me."

"Well, you're in luck." Monica smiled and drove them to the only Thai restaurant in town, the Siam House. When they got there, the parking lot was packed. Moni ended up parking on the grass next to the building. Inside, the small restaurant was so full that no booths or tables were left.

Then Tracey made an offer that was completely unexpected. Even as she said the words, they seemed to surprise her as well. "I don't live far from here. We can order and eat at my house. The only thing is, I have to get my car. We can pick it up and go back to my house."

"I like that plan."

It actually didn't take long to get their food. They were at Tracey's in twenty minutes. Monica had a tough time processing the invitation. Tracey seemed like a very private person. Though she obviously had friends, she didn't seem exceptionally close to any of them, and Moni seriously doubted she had invited any of them into her home. This woman seemed to be at war with outside perceptions all the time, even those of her family.

Monica chewed her lower lip. She didn't know that much about Tracey but she had learned to trust her instincts. Tracey's home was probably the only place where Tracey felt she could be herself. And, people didn't bring judges into their one sanctuary. Monica shook her head. She didn't want to psychoanalyze her new friend, but that's exactly what she was doing. Still…

Monica tried to be a friend without judgment or expectation. She tried to be as open as possible to show Tracey that she could do the same.

Tracey walked into the kitchen to gather plates, silverware, and glasses. Moni took it upon herself to tour the house. "This is a nice place, Tracey."

"Thank you. It belonged to my grandma up until she died and left it to me."

"I'm sorry to hear about your grandmother. How long ago did she pass?"

"Thank you. It's been years now. We were very close. This house has helped me deal with it."

Moni nodded as she came back into the living room. "Interesting. You know, looking from the outside, you wouldn't expect for it to be so plush in here."

"Don't tell the burglars."

"Is this an authentic boomerang?"

"Yeah. My dad got that a long, long time ago when he was in the service. He gave it to me when I moved over here."

"Did he give you all this stuff?"

"Most of it. Everything except for those shells and necklaces, which I got in St. Thomas, and those castanets and Spanish things I got when I lived in Salamanca. Oh yeah, and that stupid, plastic Eiffel Tower statue—"

"You lived in Salamanca?"

"Yeah," Tracey responded, coming into the living room. She set two places on the coffee table. She pulled some brown and cornflower chenille cushions off the sofa and laid them on the soft Indian-style area rug. "You don't mind sitting on the floor do you? My kitchen table is serving as extra counter space right now."

"Girl, please, I don't care."

They sat down and Tracey continued, "I lived there for a year after high school. My dad thought it would be a good idea if I took a break from school, so that was my graduation gift from him. It started out that I would live in Madrid for a year, but my mama was so mad that was already out of the question." She chuckled. "She didn't want me going. She insisted that Spain was too dangerous, I didn't speak the language well enough, and there were terrorists just waiting around every corner to sell young girls into slavery. So, my dad made some arrangements for me to attend a Spanish language institute in Salamanca for a year.

"The worst part about that is when I got there, Salamanca was ten times worse than Madrid ever could have been in all the ways Mama warned. I hated it there. Though I didn't tell my folks, I spent more of my year in Paris with some friends from high school than in Spain. I believe that was the most fun I've ever had in my life. It was like no matter where I went or what I did or who I did it with, it was all just right. Maybe it was because I barely spoke French and didn't fully understand anything. I don't know. I just had this freedom I had never felt before or really since. Oh," Tracey gasped. "I didn't mean to go on and on like that. I try not to even mention it. Most people think I'm bragging or something when I bring it up."

"No, it's okay. In fact I'd like to hear about it. My oldest, Tamia, is thirteen. Her private school takes a

European trip every year. Of course she can't go until she's sixteen, but I'd like to know what kind of experiences you had." Then Moni had to go and put her foot in it in her normal way. "Besides, I'd like to talk about this freedom you felt you had there, and why you felt that way. In my experience, when a person feels so extraordinarily free in a removed circumstance—"

"Define 'removed circumstance.'" Tracey folded her arms across her chest defensively.

Moni knew it was time to back off, but she didn't. "A place where you're anonymous. It's a place where you don't have to make any significant social contact. Well, when someone flourishes in that environment, losing inhibitions and all that, it usually means they struggle with their image of themselves." Tracey didn't say anything.

Moni shook her head and averted her eyes. Tracey wasn't ready to have this kind of discussion with her, with anybody. And, as Monica's psychological tangents sometimes did, they just snuck into the conversation without warning and took over. "I'm sorry, Tracey." She kept her voice soft. "I can't help it sometimes. Part of why I do what I do is that I've always stuck my nose into business where it didn't belong. There's something about you that seems very unhappy to me. I don't know."

"I'm not unhappy."

"Right. My bad." Moni leaned over to squeeze her forearm. They finished the meal in silence.

Before Monica left, she asked, "Hey, Tracey, did I tell you? I'm having an anniversary party in a few weeks. You want to come?"

"Sure."

Moni walked out hoping Tracey meant it.

Chapter 7

Sunday night, Garrett came back. When he came to the door and knocked, Tracey let him in. He wandered around her living room again, and sat down in her favorite chair. She was eating cubed steak steaming with the tickling scent of pepper, so tender that it was hard to keep a whole piece on a fork. On the side were mashed potatoes smothered in gravy, English peas, and the dinner rolls her great-aunt Terry was famous for. She asked if he was hungry. He told her that if he wasn't before, he was then. They ate together and chatted. She deemed the evening pleasant.

Monday night Tracey was expecting him, and he showed up around eight-thirty. He ate with her again and they talked about class. They ended up studying for midterms. They worked in silence for hours on end. It went that way that whole week, and the next. Sometimes they would take a break, have a drink, watch something stupid on television, or talk about whatever it was they were working on. Sometimes she confirmed his understanding of a business concept for corporate or tax law. And always, if she had a question about Employee Rights, he could answer it correctly and thoroughly. He answered with such a serious, authoritative tone, it was as if he went into a work mode that transformed him into an intellectual. Tracey didn't know how he managed to retain so much information, but he was really extraordinary as far as academics went.

During the day, mostly at the law library, she saw him, he saw her, but they didn't say anything more than "Hey" and they didn't always say that. He would quickly avert his eyes, or she would. Tracey didn't know how to feel about that. It wouldn't have been completely strange for them to have a conversation. For all anyone else knew, they were probably classmates. But it just felt like people would think more. It already felt like they were all watching them. Paranoia? Maybe. But he knew it, and Tracey knew it: They could spend as much time as they wanted together as long as they didn't bring it to school.

—◊◊◊—

The Omega Psi Phi pledges had just finished an unforgettable and touching step routine. It was their first appearance that year and they had *showed out*.

The young smooth-faced black youths walked up with heads shaved and backs naked save for defined muscles. The pants they wore were torn burlap and they wore chains around their throats and ankles. They dragged their chains, singing something deep, haunting, and haunted. They carried torches; some were blindfolded. The only thing saving Tracey from becoming heavy-hearted was the fact that they wore combat boots spray-painted purple and gold. She remembered one black-as-midnight back, skin stretched smooth. A horseshoe, pink and black and puffy as the brand healed, swelled on his shoulder blade, marring it. She had watched the whole show spellbound and proud and hurting all at once. And she had that feeling a person has—if that person is an average black American—when watching *Roots*, or *Amistad*, or any period piece with Denzel Washington in it. She felt briefly as if she wanted to kill every white person she knew.

A little after the show, Rett was standing with a group of his friends and Tracey with a group of hers out on the lawn.

She saw Garrett wave but averted her gaze and didn't wave back. It was just a reflex. Tracey knew she shouldn't have done it, but how would she have explained him to her friends? He passed it off as a joke to his friends. The next night around nine he showed up at her house. She didn't know what to say. She didn't know if he knew what she had done. He never mentioned it. Instead, he asked if she was hungry. She was. To avoid going out or even having someone deliver to them, she offered to cook. Again.

"I wouldn't want you to go to too much trouble. Besides you always cook. Let me do it," he insisted.

"I don't know," she hesitated, biting her lip. "My kitchen is very important to me."

"Come on, I know my way around a kitchen."

"I don't think so."

"Please," he whined, reminding her of a little boy wanting to stay up late at night watching his favorite television show. "At least let me help."

There went that tickle again. This was all unfair, very unfair. "Sure, what would you like to eat?" Tracey had a five-star kitchen. Her father had made sure of it. He had a penchant for exotic liquor, exotic music, and exotic food. He had passed it on to Tracey. She was most like him.

He was the only one who understood everything that went on inside her head. He understood it, even if he didn't always like it. So even though they were close, he spent a lot of time being angry with Tracey. But he was ever proud. He thought she was a warrior against adversity as he was. But that was before everything happened.

―――

The first time Garrett forgave her was that night after she snubbed him. After actually getting dinner prepared, a chore with Garrett making himself a general nuisance, they talked mostly about law. At some point, he tried to get her to talk about herself and the circumstances behind her living arrangements. Tracey didn't want to. She was relieved when he didn't press her. There were some things she hadn't ever talked about and never intended to talk about with anyone. She was relieved that her sophomoric behavior on the lawn had apparently gone unnoticed. Or so she thought.

The next time she saw him and they were at school, she was posted at her usual spot on the steps laughing at some guys freestyling about an Econ 111 exam. She'd always known there'd be a rap one day about shifts in the oil demand curve. She laughed so hard tears slipped from the corners of her eyes. She dabbed at them, and, when she looked up, Garrett was looking right at her, and then he was walking right towards her. Until that time, never had her knees gone weak. It was a good thing she was leaning against that pillar. Tracey watched him, her eyes locked to his, and slowly she rolled her head from side to side hoping no one would notice. He stopped in his tracks but was not kind enough to release her gaze. Tracey was helpless until, with a disgusted look, he turned and walked away.

That same night, she sat for hours slowly sipping brandy and Coke, trying for the mildly disoriented effect.

He came to her that night and asked for an explanation. He told her not to say she didn't know what he was talking about or that she hadn't done anything because it was the second time. The first time, he hadn't made a big deal about it because he hadn't wanted to embarrass her.

He didn't want to embarrass me, she thought. She wilted with that revelation.

He wanted to know why. Tracey put a cushion over her head and replied, "Because I'm stupid that way."

"That's it?"

Indignant was a good word for his tone. Drunk and belligerent did a better job. "Look, I don't even know you. You just show up here from time to time and that's it. I don't owe you anything. I don't know why you think—"

He snatched the cushion from her. "Because I never," he said through his teeth, "never would have done that to you, Tracey."

She stood to face him. "Really, Garrett? You've done it to me plenty of times before now. There was nothing different about my behavior today. The only difference was you." She poked her finger into his chest and went on. "You smile at me, I smile at you. That's the way it goes when we're in class."

He didn't say anything, but grabbed her hand, holding it still so she couldn't poke him anymore.

"What else do you want? You don't feel comfortable, and I don't feel comfortable. What do you want?" Her voice did not shake. She was lucky at times.

"I want to be friends." That just made it worse. And even though Garrett and Tracey had known each oth-

53

er only a few weeks, they had become friends the first night he'd come there, good ones. Even worse was that they both knew there was no safe friendship between the two of them. She felt helpless and tugged her hand out of his. He continued, "Listen, I don't even know why this is such a big deal. People meet each other and hang out and become friends and say 'Hey' when they pass each other in the halls. All kinds of people. But you and me, we can't."

"I know," Tracey breathed, taking her cushion back from him before slumping back down into her seat.

He sat down near her again. Neither of them asked why. Tracey didn't ask 'cause she sure didn't want an answer. They were silent. She didn't know where all that had come from. Her only defense was that she'd had too much to drink. All she knew was that somewhere under her ribs she felt a pain grow. He pulled the pillow from her arms again, gently this time, and watched her. God, he was always watching her, always paying such close attention. She felt that, somehow, he was trying to learn her.

The worst of it, the very worst of it, was they weren't exactly forging new territory. There were plenty of black and white people that hung out, that were good friends. There were even a couple in the law school. But there was that something that was dangerous for the both of them.

For Tracey it had started almost from birth. From the time she learned to talk to the time she left high school, she had people calling her an Oreo, a "wannabe," everything a person could think of to say she wasn't a "real" black person. Why? Because she spoke "proper," she was smart, she had white friends, and her parents were wealthy but from self-made wealth. Half the things she was socially obligated to identify with, she didn't, because that just wasn't where she came from.

Proud to be black? She was, but she also felt an unnatural pressure to shout it to doubters every day. As she overcompensated, she felt uncomfortable in her own skin. In truth, she never felt that she belonged to anybody or to anything other than her family. But now, even though she didn't belong, she had this tenuous grip on what was shaping up to be a new life for her. She had people to hang out with. She said the right things in the right way. She only gave when she got, as with her new friendship with Monica.

She couldn't figure out this thing with Garrett, though. She could only assume it was because he was all-American, the boy next door. He was probably engaged at birth to a girl named Susie and had a mock wedding ceremony when he was six and she was five. He was probably in his father's fraternity. He was classic and white without an ounce of "soul." Maybe their mutual affinity just confounded her enough for her to continue to be interested in it.

"Tracey, you don't seem like you care that much about what other people think."

"Good, aren't I?" she mumbled, grabbing another pillow and holding it over her face. He took that one away from her, too, then came to sit beside her on the couch, forcing her to crowd herself into the corner at the other end.

"Listen, this is stupid," Garrett grated.

She turned her head into the sofa, hiding her hot face. "Maybe, but that's my reality."

"So that's it?" he asked and then was quiet. Tracey heard him swallow deep. She felt his hand reach for her left, which twisted in the folds of her shirt. He untangled it and held it. "Yeah, I guess that's it."

Tracey nodded and sighed heavily, pained by this conversation, pained by how much it felt right to have her hand in his... They had actually agreed to deny each other. He got glasses and ice and poured more brandy.

"You need to eat something. I know you haven't eaten," he told her in the voice her mother used when Tracey was sick. He headed into her kitchen, taking her bottle of brandy with him. Tracey heard him put something into the microwave. He came back and sat upside down in her favorite chair. Blood rushed to his head. He didn't bring her bottle back. "You should stop trying to please everybody. You should stop trying to be someone you're not."

"Thanks, Dr. Atkins, but I think you should try that yourself," she returned sarcastically.

"Oh, you'd be surprised how well I'm overcoming it." He stood after hearing the microwave ping, and then he brought her a bowl of chili.

So they ended up telling each other their life stories of infatuation with social comfort and attempts to please everyone they knew. They ended up more than mildly disoriented. They ended up asleep together on her couch.

All Tracey could remember was drifting off murmuring something about pretty arms and soft hair. She awakened to a feeling she hadn't had since she was small when her father had let her fall asleep in his arms every night. Without opening her eyes, just from the sheer warmth and weight, she knew Rett was on her. She felt the arms wrapped beneath her waist and the head resting on her chest. She felt the chest spanning across her abdomen and the hips pressed against her thighs. Tracey opened her eyes—careful not to move—and could've sworn that she saw his close. She closed hers again. Nearly an hour later, he got up. She still pretended to sleep.

—∾—

Garrett kept flashing back to what it was like having Tracey under him all that next day. Clay had asked him thirty times when he got home that morning where he'd been and why he was smiling so much. Rett had answered thirty times that it was none of his damned business. Rett took a shower, got dressed and went to class, all with Tracey in his head. Even during lunch with Kim, he couldn't get her out of his mind.

Kim noticed and did the same thing she always did when she felt that he wasn't giving her enough attention. She told him she thought she was pregnant. Rett answered the same way he did every time she said it, and told her that she was not. But his heart wasn't in this monthly fight with his girlfriend of eighteen months. The phrase "bigger fish to fry" kept playing in the background.

—∾—

That night at Tracey's they didn't drink. They agreed that they didn't want to turn into alcoholics. Or rather Tracey suggested it, and Garrett went along with it. That was as good a reason as any.

When he walked in, Tracey was sitting on the floor working on her laptop at the coffee table, and John Coltrane's version of "My Favorite Things" was playing. Tracey never left her music on when he was there. She started to turn it off but Rett touched her arm. "No, leave it. I like this one."

She looked up, startled. "I thought you hated jazz."

Sometimes when Tracey was caught off-guard, she clamped her teeth over her lower lip. It was pretty damn hard for Rett to concentrate when she did that. "Truth is," Rett turned to a safer subject, "I don't know much about it. I do know that I like this song, though."

"It figures."

"Funny. It doesn't have anything to do with the Von Trapp family. I just like this song. I can get it better than a lot of that other stuff."

"Well, after classic jazz, I mean, Duke Ellington, Count Basie, it becomes an acquired taste. To get the hard-core, avant-garde styles, you kind of have to get schooled on where they come from and what the artists are trying to do, same as for any medium of expression. Listen to this." She scooted over to the stereo and changed CDs. "This song is one of my favorites and I hated it the first time I heard it. What you gotta look for is the sheer unexpectedness of it. It wants to take you by surprise, it wants you to know that it's off key at all times, but that every move is right for the music; it's all on purpose, methodical. It forces you to be at odds with it and to see how the voice of the piece is ambivalent and almost trapped by itself. Ornette Coleman, the guy who composed this, is a genius when it comes to this stuff. It's not exactly atonal, but, at the same time, it is. Coltrane's on this piece, also bringing his own special melancholy to the mix." She was silent through the rest of the song, then seemed to wait for his response. Rett smiled. Tracey noticed and said, "This song has never made me smile. I just stay still and kind of brace myself as I travel it like a roller coaster."

"That's poetic."

"Why were you smiling?"

"Because I can see it. You know, see what you see," he answered. He could also see the way the song made her feel. "I know that sounds corny, but I can. What's the name of it?"

She stopped the CD. " 'Lonely Woman.' "

Whatever they had shared was apparently over now.

Later, Tracey was bragging about her skill at playing cards. Rett decided he ought to show her how it was really done. She brought out a deck and they started off with poker. After graciously offering to deal, Rett decided to deal himself a hand just a shade better than Tracey's a couple of deals in a row. The phone rang, and Tracey, deep in thought, rose from the floor, still concentrating on the hands that had just been shown on the table. She picked up the phone.

"Hello?… Oh hey, Monica…y-no, no, I'm not doing anything. What's up?… I was planning to be there around eight…" Rett started to deal again but Tracey held up a hand to halt him. He shrugged and left the cards alone, sitting back in the armchair. "No, nothing before then… Okay, about one? Yeah, I can swing that. Uh-huh. Okay… Okay… See you tomorrow." When she hung up, Rett asked her what that was all about. "I've been volunteering at this center on the west side of town. That was one of the counselors. She wants me to help her get ready for her anniversary party tomorrow."

"That's really nice. I see that you do indeed have a soft side." Rett tried not to think about the fact that he had seen that side the night before and wouldn't mind experiencing it firsthand again.

"Not really," Tracey responded, sitting at the table again. "I just want to have something civic on my résumé."

"Girl, you don't fool me."

"No?" She smiled kind of bashfully and shook her head. "No, I guess I don't, even though you try to fool me." Garrett gave her his best "who me?" look. She went on. "For example, before I got on the phone, I was sitting here playing poker."

"Oh, really? And what do you think I was doin'?"

"Cheating."

Not born with any shame, Rett winked at her.

Chapter 8

Tracey stood for at least twenty minutes in front of the mirror in her bedroom. She wasn't used to this. In fact, she couldn't remember the last time she had actually gone to a party. Just getting dressed was taking forever. She didn't know what was appropriate. Jeans and a nice shirt? Slacks? Her tea-length dress with silver threads shooting through it? Who knew? Finally, she had to get on the phone and call Moni to ask what she was wearing.

"A little black dress." There went Tracey's standby. "What are you wearing?"

"I don't know. I can't find anything."

"I've seen your closet, honey. There's something up in there you can wear."

"I don't know, I just can't decide on what style I want."

"Well, I say wear something tasteful and sexy. It's gonna be some family and some friends, professional types, but everybody's real down to earth."

"If that's the case, I should wear some shorts and flip-flops."

"I won't let you in my house. It's dressy. Not formal, but dressy." With that she hung up the phone.

Tracey finally decided on an apple green, short-sleeved dress. The neckline scooped softly. It was long and fitted, but flowed around her whenever she turned. There was a calf-length green and violet cover over it. The ensemble, clearly Indian-influenced, had been a gift from her mother. She hadn't worn it yet. But God, it was pretty, and Tracey felt pretty in it. She donned some authentic Indian gold jewelry and parted her hair down the middle before slicking it back. She rolled her thick ponytail into a bun. With soft violet makeup, she almost looked like an Indian woman. Tracey smiled, and amended her thought: a very dark Indian woman.

She stared at herself, remembering her mother saying all the time when Tracey was a child that she was going to be a beautiful woman when she grew up. Tracey didn't know about beautiful, but that night, at least, she was almost there. Her eyes, dark brown, were wide-set and slightly slanted, her nose long and narrow like her mother's. Her lips were full, like her father's. Her cheekbones were high, which came from both sides of the family. Yes, she was fairly pleased with the way she looked, but she would never say beautiful.

Tracey was satisfied with her body. She wasn't fat, but she was no supermodel, either. She touched her tummy. It wasn't flat but slightly rounded. Her hips—her mother's hips—flared from her narrow waist. Good birthing hips, her grandmother would have called them. Her legs were long; those came from her father, and were well muscled from years of ballet. She had her mother to thank for her heavy bosom. On this night, all that was working for her. She really did look good, but even that was making her nervous.

Tracey grabbed her keys before she decided not to go at all and headed toward the front door. When she opened it, there was Garrett.

"You're going out?" He didn't even try to hide his disappointment.

"Just to a party my friend from the center's throwing. It's her anniversary."

"Oh, that's right."

"Yeah, I helped her get everything ready earlier. So what have you been up to today?"

"Not much. Just studying some. I was planning to get some more done tonight anyway."

He hadn't mentioned it, but she should have known he would come by. For a moment, she considered calling Moni. That was ridiculous. "Look, I don't think it's going to last that long. Probably no later than midnight. In fact, I'm sure I'll be home by midnight. If you want to hang out here and study, you can."

"Cool. I mean, if you really don't mind."

"No, I don't. There's an extra key in the medicine cabinet in case you need to leave or something."

"Thanks," he replied, seeing her to her own door. As she stepped out and smoothed her hair, he stood watching her.

"What?" she asked.

"You look incredible. You really do." His eyes slipped over her like heavy silk and she nearly tripped down the stairs as she left.

—∽—

It was near eight by the time she got there and her stomach was fluttering. Already there were cars parked in the driveway, on the grass in the front yard, and on the street in front of the house. The balloons on the mailbox were silver and navy blue, Monica and Maurice's wedding colors. Tracey parked and warily wound her way up the walk. There were way more people there than she had expected, although they had made enough food for a small army. Tracey neared the front door and got cold feet. She could see tons of people squeezed into the living room. She went around to the kitchen and knocked on the door.

Maurice opened it. He looked great in a pair of black slacks and a warm chocolate brown button-down. He leaned over to give Tracey a kiss on the cheek and let her in. He called for Moni. She wasn't far behind.

"Hey, Trace!" She came over to hug her friend. As she held on to Tracey, she whispered into her ear that she looked great. Immediately, Tracey asked if she was overdressed. "Yeah." Moni snickered. "But let's go make everybody else feel underdressed. Hold your head up. Square your shoulders. Take this." She put a bubbling flute in Tracey's hand and led her towards her living room. "Girl, let me tell you. I don't usually drink, but this punch Rico made has been calling to me for at least an hour and a half."

"And where are your children in all this?"

"Down in the basement playing video games, pool, doctor, and God knows what else with everybody else's kids. But I am not thinking about those children."

"Who's watching them?" Tracey inquired, aware that Moni's babies were never far from her mind no matter what she said.

"Nobody, honey," she whispered to Tracey. "I personally am hoping they pull a *Lord of the Flies*. That way we'll have fewer expenses."

"You're a mess."

"I know. Actually, my oldest, your buddy Tamia, is taking ownership of the younger kids. She'll come find me if she needs me." She stood back, taking another close perusal. "I'm not getting over this. You look so good, Tracey. Come in and meet my young eligible guests."

"Well, what do I look like the rest of the time? You haven't tried to introduce me to any eligible bachelors before now."

"Child, please. That doesn't have anything to do with anything! This was all a set-up, you see, something like a job fair, the job being finding Tracey's husband-to-be. Now, you can just pick one and stop being by yourself all the time."

Little did she know Tracey wasn't exactly by herself all the time. She thought of Garrett at her house at that very moment, studying and waiting for her. She bit her lip and surveyed the crowd gathered around. A wide range of ages from young up-and-comers to silver-haired retirees filled the room. They were all laughing and joking and singing and dancing and having a good time.

"Oh, and over here is my cousin Alex. He might as well be my big brother."

There standing before her was Alexander Burke.

Tracey smiled, genuinely happy to see him. "Hey, Alexander! Small world!"

"Tracey! I wasn't expecting to see you here." And this very stern, very serious man leaned over and hugged her hard with a big grin on his face. Tracey hadn't really seen him smile big like that before, and she was a sucker for a great smile. This one came from big, luscious, berry lips pulling back from two rows of the straightest, whitest teeth ever. His smile was really quite nice and Tracey was shocked this particular smile had never been shared with her before. But he was her advisor, substantially older than her, someone her father associated with from time to time... And—plainly speaking—he wasn't at all what she wanted.

"I wasn't expecting to see you, either," Tracey responded.

"I take it you two have already met." Moni preened, looking from one of them to the other. Tracey knew what she was thinking.

"Monica, Tracey's in one of my classes, and I'm her faculty advisor. Not only that, I was actually lectured by her father several times before and after I finished law school." Tracey was glad that he was the one to disabuse Moni of her amorous notions. She never would have listened if Tracey had told her there was no future to this particular match.

"Interesting." She raised an eyebrow. Obviously, Alexander's explanation of their relationship wasn't good enough for her.

Moni never missed anything. And, unfortunately, that meant that she had witnessed Tracey's first reaction to Alexander's smile. "My cup's empty," she whined. "And your glass is, too, Tracey."

"I can take a hint," Alexander said, taking her glass and Moni's cup to refill it.

"Don't start," Tracey warned her.

"But Tracey, just listen."

"Un-unh!"

"I'm serious. Granted, he's older than you, but hey, Rico's older than me."

"Four years as opposed to fourteen!"

"Is it really that many?" she asked, wrinkling her brow. Tracey's friend was certainly tipsy. "I keep thinking you're as old as me. Oh well. But you should consider it anyway. I saw that look you gave him. And it's *okay*. Sometimes a brother that black and sexy deserves a look like that."

"First of all, Maurice is so light, and his hair is so fine, people call him Rico like he's Spanish or something, so don't start—"

"Just 'cause Rico is somewhat pale," Tracey nearly choked on that one, "does not mean I can't appreciate a dark brother. It's apparent you can, too. And there are the added bonuses: the brother is smart, the brother is sweet, and the brother is paid."

"You can't hold your liquor well," Tracey told her disapprovingly.

"Maybe not," Moni giggled, "but I know this: he has had a thing for you for awhile."

Tracey was very smart sometimes. Smart enough to add two and two together. "If you knew that, then you knew he and I were familiar with each other before this party."

"I told you it was a setup," she announced brightly. Alex returned with their drinks.

"Don't let her have any!" Tracey motioned toward Moni. They all laughed and that set the mood for the night. Though Monica had to attend to all her guests, she, luckily, hovered around Tracey for much of the evening. She ensured that Tracey had enough to drink, to eat, and that she was forced to talk to every single person there. And in a suspicious way, Alexander was forever on hand to make Tracey feel at home, as well. She was too entertained that night to be annoyed.

Sometime during the night, the DJ broke out with an old-school song that just took everybody back, Earth, Wind, and Fire's "Groove Tonight." Even though the song was before Tracey's time, she and everybody up in the place knew it. Everybody got up to dance, partner or no partner. At the end of that song, someone played Al Green's "Let's Stay Together," and Moni grabbed her with one arm, singing the song. With arms linked they sang loudly and badly together until Maurice came up on the other side of Moni, dancing and singing, and Alex was next to Tracey doing the same. By the end of that one, Tracey had laughter pains shooting through her sides from those Al Green high notes Rico was attempting… and it was already half-past midnight. She nearly tripped over her dress. The crowd was definitely thinning out some, but she'd just had no clue that it was getting so late. Tracey excused herself to Moni, Maurice, Alex, and even the kids downstairs, then started to make her way home. Against her wishes, Alex walked Tracey to her car. He held her door open for her and closed it when she got in. He watched until she was down the street. What was she going to do about that?

When she got home she was still smiling. Her expression faltered slightly when she walked into her living room. Rett looked up at her expectantly. "Did you have a good time?" he asked. Barely noticeable was his glance at the clock on the wall that read 1:10.

"I did. I really did." She pulled off the shawl and took the binding from her hair, shaking it out. Probably not very attractive, but Tracey didn't care. She laid the items on the sofa and sat down. "How about you? Did you get anything accomplished?"

"A little, but I'm tired of it now. I'm up but I don't feel like studying."

"Well, I'm wide awake. You want to see what's on television?"

—〰—

For the longest, Tracey blamed him, blamed him for being so intrigued by their differences. That night, they watched a movie about mutant, killer vegetation eating its way down the West Coast and sucking the blood out of cheerleaders too buxom to run effectively. They lay down on their stomachs next to each other on her bed—the only television was in her bedroom—their sides touching as they nudged each other with their elbows and legs, saying something to the effect of, "I got you last."

71

Sometime during this high quality film, the smarter of the busty coeds found solace in the arms of a ranger. Solace had never looked so acrobatic. Embarrassed to say the least, Tracey turned her eyes away from the screen. It wasn't that she was a prude. It wasn't that she had some messed-up relationship with sex. It unnerved her to watch something like that with him.

Tracey could sense Garrett watching her. She looked over at him. "You know," he said, "I find this most interesting."

"What?"

"Nothing."

Garrett touched her hair. At first, she wanted to pull away quickly. She'd seen more than one white person touch the hair of a black woman and wipe their hands on their pants leg immediately after. At least if there was oil on the hair. There were other adverse reactions she'd seen as well. But he didn't do any of that. He just stroked it. Tracey waited, holding her breath, to see what he was about. "It's so soft."

"I do try." Tracey smirked. "It's a little nappy right now, though. For your understanding, let's say nappy means extra coarse. That's why I pulled it back. I need to get a perm, but my point is that it looks like steel wool at the roots right now."

"It does not look like steel wool," he argued, still running his fingers through it. She paused again, completely still, waiting for the electricity to go away, for the soft pads of his fingertips to stop running through her hair, rubbing her scalp. They didn't and he proceeded to massage her scalp then her neck, and the tingles spread down her arms. Her chest tightened.

"You're tense," he observed softly.

Tell me about it. She thought she'd kept that in her head, but his hushed laughter told her different. He got up on his knees beside her and pressed her down into the bed. He started working his hands against the taut muscles of her neck and back. Though his hands were more effective than those of any guy named Sven at any massage parlor her mother made Tracey accompany her to, those hands did not help to relax her in the least. Instead, she was being wound tighter and tighter and felt as if her whole body was just nerve endings. Everywhere he touched her, she jerked.

"I didn't know you were ticklish." Tracey could hear the smile in his soothing voice.

"I'm not usually," she answered, rising up on her elbows.

"You know," he told her a little later that night, "I get ashy."

She almost choked on her laughter. "What do you know about ash, Garrett?"

"I'm telling you, I get ashy. I've got lotion at home, in my car, in my locker. Why? Because I get ashy," he declared earnestly. He nodded to drive home his point. Tracey leaned over and bumped shoulders with him.

Chapter 9

Tracey was seeing Garrett nearly every night. He'd come after nine and always before ten. But once, he didn't show before ten or even ten-thirty. She didn't call his cell. She never did. She did text, but he didn't respond.

By eleven Tracey was angry. When he knocked around eleven-fifteen, she really, really considered not letting him in. But, she did and sat down with her arms crossed, not saying a word. When he asked what was wrong, she told him she didn't appreciate him coming over so late.

"You haven't minded before." He looked genuinely puzzled.

"Well, I do now. You can't just come over here any time you want to. Before ten is fine, but later than that…" He blinked. "I mean, I could have been sleeping or, I don't know, I could have had some other late-night company."

He stared at her for a while and she wanted to die. She couldn't tell what he was thinking. She bit her bottom lip. His gaze lowered, his thick, brown lashes fluttering down over his lion eyes. Then he expelled his breath and took off his jacket. "I hate to ask you this, but I came over as soon as I got out of intramurals. We finished late, and I really need a shower. Do you mind?"

Damn, damn, damn. She'd known he was going to be playing soccer that night. "Go ahead," she answered, thanking God she hadn't given her humiliation away.

He went into her bedroom and a beam of light briefly shone in the doorway until she heard the bathroom door close and the shower start. She pulled on the headphones lying on the coffee table and closed her eyes, wishing that he was not naked in her home, wishing that when he came out he would just go so she could be alone until she didn't feel as if she had the hormones of a sixteen-year-old.

She didn't hear him come out, but rather smelled him. He smelled warm, warm and like her when she got out of the shower. She thought of him using her soap as she slowly opened her eyes. Then Tracey burst into delirious laughter. He was wearing her very satin, very feminine ice blue robe.

She raised her hand high in the air and said, "Question." He rolled his eyes. "I just want to know why you're wearing that. You could have used the big, navy terry cloth one hanging up in there. It certainly would have been manlier."

"I don't see how you can say that. This one's got a dragon on the back. I feel like Bruce Lee," he insisted and assumed a blessedly modest position that looked something like a crane with a broken leg…or maybe hip. Tracey started to laugh from deep within. His gaze fell gently on her face and he knelt in front of her. His strong male scent mixed with her soap to make her dizzy.

"You know, when you laugh, you get weak and helpless and beautiful. I'd probably steal your books again tonight if I hadn't already." Then he got up and walked to her kitchen. She heard him taking something out of the refrigerator.

Rebelling against the tickle that had arrived in her stomach, she muttered, "He sits in my favorite chair, he eats my food, and now he's wearing my clothes. He's getting to be a regular fixture."

"I heard that," he called to her in a sing-song voice.

"Of course you did," Tracey groaned.

Later that week she waited for him, anxious to see how he had fared on an argument he'd prepared for the past couple of nights. She heard his SUV pull into the drive and opened the door even before he got to the porch. "Hey." Tracey beamed like an idiot as she opened the door wide to let him in. His lips pulled downward as he headed for her favorite chair and sat down. He closed his eyes and sucked in a long, tired breath. She waited, even holding her own breath, for him to let it go. She went to sit on the arm of the chair beside him but didn't touch him. She didn't do anything, just waited. When he was still silent, she rose. "You want something from the kitchen?"

Without opening his eyes, he nodded. "Water, if you don't mind." Tracey went into the kitchen, got a glass and rinsed it out, watching the water splash into the glass and out again, wondering what was bothering him. She put ice in the water, went back into the living room, and handed it to him. She watched him drink deeply.

"What's wrong?"

"Nothing." It was a lie. They both knew it. Standing there, Tracey propped her hands on her hips and waited some more. For someone who was always telling her to "talk about it," sometimes it was an absolute art getting him to talk about what was on his mind. So she waited. It was all she could do.

After a prolonged silence his gaze rose again to meet hers and he said, "Me and Kim got into it after my oral argument."

"You went to see her after?" The question and hurt were out before she could cut them off.

"No, Tracey, I didn't," he answered. "She was there when I got out. She walks up to me and says she's got me a gift for finishing my argument and tells me that she and my mom picked it out."

"Your mom's in town?" He shook his head at this question.

78

"No," Tracey breathed and put her hand in front of her lips. "She didn't."

"She did. Drove to my parents' this morning. Says that they went to a bridal boutique." He finished his water, then stood and walked towards her window. He pulled back the curtain and peered out into the darkness. She wondered briefly if anyone could see him there. He turned to her. "A little pushy, isn't it?"

"Yes."

He went over and sat on the sofa, leaned over, head bent into his palms, elbows resting on his knees. Tracey eased down next to him, not knowing how to help. He seemed so upset, so trapped. She was pretty sure he wanted out of the relationship but couldn't quite figure out how to go about it, especially with the way his family treated this Kim person. Helplessly, Tracey reached out and slid her hand into his soft, brown hair. She didn't expect him to turn to her. She didn't expect him to hug her to him so tight she had to catch her breath. She didn't expect him to press his nose into her neck and stroke her hair. She didn't expect him to start nibbling at her jugular, and she definitely didn't expect to lean back and let him. Tracey had the impression that everything was in slow motion. She felt removed from herself with her back braced against the arm of the sofa and the soft insides of her forearms pressing down on his shoulders. Her hands balled into tight fists because she didn't want to touch him, didn't want to let him know that she was accepting this. She heard her pulse roaring in her ears, felt his against her skin.

Garrett moved from her throat to nibble her jaw, then the tip of her chin. His eyelids were lowered as he concentrated deeply on what he was doing. As he laid those kisses on her face, that concentration slowly unfurled her fists, slowly drew her into what she wanted. When he finally pressed expert lips to hers, that slow motion she had felt in the beginning turned into flashes: him kissing her, her hands in his hair, his fingers pulling open the buttons on her blouse, his lips and tongue teasing her in the very center of her chest, her grasping him, bringing him to her breasts. But that didn't help because by then she could feel her pulse beating everywhere under her skin. Tracey squirmed beneath him, understanding that the heat of his mouth wasn't going to be enough. She knew there was only one right way to end it—and there was no way in hell she was going do that. Abruptly, she sat up and began to arrange her clothes.

For a long moment he just stared forward, breathing heavily. "I'm sorry," he said finally.

"For what?" Tracey didn't look at him.

"I don't know."

After that night, they didn't touch anymore. At all. Period. Always, Tracey wondered if he was going to make a move, but he never did. In fact, he seemed to have forgotten all about it while she couldn't get it off her mind. Once, he came over after intramural football. His hair was ruffled, there was a small cut above his eye and he was wearing those old navy shorts. She had never seen anyone so devastatingly sexy.

Though he played football, he didn't have football legs. He had tennis legs, long, slender, well-muscled and tanned. His already warm-toned skin with its deep summer tan gave him a dark buttery glow that just emphasized every single line and cut of his body. Tracey's attention span, as far as studies went, was nonexistent that night. Garrett laughed and said he was never going to study with her again because she lacked focus. Then he asked if she had been drinking without him.

Tracey wondered what it would take to get him to kiss her again, since it had taken so little encouragement the first time he touched her. Not that she wanted him to.

—m—

Rett rolled over and pulled the warm body closer to him. Playfully, he planted a kiss on the warm neck in front of him, and that woke him out of his sleep. He knew this body and this smell. And he had just been about to call it by someone else's name. Kim moaned his name in her sleep and put her hand over his, lacing their fingers together. That was sweet. Kim was sweet. He loved Kim. Yep. His eyes popped open. It had to be two-thirty in the morning. Slowly he tried to disentangle himself.

"You can't sleep, honey?" Kim asked, turning over. Her cheek was red from where she had been lying on the pillow. Her eyes were half-closed with long silky brown lashes. Her dark curls were a soft halo around her head. Rett loved Kim.

"Naw, babe, but you get some sleep."

"Okay," she whispered and let her eyes close again.

She didn't deserve this, Rett thought. He went into the kitchen and grabbed a soda. Then he grabbed a beer, too. He was only going to drink that as a last resort. However, he didn't make it back to the bedroom. He stopped instead in front of the TV. He grabbed the remote and plopped down on the couch. His eyes barely saw the flashes on the screen. Instead, he had a woman on his mind. A black woman. Things had gone way too far that last time. Sure, it was one thing to flirt. Everybody does that. But his relationship with Tracey was getting out of control. Then again, why couldn't he just have what he wanted? Really. Why couldn't he just have it? One time? Nobody had to know. Hell, she wanted it that way.

"What the hell are you doing up?" Clay asked on his way to the kitchen.

"Couldn't sleep."

"Your ass never sleeps. Well, at least not here." Clay gave him a sideways glance and sat down next to Rett. "Kim here?"

"Yeah."

"She's been here almost a solid month."

"Yeah."

"Just saying."

"Look, Clay, she's always over here."

"Yeah, but for a while there you weren't."

"What's chapping your ass?"

"Nothing much, really. It's just that when I was home last I went shooting with Charles and his dad and your dad." Clay hesitated. "You know Charles has a big mouth."

Rett didn't say anything, just went still. There was something Clay was trying to tell him, and he was guaranteed not to like it. "And just what was Charles letting his mouth run about?"

"Well, he basically was saying that you'd been away from the house a lot lately. When they made the assumption you were out with Kim, he made sure quick, fast and in a hurry that they knew you weren't out with Kim. He also made some comments about who you *were* out with."

"And who was that?"

"I don't know. And, for that matter, I don't know how he would know, either. All I'm sayin' is that he made it sound like you were goin' out with somebody you ought not."

"And how did I come up in the first place?"

"Aww, Rett, you know how it is. We were just shooting the breeze."

"It's nobody's business what I do, when I do it, and who I do it with."

"Hey, man, don't get pissed at me. I just thought you ought to know." Clay stood, getting ready to go back to bed. "I don't care what you do. I'm for real. Whatever it is, man, it's cool with me. But you might want to watch yourself."

Rett immediately felt apologetic but didn't say anything. He just watched his friend walk to his bedroom. That was a warning. Ever since they had been kids, Charles had done one thing or another to get at him. Hell, sometimes Rett returned the favor. But this was not cool. He wouldn't put it past Charles to follow him one night.

As Clay disappeared down the hall, Kim appeared in Rett's jersey. Charles was behind her.

"What is this? A party?" Charles asked, grinning. He was wearing only sweatpants. Rett noted absently that Charles still outsized him, as he always had, but Rett had never lost a fight to him.

"Naw, I couldn't sleep," Rett answered tightly.

"I just came to see where you went," Kim added, a lot more alert than when he'd left her. And she sounded guilty, too. Rett knew her too well. And he knew his *friend* too well, also.

"Well, you found him," Charles said and smacked her hard on the backside. "Why don't you go and get me some water while you're up." And there she went. Charles turned his attention to Rett then. He wanted to see if that little show had hit its mark.

It hadn't. Or if it had, Rett wasn't about to show it. He stood finishing his soda and opening his beer. "I think I'm sleepy now. You don't have to send Kim on—she always knows how to find her way back."

Charles said to his retreating back, "I hope you have a good time this weekend huntin' with Big. We sure had a good time last weekend."

Rett didn't answer. He just went to bed, barely noting that Kim was taking her sweet time to follow.

Chapter 10

Tracey was in a rotten mood, she really was. When Moni called that morning and asked why she hadn't come down to the center, she explained that she just wasn't feeling up to it. Moni asked why. Tracey told her she didn't know. Moni invited her to a matinée movie and lunch with her and her kids to shake off her doldrums. Tracey agreed because she needed the company, anything to get her mind off things.

Tracey got to the mall way too early. She slowly wandered to the area where the theater was located and eased down onto a hard bench positioned in front of a long wooden planter. Crowded shrubs strained against each other above and around her head. She closed her eyes and envisioned the greenery reaching out to wrap around her, hiding her in its lushness. When she was little, she'd imagined this kind of thing all the time. She thought that if she closed her eyes and concentrated on being part of the surroundings, making herself small, no one would notice her. Tracey would be invisible. But that was when she was a kid. Most of her friends were white, and most black kids didn't like her anyway.

Tracey hadn't seen Rett in more than two weeks. She didn't know why or why she should care. She did, though. She cared a lot and didn't know what she could do about it. He hadn't been by the house once, nor had he so much as called or texted. She'd seen him on campus a couple of times but he hadn't acknowledged her. All kinds of things crossed her mind. Maybe he had made some sort of bet and getting her to kiss him was the end of it. Maybe he had freaked out because he'd kissed her and couldn't deal with seeing her again. Maybe he just didn't care. But, dammit, she cared! Tracey hated him right then.

So when she saw him, she felt something move all over her, making her skin crawl, making her entire body warm, making her think she was losing her mind all over again. And after all that, she felt like the proverbial fish in a barrel. Garrett. He looked alive, healthy, and well. She checked his arms. They looked completely capable of lifting a telephone receiver. He was walking in through a mall entrance behind a less than beautiful girl. She had to be his girlfriend, Kim. Tracey knew she was because he had described her. In his description he was much nicer than Tracey ever would have been, though.

She wanted to be angry instead of hurt. She didn't want to watch him. But she just couldn't help herself. A person who has been starved can't help eating. Besides, she was only doing what she had always done, really: watch him and want him. There wasn't any more denying it. Whether she would ever act on it didn't matter anymore. Tracey hadn't slept the entire time he was gone. At night when she was up studying and listening to jazz, he was on her mind. She caught herself lingering around the law library. She dialed half his number and hung up. She didn't know what to do.

Tracey wondered if he would see her, and if he did see her, what he would do. She didn't know what she wanted him to do. She didn't know what *she* would do. The worst of it was that she didn't even know when this thing had happened to her. She didn't remember getting attached. And at that point, she didn't remember much of anything, except for the fact that she had never in her life been kissed the way he'd kissed her.

Maybe her thoughts of Garrett were so strong he sensed them. He glanced toward her and her heart started to tick like a bomb. Then he glanced away and that bomb exploded. How could he not have seen her? Did he see her and just ignore her?

If that was the case, the right thing for her to do would be to just roll up on him and tell him what she thought about his behavior. Tracey was no one's dirty little secret. Oh damn, that wouldn't be right either. Even if he did see her, he wasn't doing anything different than they had done before. He wasn't doing anything she hadn't asked him to do. He wasn't treating her any different than she had treated him. She started to massage her temples. Her emotional reaction was giving her a headache.

He checked the movie listings above the ticket box, and Tracey wondered what he wanted to see. Ironically, she knew his tastes. But because they had never been out in public together, she didn't have the slightest idea how he was on a date. Would he want to see whatever she wanted to see? Probably. He was always asking what she wanted to do or eat or watch. He wasn't happy with Kim before, but was he now? Had they worked everything out? Did he love her? Tracey couldn't stand the speculation. She had lost control.

She closed her eyes and hummed but couldn't distract herself. She opened her eyes again. They were standing in the long movie line. As he stood there, worry caused a tightness around his eyes. He couldn't seem to decide whether he wanted to keep his hands inside or outside his pants pockets.

When he rested his big warm hand on the crook of Kim's neck, she did not move into his touch. Tracey wondered what sex was like between them, and she felt herself getting sick again. That one night she had barely been able to resist his touch.

Then he walked toward Tracey, or rather in the direction of the concession stand. He had to pass her to get to it. She sank back into the bench and lowered her head, concentrating on the bushes and being part of them and hoping Garrett didn't see her. He passed close enough for Tracey to smell his cologne, a scent that always reminded her of amaretto and incense. His brow was creased and he was chewing at his lower lip. He passed her again carrying sodas and Kim gave him a pretty smile when he handed her one.

Moni approached with Gary, Lena, and Tam. "Tam, go buy the tickets and take your brother and sister to get something from the concession stand. Get me and Tracey some nachos." She handed her oldest daughter some money, then sat next to Tracey.

"So, Trace, Alex told me you agreed to go to dinner with him tonight."

"Yeah, but that's because we were supposed to meet yesterday morning but he got tied up."

"Uh-huh."

Tracey watched Garrett disappear into the theater. At least she knew where she stood with Alex, even if his interest in her was completely inappropriate. She decided she wanted to look *hot* when she went out with Alex.

—m—

"Rachel's sounds good to me. You ready?"

"Yeah," Rett answered. "Let's go."

When he and Kim arrived at the restaurant Rett requested a table. The thirty-minute wait marked the beginning of his irritation. Irritation amplified to something like rage when Tracey McAlpine brushed right past him. He turned to look at her and noticed her stop in her tracks. But she didn't turn around. She just went on in with…with Alexander Burke! And not only was she out with that jackass, they walked up to the hostess and asked for a table and got one right away.

Tracey wore a tight-fitting short black dress and looked like a guy's first wet dream. Not the nicest analogy Rett could think of, but he was decidedly pissed she was with Burke and didn't seem to have missed him at all. It had been more than three weeks since he'd seen her, since he'd talked to her, looked at her, touched her. And *still*, seeing her was like a guy's first wet dream. A shock to the system, for sure, but something that felt so good. Damn, he was supposed to be getting over this. He was supposed to be getting over her.

But she was so *sexy*. Before, when he saw her get all dressed up for that party, he'd thought she was gorgeous, but this? Her hair hung thick and straight, teasing her shoulders, which were bare in the sleeveless dress. Her breasts, her *perfect* breasts, were pushed up high, making two perfect semicircles just above a neckline that wasn't real low, but was definitely low enough. Her legs were so long, so toned. His body tightened painfully when he thought about folding the long limbs around his waist. Why did his shy, reserved Tracey look like that? Why was she with Burke? Why did she look like that *with* Burke?

91

"Where are you?" Kim asked by his side.

"I was just thinking about school, that's all."

"Oh."

Their table ended up being on the other side of the restaurant from Tracey and Burke, but Rett could still see them. He watched her giggle and put her hand over Burke's forearm. She'd never done that with him. He watched her cross her legs and tried to recall when he'd ever seen her in heels so high. Delectable.

Someone yelled at him for not listening. And now all he wanted to do was yell at her. "Tracey!"

"Who's Tracey?"

Rett went silent. He hadn't meant to say her name out loud, especially not in front of Kimberly.

"Rett, who is Tracey?"

He could have said right then, "Tracey is in my tax study group." He could have said it and everything would have been fine. In fact he could've said, "Tracey's a friend of my sister's. I just met her today and she really pissed me off. You know how my sister's friends are." That would have worked real well, considering that Kim hated his sister. But Rett didn't say that, either. He didn't want to save himself from this argument. In fact, he needed this argument more than Kim needed to teach kindergarten and have a little Brownie or Cub Scout of her very own. So, he didn't say anything.

"I'm not going to keep asking you. I'm sick and tired of you treating me like I am here only when it's convenient for you. I am not your toy. You can't play with me when you feel like it and ignore me when you don't. We've been together way too long for this, and I want to know: Who is Tracey?"

Rett remained silent and focused over her shoulder at the very woman she was asking about. He waited for Kim's full fury to take over. He wondered what this same conversation would be like with Tracey. She was probably too poised and too sophisticated for hysterics.

"Rett, I'm talking to you! I want to know who Tracey is and what—"

"So where were you and Charles coming from today?" That was sure to shut her up. Maybe he didn't feel like fighting after all. She folded her hands in her lap.

"Kimberly, let's just have a nice dinner. We've been fighting a lot lately. You and I both know things have changed. That doesn't mean we have to fight."

She nodded and said in a rush, "I talked to your mom today and she said she saw…"

At the end of the night, Kim let him out in front of his building. He leaned in the window to give her a kiss before she left. He could tell she didn't want to leave, but he slapped the hood of her car and she drove off. Up in the apartment he grabbed a six-pack from the fridge and sat watching late night talk shows featuring yelling and paternity tests.

—❦—

Four hours later, still wired, Rett picked up the phone and called his sister. "Angie, get up!"

"What the hell? Rett?" a deep, sleepy feminine voice asked.

"Yeah, it's me."

"What time is it?"

"Three-thirty."

"In the…what?"

"Three-thirty in the morning. I woke you?"

"No, honey, it's okay. I just laid down, really. What's going on?"

"Nothing."

"Rett, babe, you don't call me at this time of night for nothing. Can't sleep?"

"No."

"Well, come on over."

"No, you were in bed. 'Sides, my car's in the shop."

"I'll come over there. Kim's not there, is she?"

"No."

"Good, then I'll definitely come over." However, when Angie showed up at his door in flannel pajamas only fifteen minutes later—she lived a few blocks away—she said, "You have got to stop watching trash."

She cracked open a beer and took a swig before plopping on the sofa next to him with her legs folded beneath her. She asked him to talk to her, but he didn't.

Chapter 11

All Tracey knew was that the night after she went to dinner with Alex, Garrett called her. "Listen." His voice was soft and scratchy. "I want to come over."

"I'm not sure what I'm supposed to say to that."

"We need to talk."

"We needed to talk a week or so ago. We don't need to talk anymore."

"We do."

"Then come over."

"I can't. My truck's in the shop. I thought they'd finish today, but it won't be ready until Monday."

"Oh, so your SUV's been in the shop for two weeks? I suppose you left your cell phone in there all this time, too."

"No, Tracey."

"So you just can't make it here. Oh, well."

"You don't understand. Tracey, baby, I need to talk to you, to be with you. I can't stay here when all I can think about is you."

In five seconds flat he had moved her from being extraordinarily pissed to holding the phone away from her ear, clutching her stomach. He'd called her *baby*. *Baby*. She put the phone back to her ear. "Okay…"

"Could you come and get me?"

She drew in her breath and held it. That would mean going to his apartment. She knew he lived in one of the larger complexes in town, and she knew he had two roommates. Things were okay when it came to the privacy of her place. This was a whole new ball game. Her stomach began to sour. There was no way they wouldn't be seen. And it was only nine o'clock. But Tracey reminded herself that they hadn't done anything wrong. There was no reason to worry. They were, after all, just friends studying together. "What's your apartment number?"

She heard him expel his breath on the other end. "It's 415."

To avoid the appearance of a girl in a rush, she took her time driving. She also didn't want to vomit, a definite possibility, so she circled the block. She finally got there and stepped out of her car. It was late October and the night was mild, though heavy wind shook the trees. The moon looked like a pearl tucked into a slit in the sky, only half of it showing. Tracey breathed in deeply, then entered the building. Students were scattered around the lobby, but no one turned to stare accusingly at her as she had imagined in her car. She knew it was silly, but the nightmare wouldn't go away. In the elevator, she rattled the keys in her hands. When the doors opened, all she saw were the big, gold numbers, four, one, and five, looming at her.

She stood outside his door for a moment, then heard another door open down the hall. She went ahead and knocked, realizing she would look stranger just standing there. It opened and Tracey found herself staring at a short, frat-looking guy.

"Hi, I'm here to pick Rett up," she said professionally. Quickly, she added, "We're studying."

"Come on in," he invited jovially. Inside, she immediately noticed how loud it was. The TV was loud, the stereo was loud, even the posters were loud, especially that one of Lynyrd Skynyrd. He pointed Tracey in the direction of what might have been a sofa with a camouflage tarp draped over it as a slipcover, and knocked the clothes off it before they sat down. "He'll be out in a minute. He just got out of the shower."

"Oh, okay." She held out her hand, not knowing what else to do. "Tracey McAlpine."

He shook her hand. "Clay Michaels."

Awkward silence. "So, which of Rett's classes are you in?"

That threw her. They didn't have any class together. There was no way to bluff around this. Tracey tried anyway. She started to answer, then stumbled to come up with a lie. "We don't have a class together," she admitted reluctantly.

He raised his eyebrows, but let it go. "So which class are y'all studying for?"

"Uh, Rett is tutoring me in Employee Rights." Such a lie. She began to wonder about her morality. Lord, she began to worry about her soul. She shrugged it off. Her mother was always praying for her soul so she figured she'd be all right.

"Oh, I get it."

The front door opened and a very tall, very blue-eyed guy came in. Immediately, his eyes met hers, and it wasn't a nice sensation. "Hey, Big Man," he greeted Clay. "Where's our ex-roommate?"

"Getting dressed."

"Where's he going?" The guy was still looking at her. She resisted the urge to wave.

"To study." Clay nodded to me. He bit the inside of his cheek and Tracey wondered at the nervous gesture.

The newcomer still didn't speak to her. "Oh." He went to a closed door in the hallway. "Rett, boy, your daddy ain't here, so I feel I oughta—"

"Ought to what?" Tracey heard from the other side of the door.

"Give it up, man. Your study partner's here. We know you're *studying*. At least I hope to hell you're studying because if you're not—"

"Hey, man, we got guests," said Clay, trying to smile.

"Oh, excuse me." The Viking fixed her with a stare that made her uneasy.

"Come on, man." Clay stood up in front of her, blocking his roommate's view.

Her heart thumped hard in her chest. But then Garrett walked towards her, and her breath caught. His yellow eyes were on her, commanding her heart to beat faster.

"You ready, Tracey?" He stood behind her and laid a hand on the back of her neck. His warm palm and fingers flexed gently on her throat. He rubbed softly, then slid his fingers down over her shoulder. She was under the impression at the time that her shoulder would fall off if he didn't stop touching her. And he didn't. Tracey looked up at him. "Yeah," she answered, trying to read his stormy amber eyes, afraid to move. "I'm ready." She could see his jaw twitch as he clenched his teeth and his eyes blazed at her. He was positively glowering. Tracey didn't know how to act because she had never seen him that way. He came around the sofa and offered her his hand. She took it and stood, then headed towards the door. Garrett followed her, leaving a cool silence behind him.

"Well I'll be a damn—" She heard Charles hiss behind them.

Tracey didn't hear it clearly. All Tracey knew was that he'd said something derogatory. For a split second, she was trapped between saying something to him, standing up for herself the way a proud black person would, and fear about what would happen when she did. But before she knew it, before she even had a chance to react, Garrett had turned around and was emanating anger, arms wide, fists clenched. He didn't say anything, just pointed at Charles, who turned as white as a sheet. Then Garrett said in an even, soft voice, "You show some respect when I bring a friend to this house. Especially this one. Or I swear to God I will mess you up." Then he turned and ushered her out the door. They got onto the elevator in silence. They got off the elevator and Tracey walked ahead of him out of the building. In the car they said nothing. Back at her place, she finally caught her breath and stopped shaking. And, eventually, they spoke.

"I'm sorry about that." He sat forward in her favorite chair. His hands were clasped and hanging between his widespread knees. His eyes on her were intense.

"Which part?" She sat back on the sofa with her legs crossed and her arms folded. She felt cold and impotent. She felt rage and devastation. What had just happened had left her world feeling ugly and raw.

"Charles is a jackass."

"I gathered as much," she said dryly. "So that's all you're sorry for?"

"Yes. You had to know they suspected something."

"There's nothing to suspect, actually. But now, now that you put on that little show, there's no telling what they're thinking."

"Do you care?"

Tracey lowered her eyes. "I don't care about your roommates, I don't. It's just…"

"Yeah?" He raised an eyebrow at her.

This was the point at which she changed the subject, revealing a little more than she wanted. "I saw you at the movies with Kim."

"I know. I was the one trying to figure out whether it was legal to say hello to you in a mall or not!"

"Whatever, Garrett," was her very mature response. "You didn't say anything to me because your girlfriend was there and maybe 'cause you knew you were wrong."

He ignored this and gave her a look. It was almost "the look." There he was switching modes in the middle again. Tracey could have sworn someone had run a feather up her spine. "Maybe I haven't cleanly cut ties because I need something or someone worth cutting them for."

"That's ridiculous," Tracey countered with more bravado than necessary. "If you don't want her, then you shouldn't be in a relationship with her." He leaned over, picked up the fetish he'd been so fascinated with that first night, and began stroking it as he considered something. He was making Tracey nervous. She had thought that feeling she'd had in the pit of her stomach would go away as soon as she got home, but it hadn't, and he was just making it worse.

"Maybe so." He put the fetish down. "I guess we're goin' to talk now."

"Isn't that what you came here to do?" Tracey folded her arms across her chest.

He grinned at her, actually grinned at her, at a time like this. "No, but I guess we need to do that first."

She swallowed. Tracey had been planning what she would say to him for a while. She had planned to read him the riot act, back and forth, up and down, side to side. She was going to light into him in a way he'd never experienced before, and yet here he was, grinning at her and spouting innuendo. She couldn't think of anything to say.

"I suppose I should explain why I haven't been around."

"Do what you want." She was proud of her nonchalance.

"Listen to me. I'm not goin' to lie to you. I spent the past couple of weeks mostly with Kim."

"Yeah."

"First, I want to tell you, I didn't have sex with her."

Tracey's face burned. "That's really none of my business."

"It is your business, and you know why, Trace," he countered. "What I want to tell you is that I spent the past couple of weeks with Kim to see…" He didn't go on.

"To see what, Garrett? What did you spend those *celibate* weeks with Kim to see? What were you seeing that stopped you from calling me or coming by out of common courtesy?" And when did he begin owing her that? It was the first time she'd actually wondered. Tracey really didn't have any right to ask him any of those questions. She was halfway expecting him to say something to that effect.

"I was seein' if I could stay away from you."

Wrong answer. This was the first time they had talked to each other this way, and she could actually feel the beating of her heart in all her extremities. "Well, now you know you can. So why don't you?"

"Is that what you think?"

"You seem to have managed just fine."

"If I had managed, I wouldn't have driven by your place every night. I wouldn't have gone to the ANM every night hoping you would show up there. I wouldn't have followed members of your study group around the library hoping they would lead me to you. Hell, I wouldn't have begged you to come get me tonight." Tracey didn't mention that he'd never actually begged her to do anything. Rett was not the begging sort. "What I'm telling you, Trace, is that I can't stay away from you. And I have this feeling that it may be the same for you."

"That's pretty conceited of you."

"Deny it," he dared her. She hated when he was like this. So aggressive, so smug, so…sexy.

Tracey loved diversionary tactics. "You hungry?"

"No, but I haven't eaten all day so I guess I should have something."

She got up and went into the kitchen. He followed her.

"Why aren't you eating?"

"I don't know, I guess I've just had a lot of stuff on my mind."

She glanced at him, then opened her refrigerator and stared, not really seeing the contents. She just needed somewhere else to focus her attention. She grabbed a beer.

"Can I get one?"

She tossed him a bottle. He tapped the top before he opened it. He still stood there staring at her. Staring at her and drinking. "What is it?"

"What?"

"Why do you keep staring at me?"

"I can't help it."

Tracey ignored this. "What do you want," she hesitated, "to eat?"

He paused for a millisecond. His eyes were lazy on her. He smiled. "Doesn't matter. Like I said, I'm not really hungry."

Tracey thought about the pre-packaged tortellini in her cabinet. Quick and easy. The problem was that

Garrett was standing beneath the cabinet and she wasn't too keen on being close to him right then. The way he watched her was downright feral.

"When you asked me if that was all I wanted to apologize for—Charles, that is—was there something else you had in mind?"

"Nope," she answered.

"Was it my absence?"

Tracey shrugged.

"Did you miss me?"

She bit down hard on the inside of her cheek.

"Was it the way I touched you?" he prodded gently. She didn't look at him. Her stomach tied itself in knots and she developed an obsessive desire to wipe the blurry spots off the side of her chrome toaster.

"No."

"I think it was." His voice was low, caressing. "I think the way I touched you made you nervous, the same way I'm makin' you nervous right now."

"You're not making me nervous," Tracey retorted. And, as if to prove it, she decided to go for the pasta. She didn't care how close she got to him because she was not one to back down from a challenge. She should have been. When she brushed against him, her breath caught for the nth time that night and her eyes sought his.

"You're surprised?"

She could barely speak. Her whole body sang with electricity and she thought she was going to melt into a warm puddle any second. She stared at him a tense moment and finally said, "How long have you been like that?"

"I think maybe ever since I met you. I know I've been like this ever since that night. You remember, don't you, Tracey? The next morning we woke up and pretended to be asleep. Or that other night, the night when you finally let me touch you after I had waited for so long. The same night I wanted to make love to you so bad I could taste you."

Mute, Tracey just stood there with an ache and fire building between her legs.

He moved closer to her and she waited for him to kiss her. "Can I, Tracey?" he begged. She looked up into his beautiful eyes. "Can I taste you?" Tracey began to shake her head, but he didn't allow her to. He chose that time to kiss her. His mouth was so warm, too warm, hot. His hands, however, were cool. He laid one on her back beneath her sweater, and the other beneath the waist of her skirt. He was trying his luck at a surprise attack. It was working. His soft tongue flicked, then teased. His lips sucked softly on hers. His teeth nibbled gently, and then he sat back and looked at her expectantly.

Tracey finished the rest of her beer, then, spying his on the counter behind her, finished that one, too.

He grinned slyly. "What are you afraid of, Trace? I'm not gonna hurt you."

"You sound like a pedophile. 'Come on in, little girl. I've got some candy.' " He laughed again—she was glad to know she was amusing him—but Tracey was a little terrified. "I mean, do you really want to do this?"

He pressed the whole length of his body against hers. "Can't you tell?"

"No, that's not what I mean, I mean, you know what I mean...I mean this is not... You've got a girl-friend."

"Come on, Tracey. Kim is sleeping with Charles, for one thing, and I don't even care. And why is that? Because I don't want her. To be honest, I haven't wanted anybody but you for God knows how long, and I know you want me."

"I don't," she lied. He responded by licking a moist line from her collarbone to her throat up all the way to her chin and over her lips. Tracey felt like she was having a heart attack. There was no other explanation... well, maybe a stroke. A chill ran right up her spine, she could barely stand, and her breath was ragged. Something had to give. She tried to ignore him, just not respond. Maybe then he would leave her alone. No such luck. His hand tangled in her hair and he kissed her again, making her altogether dizzy.

This time, she had the strength to pull away. "Listen." He started in on her neck. Her neck was her weak spot and he seemed to know it. "What'll we say?"

"Nothing, it's our business." He did not let up on her neck and she found herself squirming. Tracey was not being very assertive. She didn't *want* to be assertive. She wanted everything he wanted. She wanted to be a consenting adult. "Don't make me stop," he murmured, "please don't."

Tracey didn't answer him. She just led him by the hand out of the kitchen and into her bedroom. Inside, she turned and slipped his shirt over his head. Garrett didn't hesitate to put his arms up and allow her. When she dropped it to the floor, her lips pressed to the chest she had wanted to touch ever since she'd first seen him without a shirt. Her fingers caressed the hard muscles lined up and down his stomach, and electricity seemed to leap from them into her hands as she felt them contract involuntarily at her touch. And those arms, those beautiful arms. Tracey slowly sank her teeth into the firm flesh, running her tongue over the skin trapped between them. She crawled over him as he lay back on her bed. Then she slipped his pants down his long, pretty legs. She decided that they were actually more like soccer legs than tennis legs, either one just as appealing. She slid back up towards him, letting her hands explore the silky down covering him. She stopped midway and gave him a delicate lick.

He groaned and his hips flexed.

She slithered up his body and kissed him softly, . tentatively. Without hesitation, his lips responded to hers and his hands clasped her face to his. Again, fear roiled hotly in her stomach. He rolled on top of her, and there was nothing tentative about it.

Slowly he started to undo her shirt, and that's when she started talking, "I cannot believe we're doing this. I don't even—"

"Quiet, Tracey," he grated and slipped the shirt off her shoulders. He unbuttoned her pants and pulled the zipper down. "Lift up," he said in a sort of doctorly tone. She closed her eyes. He pulled her jeans and panties down. Then he ran his hands reverently over her legs.

"You have gorgeous legs, baby. You should wear skirts every day."

He slipped up her body, kissing her belly, then the skin above the line of her bra while he pressed his thumb into her heat. "Scratch that. Your whole body is so sexy, you should stay naked." He reached over to his pants, which were lying on the floor, and pulled a condom out of his pocket.

"I see you came prepared."

"I haven't come at all yet," he returned huskily. He kissed her stupid while a hand slipped between her legs to promote liquid acquiescence.

When she moaned out loud, unable to stop the sound from bursting from her lips, he smiled widely. If she weren't already lying down, her knees would have buckled and Tracey would have fallen down. She felt her stomach wobbling.

Within seconds he had covered her body with his, and she burned and stretched as he pushed inside her slowly, filling her. She let out a moan; it felt so good she couldn't help it. Then when he moved, God, she couldn't see, couldn't hear, she couldn't do anything but feel it. It was like nothing else in life. In a single moment of clarity, her eyes widened and she could see him lick his lips, could hear the rush of his breath. Reflexively, she started to wind her waist and hips, meeting every delicious gift of his body with passion. His pale skin pressed into her dark skin and she saw that she still wore her bra. That erotic picture playing in her mind made it difficult to breathe. Every time he retreated, only to bury himself deeper and harder within her once more. He tore her soul apart and all she could do was make it easier for him to do it.

And when she felt it start—when she felt herself reaching that precipice, her cries shrill and broken, every nerve in her body singing with glory—she tried to slow it down, she tried to hold out, but she couldn't. She dug her fingers into the small of his back and rocked against him as hard and as fast as she could.

He wrapped her hair in his fist and pumped harder, taking everything until she arched like a bow, every muscle in her body squeezed, paralyzed, until she started to shake from the violent climax. But he didn't stop. He kept going until he grunted hard and his movements became shallow. Then he collapsed over her from his own orgasm.

Moments later they were lying side by side, breathing heavily, and sweating. "That was... I haven't... I mean, it's been a while." Tracey didn't know *what* she was saying.

"Me, too," he said.

They lay there for more moments than she could remember. The silence didn't break until she got the giggles.

After giving her a brief, lovely kiss, he asked, "What's so funny?"

"Whatever happened to foreplay?" Laughter bubbled all the way up out of her stomach.

Garrett scratched his head and licked his lips. "Hell, Tracey, I thought that's what we've been having for weeks."

He rolled over onto his side to face her. He studied her intently before bending his head toward hers and pressing his lips to her lips, softly, as if he were kissing a baby or some other something that was more precious and more fragile than Tracey ever imagined herself to be. And she felt her eyes close, the breath ease all out of her again, and her limbs became warm liquid. He kissed her long, without the hurry of only moments before. His hand found its way up to lie against her cheek. His gentle licking and sucking made her want to—at once—show him how much he was making her want him all over again and to be still so as not to upset this tenuous, surreal atmosphere. Just as gently as they came, his lips retreated and for hushed seconds he only looked at her. Then one hand, one smooth hand was placed flat against her stomach. It stroked her flesh, leaving tingles in its wake. Slowly, that hand moved down to fit over the curve of her hip, down further to grasp her thigh as he slid it up to lay over his. They both watched his hand there playing against her sensitive skin.

His lips found her collarbone and gently traced it. They moistened a path down the center of her chest as he unhooked her bra. Her breasts were heavy and sensitive, anticipating the attention he would pay them. Reverently he pressed his cheek against them. His bristly jaw was rough, causing her skin to prickle. She felt her nipples growing taut, and he saw it. It was as if that was all he was waiting for. His tongue flashed out over one tip, then the other, making her back arch involuntarily. With torturous focus, his tongue circled each nipple, still not taking them fully into his mouth. He raked his teeth over her overly sensitive peaks and the gasp slipped out before she could stop it. Her hands automatically clung in his hair and finally, finally he stopped teasing her and kissed her, creating a new throb. As he drew her in with his mouth, his deft fingers slipped beneath her thigh and he cradled the heart of her in his hands, frustrating her as his palm moved tightly against her. Her thigh slid higher on his hip to give in to him even more. Then his mouth left its torturous post at her chest and came again to claim hers. He held her tightly as he kissed the life away from her and performed black magic between her legs. Tracey groaned when he pulled his hand away and stopped kissing her.

He turned her over so that he was presented with her back and moved close enough to her for her to feel the lines of his body against hers. She felt his love bites all over her shoulder blades. She felt his moist, hot tongue travel the length of her spine, moving low against her body. She felt his kisses on the backs of her knees, on her calves, and she found that she could no longer be still.

When he moved up her body again to kiss her neck, she raised her body up to meet his. In a motion as natural as time, he slipped inside of her and she arched from the pleasure. He pushed again and she tossed her head back. One hand slipped beneath her to cup one of her breasts and he bent low to kiss the back of her neck. She tilted her hips back against him more, so that she kept him with her. She twisted her head and he captured her lips in a quick kiss before he pulled back and grabbed her hips. His next stroke was so deep that she shrieked. The next was still deeper. Tracey closed her eyes and bit her lip, sucking in at the pleasure ricocheting through her body, at the feeling of Garrett within her.

―――

"No," Tracey breathed, moving his hand from her hip. She couldn't be touched anymore. She felt like she had no skin. Her whole body was a bundle of raw nerves and every touch, no matter how light was too much to process. She put a hand to her forehead, smoothing her hair away from her sweaty brow. Her whole body was hot and sweaty and Tracey had a feeling that those sheets were just as damp as she was. Finally, her breathing returned to normal.

"Is it okay to touch you now?"

"I don't think so," she teased. His response was to lay his big, wet body on her and nearly crush the life out of her. She gleefully pushed him off.

"Don't ever ask me for foreplay again. Ever. You don't really want it. I mean, I was just getting warmed up and what did you do?"

She put a pillow over his head and turned her back to him. It wasn't long before his arm snaked over her and he pulled her close. In the perfect fit, it didn't take long for sleep to set in. The last thing Tracey remembered was Garrett pulling the covers over them and turning out the light. The next thing she knew, it was four-thirty in the morning and he was gently nudging her awake.

"Tracey," he whispered. "I need to go back to the apartment."

She turned over groggily, trying to make out his features in the dark. "Why?"

"I don't have a change of clothes, for one," he replied. Then, adding venom she didn't know he possessed, he added, "And I know you're not going to want to take me to school in the morning."

That sound, the sound of his voice, the edge of anger, glazed her over in ice. She shook away that feeling and the quick stinging in her eyes and sat up. She slowly nodded. Even in the dark, she could feel his eyes. It was a timeless moment as he pressed one hand to her left breast, rubbing a thumb gently over her puckered nipple. Tracey moaned. He leaned down to taste it once more. She slipped her fingers into his hair.

"Damn," he grunted before he pulled away. Then he stood, and seeing his beautiful body again—that perfect V from shoulders to waist—Tracey felt her own response. She balled her hands up into fists as her fingers itched to touch him. She needed him again, but for the life of her, she couldn't say it. She couldn't let him know how much she wanted him, couldn't move those few feet to touch him and be touched. It was ridiculous, she knew. They had just been as intimate as any woman and man could be, and yet there she was, in the grips of a psychosomatic paralysis. And Tracey knew what it was that held her back: she had no right to promise something for which he'd been wise enough not to ask. And that was the very moment, she could pinpoint it, when her heart started breaking.

Chapter 12

They didn't say anything to each other on the way back to his apartment, nor when he got out. Tracey watched him go. He walked into the building without turning back. She didn't pull off right away, thinking he might just get inside, then come right back out again to come home with her. Foolish thought. She pushed back in her seat. Thoughts came and went. She rolled down her window and smoothed her hands over her face. The air was frigid, the sky featureless, the moon and stars having been pocketed by the late autumn dark. Tracey could still feel him in there. Inside her. Soreness and lingering pleasure combined at her core. She listened carefully. There was a train somewhere. Its soft moaning lulled her. She heard cars purring softly into the lot.

Flashes of that evening ran through her mind: the phone call—specifically, the sound of him calling her baby—the way he'd shielded her from his roommates, the way he didn't allow her to deny herself. The force of the first time they came together, the sweetness of the second, and the way falling asleep in his arms felt like forever. But she couldn't stop the chorus looping in the back of her mind. *I don't want this to be forever. This cannot be my forever.*

Finally, it seemed to dawn on her that in all probability, someone was out there wondering what she was doing. She pulled off. By the sheer grace of God, Tracey was able to fall asleep once more that night when she got home.

She didn't see Garrett at all that next day. Usually on Tuesdays and Thursdays she would at least see him out on the lawn, but that Thursday it was raining harder than it had in a very long time. Heavy, swollen drops pounded down on her car as she tried to ease her way home through heavy and relentless after-school traffic. When she got home, she was soaked but didn't change right away. She sat cross-legged on the bathroom floor in her damp clothes with the window open, enjoying the scent and sound of the rain. Tracey tried to ignore her skin, cold and raw and wrapped in the wet and abrasive cloth. She tried to lose herself in the perfume of wet earth and bark, the constant drumming, like a mother's heartbeat. She needed to accept that she had officially crossed a line with Garrett and that it was best they never make love again. Is that what they'd done? There was a part of her that had been wondering where he was, what he was doing, and who he was doing it with all day long. But she didn't text him, and she found herself depressed that he hadn't texted her.

This was making her nervous, not nervous as in anticipation but nervous as in breakdown.

After maybe half an hour, Tracey mopped the glistening floor and put on some sweats. Then, just as with the night before, her stomach was in knots. She didn't know if he would come to her, and even if he did, what then? Would he want to talk about it? Would he act as if it had never happened? Most importantly, what would she do? And, as an afterthought, why was this such a big deal for them? She drank tea in an attempt to steady herself, but when she heard the familiar sigh of his motor she felt it all again, ten times what it had been.

As he entered, she noted the leather bomber jacket pulled up at the collar against the rain. He wore dark blue jeans that concealed the thighs she had run her hands over the night before. She saw the dampness of the rain in his hair, making it a dark, curling auburn, and learned what it meant to go weak in the knees. She almost felt as if her man had come home from the war. He said hello and then sat down, declaring that they had to get some work done since they hadn't the night before. She sat next to him as she normally did when they studied. She truly tried to concentrate, but then his scent, God, his scent…

"What do you think, Tracey?"

She heard him ask, but had absolutely no idea to what he was referring.

"I was asking you something," he said with yellowy eyes flashing. It made her positively dizzy.

"I'm sorry," she offered, shifting her eyes away. "I guess my mind was somewhere else."

"Is that right? Probably where mine has been all day." He chuckled huskily. Her eyes snapped back to him. He closed the book he'd been flipping through and watched her in that intense way of his and she couldn't think of anything else or deny his words. She just sat there staring. "Wow, Tracey," he chuckled, "I found a way to stifle that smart little mouth of yours."

"I don't know about that."

"Just my luck." He drew her close as she laughed. And then his fingers were pulling her shirt up. "Now, excuse me for saying this…" There went her sweat-shirt. "…And I by no means want our friendship to turn into some dirty sexcapade." He was easing her pants down her hips. "But I really want you right now—I have since I woke up this morning—and I was wondering if you wouldn't mind…" He was kissing her as he took off his jacket and shirt. She wrapped her legs around his waist and he didn't have to tell her what he was wondering.

Later, they lay on the sofa on a pile of clothes and on class notes that had somehow found their way under them. He cuddled her up in his arms, cradling her like a little baby. She closed her eyes.

"You know, I was worried about tonight," she confessed, feeling the soft silkiness of his hair between her fingers. "But I guess things worked out okay." Tracey opened her eyes.

"Yeah, I guess." The creases around his mouth showed his amusement. His laughter continued as he attempted to dislodge the papers beneath them without letting her up out of his lap. Somehow he succeeded. "Hmmm, let's see. Page 233, page 234, page 236, page 238... Well, looks like I have to go digging some more." And his hands began to move over her body again as he pretended to fumble for the rest of his notes. He was making her squirm, and the more she moved, the less interested his hands seemed to be in contract law. In moments they were kissing again. She pulled back and shook her head, trying to get through to him that they really needed to get some work done, but he only smiled his incorrigible smile at her. Tracey paused, the thoughts tumbling clumsily from her head.

"What is it?"

"I do love your smile."

Every time they kissed, Tracey breathed out heavy like a baby sighing as it nestles into its mother's arms. "We have got to get some work done."

"Yeah, I know," he agreed ruefully and let her slide up out of his lap.

122

She had started to retrieve her clothes when she noticed he wasn't doing anything, was only staring at her. She stood holding her clothes in front of her. She'd never been a modest woman, but the way he was staring at her, *Lord*. He was studying her again, and she was beginning to hate that. He leaned forward and took the clothes from her hands. Still, he did little more than stare.

"What?" Tracey demanded.

"Nothing. I just like looking at you. You may love my smile, but this body, this face, this woman..." He stroked his hand over her hip and placed a dry kiss on her belly. She felt heat surface, in her face, in all the parts of her body he had just scrutinized so thoroughly. Did one say "thank you" at a time like that? Tracey didn't. Instead, she went into the bathroom to wash up, then to her bedroom to put on some more unattractive sweats. When she returned he had washed up and dressed as well and actually opened a book. They began to study.

"You know what?" he asked her somberly at one point.

"What?"

"You got a lot of damn trees in the yard."

"Huh?"

"You got a lot of damn trees in your yard. A tornado comes through here and you're done for."

"This house has stood forever and those trees have been out there forever and I *like* those trees."

He raised one eyebrow. "Just saying."

—∽∾—

"There's only one thing."

Oh, no, here it comes.

"What does this mean? What are we?" He pulled Tracey down into his lap—his new favorite way to sit.

She thought it best to point out, "That's a woman question."

"I don't disagree," he drawled.

God, I love that accent, she thought.

"What are we?"

"We're friends?" she offered tentatively. It had barely been two weeks.

"We were friends a month ago." He hesitated. "I think we're past that, sweetness."

"I guess," Tracey demurred, pressing her head into his chest where he couldn't see her face-to-face. They were quiet for a moment.

He cleared his throat. "Tracey, I don't want you to think it's just sex for me."

"I don't," she returned, not sure if it could be more than that.

"Because if I'm honest, I know that the way you make me feel… God, Trace. I've wanted to be with you like this for so long."

She propped her head up to look at him. "Really?"

"Really. I mean, I was attracted to you right off. That first day."

"You thought I was a janitor."

"A cute one, nevertheless."

"Can I ask you a question?" Her eyes met his.

"Yeah."

"I know you haven't dated a…a…well, you know. But have you been attracted? I mean, before me."

He shifted under her. His arms held her securely as he did. He was thinking. "I have. That's no lie. But I never really thought anything about it, you know? It didn't seem like a possibility so I just didn't think about it." She chewed on that. "What about you?"

"Me? Oh, I think it's the same thing. I never really considered it. I mean, when I saw you that day, I didn't even pay you any attention until you actually spoke to me. Then I was pissed at you. And then after that when I saw you around I became attracted, really attracted. But, like you said, it just didn't occur to me."

" 'Til when?" he asked.

" 'Til the next time I saw you."

"Me, too," he said and gave her a brief, smiling kiss. Then he leaned back and his face was serious again. "And now I can't think of anything else I want more than for us to really be together." Tracey started to move away from him in protest but he shushed her, holding her tight and continued, "But I know how you

125

feel about it. And I don't think I'm ready for that, either. It'd be hard. I'm not pushing. What we have is fine the way it is."

It was a relief, she thought, that they were thinking along the same lines. They could have a relationship, but would keep it in her house.

Chapter 13

Big, Rett's father, lay in his bed for a second, feeling warm and toasty. He didn't open his eyes. It was 3:00 a.m. He could feel it. He sat up and looked over at the clock: 3:00 a.m. Hot damn, he had a gift! Big looked over at his wife. She still was a fine-looking woman. And when she slept, she was a saint, too. Big smiled at that. He'd have one hell of a marriage if she'd just stay asleep one or two more hours every day. Then he actually chuckled and smacked her soundly on her rump.

"Damn, Big," she moaned in a muffled but squirrelly voice. She sure as hell knew how to say his name right. She said it like syrup getting tipped out its jar: really slow, in a steady, warm stream. He smacked her again, even more firmly than the last time. She rolled away from him, taking her pillow with her. "Dammit, Big, why don't you just go on and go kill something already?"

Big grinned wide. He stood and stretched, touching the ceiling as he clasped his hands above his head. His height was how he got his name. By the time he was knee-high to a grasshopper – well, hell, that was the point. He never *was* knee-high to a grasshopper. He had always been the biggest boy and man around.

In college he played football for the Tide, and everybody was scared of him. A six foot, six inch man carrying more than two hundred seventy-five pounds of muscle on him makes anyone pause. Still, at fifty-five years old, though his stomach and chest had grown into a soft barrel and his back and knees hurt every time he moved, he was the man you asked questions in any given room. He put on his clothes, checked his guns, and went down the hall.

He pushed open the door to his son's room, went over to the bed and looked down at Rett. Big shook his head, more and more confused the more time he spent with his son.

"Why are you standing over me watching me sleep? I said I'd be up at 3:30." Rett grinned before he opened his eyes. When he finally did open them and sat up, Big saw that he had slept in his camouflage. "Thought I wasn't going to be ready, huh?"

"That's my son!"

—〰—

After he and Rett had been out for about an hour, he began. "Yeah, so…" he started, taking a swig of beer.

"Yeah?" Rett returned, drinking his own.

"Yeah. I was out in the plant yesterday with Brandon." Big glanced sideways at his son. Rett's jawed twitched. Big knew he had him, but the boy didn't say anything. "We had a long conversation about this and that." He glanced over again. "Yep. Just shooting the breeze, you know."

"Yep," Rett said hesitantly.

"Yeah, you know, Charles, that son of his, your friend, yeah, that boy can talk."

Rett didn't say a word. He didn't even move. He was still enough to tag a nearby wild turkey, but he didn't even see it. Even though he wanted to, Big didn't think it was a time for him to tag it, either. Then he saw the thing take off. Just the thought had it on the run. Big smiled, then went back to the task at hand. "Yeah, he talks a lot. You have to watch out for people who talk, and especially what they talk about. Some things you do behind closed doors, and you should keep 'em there. "

"Oh, yeah?" Rett pulled his trigger, but missed what he'd been intending to hit.

"Yeah," Big told him. You had to give it to his son. He was going be his own man regardless. "Son?"

"I hear ya, Dad. All right? I hear ya."

Chapter 14

One Tuesday night, Garrett called to say he wouldn't be there early enough for dinner, something had come up. So instead of having dinner at home alone—something Tracey had never had a problem with before—she went over to Monica's. By the time she got there, Gary and Lena had already eaten and were getting ready for bed. Maurice had gone back to work to prepare for an audit. That left Moni and her thirteen-year-old, Tamia.

As they sat there talking over the kitchen table, Tracey had the longest conversation with a teenager she'd had since she *was* one. At the center, she did what she could to listen and connect and be there for the girls in her group. However, more often than not, she still felt like an outsider. Was she supposed to relate to them just because she was black? Never mind that the way she grew up was grossly different from the way they did. But talking to Tamia was different. The girl was so sensitive and intelligent and inquisitive. She reminded Tracey so much of herself at that age it was almost uncanny.

Tracey enjoyed talking to her and would have continued if she hadn't glimpsed the clock on the microwave. It was nine-thirty.

"Yeah, well, I think I'm going to head home," she breathed.

"I do have to work in the morning," Monica agreed, yawning. Tracey gathered her things. "You know, Tracey, Tam reminds me a lot of you," Moni told her as they stood in her driveway. It was a very warm night for the beginning of December, even though strong wind blew against them.

"How so?"

Monica smiled almost wistfully. "Because she doesn't fit anywhere, either. Or at least she doesn't think she does. She's unhappy, too." There was nothing for Tracey to say. She put her arms across her chest. "She never got along with any of the kids in public school," Moni continued. "She cried all the time that nobody liked her, mainly other girls who got a kick out of ganging up on her. I love my baby, but she is such a gentle soul. There was nothing I could do. Me, a psychologist, nothing I could do. This new school's better for her. She's got friends. A bunch of little white girls, but friends. I think the hardest part for me is that I don't really understand where she's coming from sometimes. I was born and raised in the projects. I had five brothers and sisters that went down the road before me. They lit the path so I never had a problem finding my way. And not just that. Everybody I knew had the same life I did. Rico has a similar background, too. That helped."

"But you and your brothers and sisters went to school and you got a medical degree and—"

"And those were things my parents insisted that all of us do. And even in college, I knew plenty of people in the same situation. Around here Tam's been the exception. Kind of. Rico and I have plenty of people we associate with that have kids with similar backgrounds. But Tamia doesn't get along with any of them, either." Tracey nodded. It all sounded too familiar. "She likes you, Tracey. I really haven't seen her connect the way she connects to you."

"Thank you."

"Nothing to thank me for."

—∽∽—

Heavy thoughts followed Tracey home but dissipated at the door. Rett was already there listening to music they both enjoyed. Tracey joined him. He snuggled close to her, sometimes putting his arm around her, sometimes kissing her. It still scared Tracey how her body responded to his. She wondered when she would get used to it, when he would touch her and she would feel warm, not hot.

She could barely keep her mind on anything as he did this, and he seemed so comfortable about it all, as if it was the most natural thing. And then, as she always did, she got caught up in the way he smelled. His own special and irresistible scent reminded her of how his lips kissed hers and saturated her mind with visions of the night before. Like always, she couldn't tell him what she wanted, but he looked up at her and stroked the side of her arm. When he stood, she followed him into the bedroom.

—∽—

Walking through the ANM that Friday evening, Tracey saw a girl about an inch shorter than her, maybe five feet, nine inches, with ash blonde hair almost down to her waist. She had pale hazel eyes and was pin-up girl pretty with naturally pursed lips and a healthy blush on her cheeks. She had a little silver stud in her nose and a tattoo on the side of her arm that looked like a dragon climbing through a flaming number seventy-six. She caught Tracey staring and smiled curiously. Tracey smiled back, then averted her gaze.

The blonde girl walked up to the counter with her selections and a conversation started between her and Jenna, the same girl that had nearly thrown her panties at Garrett the last time Tracey was there.

Tracey didn't intend to eavesdrop.

"Jenna," the blonde said, "you are so not his type it's ridiculous."

"I could be his type," Jenna retorted, licking her highly glossed lips. "I could be whatever he wanted me to be, he's so damn sexy."

Uh, hello? Tracey thought. *Customer standing here.*

"Trust me. You wouldn't get anywhere." The girl leaned over and put her hand on Jenna's shoulder.

"Why? You think I'd have a problem kicking Kim's ass?"

"Jenna, you couldn't kick a blind, deaf, and dumb four-year-old's ass. This is Angie you're talkin' to. I know my brother."

Tracey's eyes zeroed in on the girl. Pale hazel eyes, lazy smile, same accent. Tracey couldn't figure out which emotion had her pulse racing. Anger? Indignation?

Angie returned the smile and handed Jenna her check. She grabbed her videos as Jenna began to ring Tracey up.

"Student ID?" Jenna asked her politely. She told herself she shouldn't care that she didn't remember her. Of course she didn't remember her. She probably had a brain tumor from hyperactive cell phone usage.

Angie continued, "I'm actually kind of worried about him. Something's up with Rett and I'm not sure what it is."

Tracey's knees buckled.

"Hell, it's probably law school, Angie. Did you think about that? I mean, from what I hear, nobody's seen him around lately since he's been studying. Clay told me he's at the library late almost every night."

"Yeah, I guess, but we had dinner last night and he was just so distracted. And speaking of Clay, your brother is out of his mind...."

Tracey didn't start to breathe until five minutes after she got home. She dialed Rett's number. In two seconds she hung up. What was she going to say? Was she supposed to ask him why he hadn't mentioned that his sister was in school with them? Did it matter? Was she angry? Tracey didn't even know if she had a right to be angry. Did she have any rights where he was concerned? At the very least she was hurt, but... She turned off all the lights in her house and went in the bathroom to think, or maybe sulk, but not to cry. She refused to cry.

Tracey heard him pull up and the motor of his SUV die. The quiet in the house was so pure that she could even hear his footfalls on the gravel in the drive. He came to the door and knocked. She hoped he would go away. She really hoped he would just think she was gone away with a friend and leave. But then she heard the sound of his key click in the door. Tracey regretted the day she let him have it. He came in calling her name. She didn't call back. Tracey saw yellow light seep in beneath the door. She would have to live through the moment. She stood up, trying to calm herself enough to walk out a rational, thinking person.

Just before she could act and open the door, it was opened for her and light rained into the small chrome and white linoleum room.

"Why are you hiding in the bathroom?"

"I saw Angie tonight. At the ANM."

"Baby," he breathed. "I was going to tell you about her. I was."

"You don't have to tell me anything."

"I don't have to, but babe, I know I should have."

"Go, Garrett. Just please go." Her voice was so choked, she barely heard it herself.

Thirty minutes later, headlights flashed through the window. Rett's SUV pulled into the drive. Tracey couldn't believe he had come back. She went out of the bathroom and stood in the living room facing the door. He came in, followed by his sister, Angie who was wearing combat boots and pajamas. She looked over at Tracey, then at Rett, as if looking for reassurance.

"Angie, this is Tracey. Tracey, this is my sister Angie." He closed the door, then sat down on the sofa rubbing his temples.

She couldn't believe he had brought his sister over, introduced them.

Angie cleared her throat loudly into the silence. "Uh, hi. Tracey, is it? Do you happen to know why my brother got me out of bed to come over here, even though he knows I have practice at six o'clock in the morning?"

"You didn't say anything to her?" Tracey asked him, upset that he seemed to be leaving this for her to explain.

"Wait a minute…wait a minute," she gasped. "You're that girl from the video store yesterday… Are you *dating* my brother?"

Tracey didn't know exactly how to answer since they had never technically gone out on a date. She didn't think it'd be appropriate to say that she was potentially in love with and sleeping with him, but no, they weren't dating.

A light dawned in Angie's eyes. Then she sat on Tracey's sofa and stared at her brother with her mouth open.

Garrett ignored her. "Tracey, I've always meant to tell you she's an undergrad here. I wanted to introduce you before now, but you didn't want—"

When he didn't finish his sentence, Angie looked from him to Tracey, then back again. "She didn't want what?"

"None of your business," he growled, protecting Tracey.

"Hey, you got me out of bed to come here, not the other way around. *Something* is my business."

Angie was here now. She knew the most important part. She might as well know everything. "He was going to say that I didn't want anyone to know we were together."

"*You* didn't want anyone to know?" she questioned incredulously.

"I don't like the way you said that."

She laughed. "Well, I'm sorry. But it's usually the other way around."

"I don't know who *you* know or what you think your experience tells you about me, but that's the situation."

"I didn't mean to offend, I just know my brother and he's more likely—"

"Angie," Rett warned.

"Whereas I am the reject of the family and will date whoever I please—" *That was interesting news.* "—my brother is the most clean-cut, All-American, wannabe Southern gentleman you will ever meet. He hangs out on the strip. He wears khaki pants, tucked-in plaid shirts, and *duck shoes*, for Chrissakes. That's the way it's been in my family for generations. He played football in high school. He and my dad go hunting every fall. He goes to church every Sunday, even here at school. He's got friends named Clay and Hunter and, yes, one they call Bubba. Even if his skin's always tan, he's the whitest white boy I know. Hell, his name is Rett, and you're sure as hell not Scarlett. I mean, I can't see him with a black woman without him being called 'Massah Rett' somewhere in the process!"

"Will you just shut up, Angie?" he roared at her.

She rolled her eyes at him. "Tracey, I was just tryin' to explain to you why I was in shock. I'm sure you know what I'm talkin' about."

Tracey didn't answer her. Just like that, she hated Garrett's sister. In fact, Tracey got up and left the room. She went in the bedroom and held her breath. She counted to ten. She could hear them in the living room bickering. Tracey didn't like Angie's quick and surgical verbalization of the situation. It was all too true. But where Garrett and she had settled into things, never even saying the words 'black' or 'white' in that respect, she was putting everything out on a platter in front of them. This chick wasn't pulling any punches.

Tracey breathed out slowly, then counted to ten again. The counting and breathing thing was way overrated.

"Tracey?" It was Angie.

She turned to watch Angie enter the bedroom. "What do you want?"

"To apologize. I get carried away sometimes, and I forget. Rett's used to me, but you're not. I shouldn't have said all that. But can I tell you something?" she asked, coming to stand in front of Tracey.

"I don't know…."

"Please, just hear this. Be careful. My brother is very charming and persuasive and selfish. He doesn't have a chivalrous bone in his body that's not connected to the 'him-getting-what-he-wants' bone. Don't get wrapped up in him."

"Huh?"

"Don't get pissed, but I don't see him being in a long term relationship with you."

Hurt pelted Tracey's insides like hailstones. "As he said, I'm the one who wants the relationship to stay the way it is. Not him."

"Or so you think. Don't take it to heart that I'm here, that he introduced me and you. I know it seems like a grand romantic gesture, but I'm his sister and I'm the black sheep. I am the *only* one who he's been one hundred percent honest with. I am the only one he could trust with something like this without worrying about what I'll say or do or think. He can tell me anything and I'll love him no matter what. That's how close we are. It doesn't mean he'll ever acknowledge—"

"I don't need him to acknowledge me!"

She placed her hand on Tracey's arm. Tracey shrugged it off roughly. "I'm sure he cares about you or he wouldn't have bothered. He wouldn't have gone to this kind of trouble. Especially not if he'd slept with you already, but I'm right about my brother."

Tracey's bottom lip trembled and she tried to think of something to say.

"You don't know me. So why are you telling me this?"

Garrett walked into the room, and his sister went silent. Tension marked every stiff movement and there was a tick in his jaw. His eyes held hers.

Tracey had never been as quick as she wanted to be in these situations. She was always that person who thought of something brilliant and life-changing to say three days later. She wanted to ask him about what Angie had said. That or to kick him out of her life because if there was a time to end this cleanly, this was it. But, sadly, she was not quick and she would not break up with him in front of his sister. Tracey felt angry, pathetic, and alone, and still he watched her. She wanted to believe he was not the way Angie described him.

He remained silent, watching her.

"How long have you been dating?" Angie asked.

"We've been friends since August," he answered without shifting his gaze.

"How long have you been sleeping together?"

"Now, that really isn't your business," Tracey mustered up the spirit to say.

Angie smiled Garrett's smile at Tracey. Then looked from Tracey to Garrett and back again. In the silence, she left the room.

The pair stared at each long enough for Tracey to feel a tear in the corner of her eye and for Garrett to come forward to wipe it away.

"Don't." She stepped back and away from him.

He moved forward again and grasped her upper arms gently in his hands. "Tracey, I love you."

More tears slipped from her eyes.

"Angie knows me for sure. I don't know what she said to you, but she's honest to a fault. I can't say she wasn't right about the… the convenience of keeping this quiet. But *you* didn't want anyone to know. That wasn't me alone. And she's right, I can trust her with any secret, but who better to start opening up to? Who better to be the first person to know us, *together*?"

Tracey didn't say a word. It amazed her that she was so eloquent internally.

He came forward once again. His arms slipped around her and held her tight. He held her so tight that she felt a sob deep in her chest.

"I love you," he whispered.

Tracey hugged him back.

—◊—

"Hmmm. So my brother's dating a black woman. I think I'm going to lay down and die." Those were the first words out of her mouth when they went, hand and hand, back into the living room.

142

"You got practice in the morning?" Rett asked his sister, ignoring her comment. Angie nodded. "I'll tell you what. You can take the truck back and drive it to practice in the morning. Just come get me when you're done. Really, any time tomorrow is fine. I'll be here all day." He turned to Tracey. "If that's all right with you?"

"Actually…" Actually, she wanted him to stay there and tell her he loved her again while he *made* love to her and exorcised her of reborn insecurities. "I still have some things to sort out. I think I'd rather be alone tonight."

He sighed deeply.

Garrett led Angie towards the door. Even then, Tracey chose to believe the girl just didn't know her brother as well as she thought, that the fact that he loved her—and she knew he loved her—would overcome any bad behavior on his part. Tracey would find out later that you didn't grow up in a house with someone for twenty-plus years without knowing him almost better than anyone else ever could.

"Just one thing." Angie glanced back and forth between the two of them as she stood to leave. "Can I see you kiss?"

"No," they both said at once.

Chapter 15

Angie crossed her arms in front of her as her brother escorted her out. They stood on the porch staring each other in the eye. "So?" she challenged him.

"So what? So you're going to tell me why you just tried to ruin what I have with that girl?"

"I didn't try to ruin anything."

"I brought you here just to prove to her that I wasn't hiding you and that I didn't *want* to hide you. I'm not saying you didn't make a point, but I brought you here to put her fears to rest. And what did you do?"

"Yeah, what did I do?" She got in his face to ask the question.

"You went in and tried to ruin it." He shrugged his shoulders the way he always did when he was trying to make her feel childish.

"How in the hell did this all start?"

"I don't know. We met and kept running into each other and one thing led to another."

"Uh-huh."

"Uh-huh." Garrett started to hand her the keys to his car.

Angie didn't take them. "Rett, I don't think you should hurt that girl."

"Why do you think I would?"

She cocked her head to the side. "I mean, you know what Momma always tells you about you and Kim. 'Don't play house if you're the only one who knows it's a game.' "

"This is not a game to me. I'm in love with her."

"Well, I hope to hell not." She cocked her head to the side.

"What do you have against this? Aren't you the one who wanted to date that boy with all those dread-locks?"

"Yep, but I'm also the one who doesn't give a damn what anybody thinks about me. I date who I want to when I want to, I just don't take them home to Momma and Daddy. And usually I don't even let my brother Rett meet them 'cause he's just as bad as Momma and Daddy. But you can't do what I do. You're the Golden Boy. I don't know if you're in love with her, or if she is in love with you. But I do know she's not Juliet, and you sure aren't Romeo."

"What's that supposed to mean?"

"I think you know what it's supposed to mean. Even if you love her, in order for you two to be a real couple, your *whole* life has to change. I'm not being dramatic, Rett. You can't hang out with the same guys. You can't go to the same places. You *can't* bring her home. Momma only tolerates me in the house these days because Dad makes her. But she can barely stand me."

"That's not true."

"It is." She put a hand to her chest. "But *I* have come to accept that. I've had to build a whole other network of people who care about me to make sure I stay happy."

"Dad cares about you, no matter what."

"I know."

"I care about you, no matter what."

"I know that, too." Impulsively, she hugged him hard. "Clay knows somethin's up. So does Charles, he said."

Rett ignored her comment. "Just take the keys. Come get me in the morning."

"She said she wanted to be alone."

"She'll change her mind. See you tomorrow, Angie."

"Yeah, yeah, yeah, *Garrett*."

Rett waited until Angie pulled off to take a deep breath and go back into the house.

Tracey was still sitting in the same place and she looked up at him as he entered. She had a look on her face that was like...like...it was just horrible.

"What are you doing back?"

"I wanted to talk to you."

"So you ignored me."

Rett couldn't help himself; he grinned and nodded. Tracey rolled her eyes. But he saw a little smile,
which meant he was just this side of home free. He
sat down on the sofa beside her. She crossed her arms
over her chest. He put his arm across her shoulders
and pulled her close to him. She was nice and warm
and soft. At that precise moment, talking was the last
thing he felt like doing, but he couldn't get to point C
from point A without hitting point B first. "Tracey?"

"What?"

"We're both adults who care about each other—"

"You don't understand. There's more to it than
that. Angie knows what kind of person you are. She
knows how potentially bad this could be." She paused.
"And, Garrett, I need to know. Do you have a problem
with me? I mean, who I am. Do you have a problem
with me being black?"

"If I did, I wouldn't be here."

"Not necessarily true."

Okay, not as home free as he'd thought. "Well, do
you have a problem with me being white?"

"I don't—"

He didn't let her finish that thought. It was either
going to be "I don't think so" or "I don't know," neither of which he wanted to hear right then. "Or maybe
you're just tolerating me because I'm so talented in
bed?"

He nipped at her neck, and Tracey squealed a little, trying not to laugh. "Don't do that. I told you I need to sort things out. " Garrett took that opportunity to pull the front of her shirt down, along with her bra, exposing one plump breast, which he seized with his mouth. He heard her moan above him and knew that no matter how much she fought, they were done talking for the night.

—◊—

The very next day, he tackled changing their relationship.

"Hey, Trace, read this sheet and let me depose you." Garrett handed her a piece of paper. She sat up in bed to take it. Tracey had been lying down all day because she hadn't been feeling too well. Granted, that hadn't prevented him from forcing her into rigorous physical activity just moments before. He said he didn't care if he caught her cold. He was so affectionate, his hands and lips everywhere. When they realized they were out of condoms, he nearly went into apoplectic shock, until Tracey reminded him she was on the pill, and they had established that they both had clean bills of health—despite her perpetual cough. The sex had been, well, *yummy*.

"Hmm." Tracey studied the paper. "Depositions." It had been an interesting case minutes ago, but she didn't remember at all what it was about.

"Tracey?"

"Yeah, Garrett?"

"I don't know how to say this." He leaned against the wall.

"Tell me what?" Tracey glanced up from the page.

"I don't want us to see other people."

She lowered the paper in her hands and looked up at him. "What?"

"I mean, well, just what I said. I don't want us to see other people."

"I didn't know that we were seeing *each other*," she countered.

"Well, what do you call it, Tracey?" His jaw flexed as he clenched his teeth.

She didn't answer. Instead, she changed her tactic. "Besides, I'm not the one who's in a relationship."

"Well, babe, neither am I," he said pointedly. "If you'll recall, I broke it off with Kim."

"Then it's settled, isn't it? I'm not seeing anyone, and you're not seeing anyone." Tracey tried again to focus on the case but found it impossible—especially with him standing there deeply studying his coffee, obviously dissatisfied. She sighed impatiently. "What is it, Garrett?"

"Tracey, listen. I see you almost every day out there on the lawn with your girlfriends, and there's always some guy or some guys standing there talking to you, looking at you the way I look at you. I can't stand it.

I know that some of them probably put the moves on you, and it just drives me crazy."

"What are you saying? I mean, guys always hit on girls."

"Including Dr. Burke? It looks like he's got more on his mind than Legal Action in Labor Disputes."

Why, oh why, was it so obvious to everyone in the world that Alex was interested in her? Tracey hadn't noticed any real change in his behavior when he was around her. He hadn't once offered to do her thesis for her, which certainly would have been an excellent come-on. At dinner that same night she saw Garrett at the movies, Alex hadn't so much as tried to hold her hand. She wouldn't have let him, but he didn't even try. The majority of their conversations revolved around what was happening at school. Granted, he held her coat for her, opened the door for her, and afforded her the random long look, but it all just seemed routine. To Tracey, he just seemed like a really nice, somewhat lonely man, despite going out to dinner with a female student.

"Whatever, Garrett," she gasped. She wished she could come up with something wittier.

"It's true, Tracey. I saw you at Rachel's."

"You saw me at Rachel's when?"

"That doesn't matter, but I saw you and Burke having dinner at Rachel's. I could tell it wasn't just business just by the dress you were wearing."

"Since I've had dinner alone with Alexander exactly once, I can only assume that the time you saw me with him at Rachel's was the night before you came over and forced yourself on me."

"When did he become 'Alexander'?"

"Don't worry about it. My question is this: Did you come back after those two weeks just because you saw me having dinner with Alex?"

"Oh, it's 'Alex' now, is it? You don't even call *me* Rett."

"Do not change the subject, *Garrett*! I asked you a question. Does 'I couldn't stay away from you' really equal 'I couldn't stay away from you if somebody else might want you'?"

"Jesus, Tracey!"

"Answer me!"

"I didn't have to be jealous of Burke to come back to you. But, yeah, I wanted to know why you were dressing up for him like that."

"I wanted to."

"Why? You don't show that much cleavage and leg even here, when we're home. Did you plan on sleeping with him? I mean—"

"What does it matter? You had a girlfriend. It's not like—"

"Tracey!" he growled at her. She jumped.

"No, Garrett, I didn't sleep with him, okay? I was mad at you for not coming around, and sure I wanted some male attention, but I didn't have any interest in letting anything happen."

He was silent for a moment, then gave her a lop-sided smile, "Hell yeah, I was jealous, baby. But I didn't figure it was going anywhere. I saw you yawn that night and stare into a drink you never finished. I watched you giggle, and Tracey, you don't giggle. You full out laugh, at least you do when you're with me. I knew, sure as I'm sitting here, you weren't going to sleep with him. I mighta been a little jealous, but I won't worry about you and another man until that changes."

"You're so cocky."

She put a hand over his mouth to prevent him from saying something perverted and incendiary. "I'm trying to figure out what your point is. If you're so confident you're the only person in the world I could be interested in—stupid, I know—then why would it matter if—"

"It's a man thing." He chuckled and leaned over to kiss her.

"Whatever that means." Tracey rolled her eyes, try-ing to stop him from charming her out of her mood. He snuggled next to her in the bed but was pensive again. "I'm really just saying that…ah—" Garrett hardly ever had a problem saying what was on his mind. That worried her.

"God," she breathed, exasperated. "What is it, Garrett?"

"I just want people to know."

Tracey had been walking underwater for those past few weeks. She was admiring the view, calm but holding her breath all the while. This was her inevitable resurfacing. She ran her tongue over the front of her teeth. "What's to know?" she asked.

"What I mean is that I don't want to be strangers every time we leave this house. We spend all our time together; I practically live here. You are my best friend, Tracey. Besides, Angie knows and nothing terrible's happened."

"Angie's not like the rest of the world, *obviously*. You know that. She took care to give me a whole diatribe about that very fact the first night, remember? She doesn't care. Apparently, she does and says whatever comes to mind and somehow seems to get away with it. We're not like that."

"Yeah, but still, she knows."

Tracey swallowed hard, but could not rid herself of the guilt growing into a knot in the back of her throat. She wiped the sweat from her forehead. She was panicking, "What are you saying? What happened to 'we won't say anything; it's our business'?"

"That was just a ploy to get you into bed," he said, laughing. She whacked him in the stomach. "I want us to be together. You know, not seeing anyone else, showing each other some respect. And I don't want any other men wasting time with a woman who can't stop thinking about me."

She punched him squarely in the chest. She did it again. She did it once more for good measure. Then she grabbed her mouth and ran.

Tracey found herself in the bathroom losing every bit of food she'd had over the last couple of days. She heard him come to stand outside the door. "You could really wreak havoc on a man's ego, you know."

"Oh, no! Not yours! It's completely safe and sound," she assured him. Tracey rinsed her mouth, brushed her teeth, and gripped the sheet around her body, which was suddenly cold. She opened the door. "You know, I haven't been feeling too well for the past couple weeks. I've been on and off antibiotics since forever."

He drew her into his arms and held her. "I'll take care of you, girl."

Tracey sighed at the way they fit, at the way he smelled, at the way when he held her; she felt like she had everything she ever wanted or would want in the world. "Do you think I could just have a little time? I promise it'll happen, I just need some time."

"Okay, Trace," he agreed. Tracey liked the way she could feel his voice when he held her, feel it come all the way up from within him. "Anything if you'll just let me…" His voice trailed off but it wasn't necessary for him to go on. He held her there forever.

—m—

It was about seven in the evening when Angie pulled into the drive behind trees that were still green in the middle of November. It had been easy enough to find the place after last night, even though she wouldn't have been able to get in touch with her brother for directions even if she wanted to. He had left his cell phone in the car and he hadn't been in too much of a mood for particulars the night before.

She still couldn't believe it, though she knew it was true. But still, not her brother. No, she wasn't going to think about it. She was just going to see how things went down. Rett came out to meet her, then took the keys from her hands and settled in the driver's seat while she got in on the other side. He didn't say anything. Angie just waited, knowing that wouldn't last long.

"Angie…" Yep, she knew her brother. "I brought you here last night because—"

"I know, I know. You brought me here because you thought she thought you were hiding her from me. You wanted to put her mind at ease. And I screwed it up."

"No," he shook his head slowly. "You're right so often you have no idea how to handle it when you've got it all wrong. I brought you here because I really care about her and I wanted you to get know her. Period."

"You wanted me to—" She cut her own words off and frowned thoughtfully. "Rett, hon, I know we started talking about this last night, but if you're this serious about her, that's all the more reason why you want to think—"

"I don't care," he answered solemnly.

"What?"

"I don't care right now about what anyone thinks. I know what I want and I don't care if anyone has a problem with it."

"You should care, Rett. That's all I'm saying. And what if Momma and Dad—"

"Dad knows."

"What?" Angie knew she didn't just hear that.

"He knows. Oh, we haven't talked about it out loud or anything, but he knows."

"But not Momma."

"No, not Momma."

Angie didn't say a word. Rett went on, "I just wanted you to get to know her, that's all."

Oh no, brother, Angie thought, *that's not all.*

—m—

"Angie, would you like something to drink?" Tracey offered.

It was a few nights later and Angie had just gotten there with Garrett's SUV. This time, she'd borrowed it to go home and pick up her futon. Tracey took the keys from her at the door and told her Rett was in the shower. Angie went on in, carrying a bag containing a burger and fries. She sat down in the living room without anybody inviting her. She figured since Tracey was so stiff, she probably wouldn't have ever gotten around to it. In fact, Tracey seemed frustrated as Angie sat on the floor at the coffee table and made herself at home.

"Yeah, what you got?" Angie asked.

"Probably whatever you like."

Just at that moment, they both heard the bathroom door open in Tracey's bedroom. Rett was singing. Since Tracey was sitting in the leather chair by the wall, she could see him down the hall before Angie did. She nearly choked when she saw him. She shrieked, "Rett! Angie's here!"

It took a second for him to appear. He peeked around the corner and grinned at his sister. She could see his wet hair as he came into the hallway wearing nothing but a towel around his waist. "I didn't hear you come in."

"I just got here," Angie answered, biting into her burger. "Besides, I was just about to get a drink before you came parading around, tackle out."

"I'll go ahead and take her home soon as I get dressed, Tracey," he said before he leaned down to give her a quick kiss.

That was when Angie figured out what was eating Tracey. The chick didn't want her there. Unfortunately, she hadn't yet realized that Angie couldn't leave any sooner, even if she wanted to. She had no way to get home. Apparently, Garrett mentioning it eased her tension some because she looked a lot less stricken and wasn't staring at Angie as if she wanted to scream, "Interloper!"

"No," Tracey answered, surprising both Angie and her brother. "She can stay for a drink."

"How about a rum and coke," Angie asked and stuck her tongue out at her brother.

"Dark okay?" Tracey asked.

"But of course," Angie answered.

Tracey started to get up, but Garrett stopped her. "I'll get it, hon. What do you want?"

"I'll have the same."

He passed her and stroked her face.

Angie felt as if she'd swallowed down the wrong pipe. There was her brother behaving like a sensitive, caring man again. Who knew he could do it?

"You're on the swim team, right?" Tracey asked her.

"Yeah. And, since I am one of the few people on the team who is *not* an Olympic hopeful, I've found it best to just show up on time every day and keep real quiet."

"You're capable of keeping real quiet?"

Angie laughed, feeling that at last they were starting to warm up to each other. Then she remembered something. "Oh," she yelped, finishing her burger and wiping her hands. She reached in her purse. "I have something for you."

It was a teeny tiny gift bag with delicate teal and lilac tissue peeking out from it. Inside was a silver coin charm. It was about an inch-wide circle with a fighting tiger embossed onto it. Tracey held it in her hand as if it were the most delicate something she'd ever seen. "I don't know what to say."

"Nothing, I saw it and thought of you," Angie answered before starting in on her fries. Eating like that was going to totally mess up her training.

"I don't think I can accept this. I mean—"

"Think of it as an apology for our rocky start the other night and, well, rocky times to come. You know, I have a problem thinking before I speak."

"Think so?"

"Sarcasm." Angie smirked wickedly. "I like it."

Rett sauntered back in, still wearing his towel, and handed Angie her drink. She sipped liberally. After swallowing she closed her eyes and licked her lips, then let out a moan of appreciation and opened her eyes again. "Maybe I shouldn't have offered you a drink," Tracey quipped, laughing.

"No," Angie declared. "I'm not a lush or anything. I just have an acute appreciation, that's all."

"I see. Your brother has an acute appreciation, also."

"Don't I know it? We get it from our mother, who swears to this day she can't drink." Tracey asked her why. " 'Cause Dad can't and God forbid she out-man Dad."

They both laughed over that as Tracey's phone rang. She answered it. "Hey, Moni. What's up?... Hmm, probably around six...." She cleared her throat. "Can't...studying...all right, see you tomorrow."

"Monica?" Rett prompted. Tracey nodded. Angie knew he wanted to meet this friend of Tracey's as she had met his sister. Tracey had told him no. Angie glanced back and forth between them, sensing the tension.

"Are you pressuring Tracey to shout from the mountain top that you're her boyfriend again?" she asked her brother. He didn't say anything. Tracey didn't say anything.

—∾—

As much as Tracey and Rett were probably hoping for Angie's appearance not to interrupt the dynamic of their relationship, it had. She called often. She came over even more often. And she learned more about Tracey and vice versa than either of them had predicted. Tracey figured out that part of the insane banter Angie spewed out all the time was just her sense of humor. She learned that whenever Angie felt bad about something she'd done or said, she tried to do something right away to fix it, like the charm she'd given Tracey that night. Angie learned that Tracey had traveled all over the world and had a story for every occasion. More importantly, she had a subtle, dry way of turning a phase that just had to make you laugh. In the end, Angie knew that though Tracey didn't want to, she was starting to like the lesser Atkins.

And Angie really liked her. That was why she worried over the mounting problems between the two.

One night she came over to work on a final project. They moved the coffee table into the spare room so she could spread out on the floor. In five minutes her supplies were all over the place, from foam core board to epoxy to a T-square. With her hair held fast in a tortoiseshell clip and her wire-rimmed glasses slipping on her nose as she bent over her work, Angie figured she looked damn scholastic.

In the middle of working on the project, she looked up at Tracey. "I don't suppose you have a three-millimeter technical drawin' pencil anywhere in the house?" She screwed up her nose hopefully.

"No." Tracey shook her head. "Unfortunately, I don't."

"Mine's broken and I just can't work with it anymore. I'm gonna have to go to the ANM. You need anything?"

"No. Garrett," Tracey called to him. He was in the bedroom watching a court case broadcast on public television.

"Yeah, baby?" he called back and came down the hall to join them in the living room.

"You need anything from the store? Angie's going."

"Which one?"

"The ANM."

"Actually I need to pick up a case for Monday. I'll ride with you, Angie." He went back down the hall, then reappeared wearing sneakers, a jacket, and a navy baseball cap.

"You want to come, Tracey?"

Angie noted how Tracey looked at them. She tried to imagine what she was seeing. Rett looked the preppie frat boy, as usual, but probably more so next to Angie, who looked deceptively normal in her studious glasses and Penn State sweatshirt.

"No, thanks, sweetie, but you can bring back a loaf of bread. We're almost out."

He goaded her. "Come on, Tracey. It'll be fun."

"Garrett," she answered warily, "really, I don't feel like it."

"You know what, Tracey? Screw it," he lashed out. Then he shook his head and spat out, "As if anything would ever be any different with you. Look, I'm not sure I'll be back tonight." He stalked out of the door.

Angie followed him but turned back to Tracey to mouth, "I'll talk to him."

Tracey only nodded at her.

Outside Angie started in on him. "At least you could have given some warning. All I knew was that one minute you were asking her to go, the next you were teasing her about it, and in the next, you were so mad you were turning red and looking like you wanted to kill her. I know how much stress you're under, but was all that necessary?"

"You don't understand," he grumbled.

"Then enlighten me."

Rett swiped at his eyes, but thankfully Angie didn't mention the glistening tears.

"It just seems like this is getting old fast."

"What? Being in love with her?"

Surprisingly, Rett nodded.

"That's not even the hard part." Angie knew he needed support, but it had to be said.

Tracey was in the same position when they got back. Angie came in with a smile for support. Rett followed her with a frown. He didn't say a word to Tracey. He just plunked the loaf of bread he was carrying down on the kitchen counter, and went back into the bedroom.

Angie settled on the floor again. "He'll be all right."

"But, I—"

"Listen, Tracey. I talked to him. He loves you. No matter what I used to believe, I don't think anything could change that. He'll be all right."

Chapter 16

On the night before Tracey and Garrett left for Christmas break, they exchanged gifts. Because she had already handed in all her work, Tracey volunteered to make dinner that night. By the time Garrett got into the house, her whole body tingled with hypersensitivity. She was breathing fast and the adrenaline was pumping. She wanted so much for that night to be beautiful and for it to please him. Lately, she hadn't really done anything, it seemed, that pleased him. She knew she loved him, though she had never told him. She knew he loved her, though he had stopped saying it. But it wasn't enough.

More than anything, she wanted this night to be special. So she wore that short, fitted black dress for him, despite feeling a little heavy. She flat-ironed her hair and let it hang against her shoulders the way he liked. She wore heels and makeup.

Standing there in the living room in a coal black suit, a soft grey shirt beneath, a bottle of champagne in one hand, and flowers in the other, he stared at Tracey long and hard. "Baby." He swallowed. "Baby, you look so good."

"How'd you do?" She asked him about his paper, barely recognizing her own voice.

"Fine," he answered absently as he came forward to kiss her softly. They had always been so aggressive with each other and, now that she was getting used to the mild cardiac disturbance she got when he kissed her hard, he was changing things. Now he was kissing her softly and she felt like someone had a jackhammer smashing her in the sternum.

"I'm sorry I'm late." He handed her the bouquet of fragrant wildflowers. She wondered briefly if anyone could get fresh wildflowers in December anywhere else but in the South.

"I hadn't noticed."

"You always notice," he answered wryly. She recalled that first night he'd come in late from intramurals and how angry she'd been.

"There's dinner in the kitchen."

"I can't get over how beautiful you look."

Tracey smiled. She couldn't help it.

"Are you blushing?"

She didn't say anything.

"You are! You sure picked a funny time to get shy." He couldn't stop staring at Tracey. She felt giddy. He patted her on the bottom and said, "Hey, Angie told me what you got her for Christmas."

Earlier that day, when she was handing her the envelope, she told Tracey, "I would just like to thank you in advance. I already know that this is going to be an excellent present because you have such good taste. But if it isn't," she raised her voice, "then by God—"

"Just open the present, silly." Tracey laughed. She had only known her for a couple of weeks, but the more Tracey got to know her, the funnier and more adorable Angie got.

"My God, you didn't do this. Not for me, you didn't!"

"I believe I did."

She nearly tackled Tracey as she hugged her. "Ohmigod! Ohmigod! Ohmigod!" Angie squealed as she jumped around the living room. "You don't understand, Tracey. Fitts & Mahler is one of the best architectural firms in the country. They are at the very least, the best out of the South. I would be honored to kiss the feet of anyone there. I couldn't say 'no' to this. How? How?"

"My mom does a lot of work with that firm. I've known them forever. I beat Brennie Mahler up in the first grade." Tracey chuckled, remembering. "They needed an intern."

Afterward, Tracey opened Angie's present. Wrapped in a soft silk scarf that faded from eggplant to lilac was a book of Tibetan proverbs.

"You know what she got me?" Garrett asked. Tracey shook her head. "A hardbound copy of the writings of Frederick Douglass."

"Just a little heavy-handed of her."

"A little." He kissed her again. "Where's my present?"

Tracey smiled and handed him the only box beneath her tree.

While she was trying to figure out what to get him for Christmas, extravagant things crossed her mind. She thought about a cruise or a laptop or a car or something. She was going through a guilt thing at the same time she was going through an insane love thing. She wanted to get him something that would make him forget all the tension between them. Unfortunately, the gift she ultimately decided on made her even more guilty. He opened it. It was a supple, chic brown leather jacket made of the softest Italian leather she could find. It never really got cold enough for a heavy leather jacket, but this one he could wear all year round if he really wanted to. And she thought he would look a lot less "frat boy" in it as opposed to the bomber. A lot more metropolitan. This was why she felt guilty. Still, his eyes were big as he pulled it out. He looked like a little boy as he held it. He slipped it on. He definitely looked like a full-grown man. Tracey didn't know he would look so damn good in it. Guilt gone.

At that moment her heart started breaking in her chest. Garrett went through the pocket of the jacket he'd taken off and produced a box that couldn't be anything but a ring box. Tracey started shaking. Her whole body just started shaking. She took the box in trembling hands, already thinking to herself that she had to find some way to give it back to him. She didn't want to give it back, but she certainly couldn't accept it, no matter how desperately she wanted to say yes. She felt tears welling up and she could barely open the box.

When she managed it, she started bawling out of just… The ring was an amethyst surrounded by citrines. Her birthstone surrounded by his. The lilac and gold gems were set in a thick gold band and the ring looked like an antique. She took it and held it in the palm of her hand and just cried like a baby. Finally, he took the ring from her palm and slipped it onto the ring finger of her right hand. The way he looked at her as he put that ring on her finger said more to her than the position. She couldn't breathe. She grabbed onto him and kissed him so that he could give her life.

Afterward, they shared a virtually silent meal. He cleaned up the dishes, and Tracey waited on him with remote in hand, pretending to watch television. He walked in and gently took it from her. He turned off the set, and then took her into the bedroom laid her on the bed. He pulled his shirt over his head then lay down next to her. He rubbed her cheek with the backs of his fingers and said, "I'm officially off the lease at Woodlands."

Tracey swallowed. Whatever her parents would think if they found out, whatever the world would think, it just didn't matter then.

"I'm glad."

They lay there in silence until he put his arms around her and squeezed tight. Tracey held him hard and for some reason wanted to cry. "Tracey, I love you," he whispered.

She whispered back, "I love you, too." It was as if those words had to be kept in hushed tones so that there was no possibility of anyone else ever hearing them. But Tracey didn't want to think about that, and she didn't have to because he was kissing her softly again, and making love to her like a man in love.

—∽—

The following morning, Monica stopped by to give Tracey her gift before she went to her parents'. Tracey had completely forgotten she was coming and so, even though Garrett had cleaned up her kitchen the night before, a champagne bottle and wrapping paper were still laying in the living room. Moni noticed.

"Girl, my feelings are hurt. Looks like you had a party here last night and didn't invite me." Though she was smiling as she spoke, her voice told Tracey she truly was disappointed.

"No, it was really just my study group. We met over here last night and gave each other some gag gifts, that's all."

"Oh," she answered, but hurt and suspicion still creased her brow.

They exchanged presents then. "I didn't know what to get you," Moni complained. "You have everything! So I have to admit that Rico picked it."

Tracey started laughing even before she finished unwrapping the box. She leaned over to hug Moni, still laughing. "Why on earth did he get me a hand-held gaming system?"

"He said he saw you playing video games with the kids. You looked like you were having fun. Besides, he enjoys his, too."

"I was, and you're right, I don't have one. Woo-wee, I can't believe you got me this. I love it. It's going home with me."

"So you like it? I can take it back if you don't."

"No," Tracey yelped, more pleased than she should have been to get the system. She got three games with it to boot. "I want it! Open yours."

She opened her present, an envelope. "Oh, my! Damn, Rico's gonna die! Thank you, Tracey!" She hugged Tracey and kissed her on the cheek.

"Every time I come over there, you and Rico are arguing about this, so I'm helping you out. Now he has to do it." Tracey had decided on twelve weeks of ballroom dancing lessons with a Latin specialist. "And take these for the little ones. Give them my love."

—∽—

When she was a teenager living at home, it drove Tracey crazy that her mother was always in her room doing something. She was always scared Carolyn was in there reading her diary or snooping for God knows what. By the time she went away to college, Tracey was over that. As nosy as she was, her mother had a serious respect for the privacy of others, even her daughter's. She came in there because it was her way. Compelled to assess the aesthetic, she was always changing color schemes, changing styles, changing everything in the house. She'd gone through every style except French Provincial. "I can't stand French Provincial!" she'd said. Whatever the genre, she always refined it to her own clean style.

Now Tracey's room was completely blue. Almost electric blue. The hardwood floor was now stained blue. The walls were covered in light blue satin with a *fleur-de-lis* design that appeared when you moved a certain way. The dresser was blue. The chaise positioned under a window and beside the television, was blue. The table the TV sat on was blue. Tracey's bed, which was thankfully the same bed she had always had and always loved, was now covered in linens of bright, robin's egg blue with muted blue stripes. The only other colors in the place were some hints of white and silver. It was gorgeous, fit for a magazine, but not for a person's actual bedroom. Shrugging, Tracey reminded herself that no matter what color the lines, that was the most wonderful bed ever created by man, and it called to her. She went to lie down. She didn't expect to sleep into the next day.

—∾—

"Nice to see you decided to join the living," her mother said to her before cutting into a pancake. Carolyn sat at the table in the kitchen wearing a soft yellow and red floral shirt over dark green yoga pants. The sun filtered through the window into a room completely decorated in forest green, lemon, and tomato. Completely coordinated with the room, she looked perfect, as usual.

Tracey grunted at her in response. As soon as her mother got tired of wearing green to breakfast, she'd probably change the kitchen again. How practical was that?

"You must have been very tired," her mother started again. Regular old pleasant words, but Tracey knew her mother. She was like a bull scratching at the ground.

"I was," Tracey answered, sitting down next to her mother. "Thank you, Petey."

Petey, the jack of all trades at their house since Tracey was little, set a warm plate of eggs, bacon, and grits in front of her. He knew she saved her pancakes for last.

"You've been tired a lot lately, apparently. You've been too tired to come home in the past three months. You've been too tired to call like you should. And I mean on a day besides Thanksgiving. You've been too tired for a lot of things. I hope you're not too tired to graduate this spring."

"Mama—"

"Don't *Mama* me. Eat your breakfast."

"I'm a grown woman—"

"Don't tell me what you are. I'm the one that gave birth to you almost twenty-five years ago. You would think that a grown woman would be a little more thoughtful. Now *eat* your breakfast."

Tracey finally dug in, but her mother kept watching her. "Slow down, Tracey. You're eating like you're starving and I can tell by the two or three extra pounds that you aren't starving."

"Mama!"

She shrugged one shoulder and tried to assuage Tracey's outrage by saying, "You're fine, baby, fine."

She was surprised when her mother only raised an eyebrow when Tracey went back upstairs to lie down again.

—∞—

On Christmas Day Tracey opened her present from her daddy, which was an envelope. Inside, she found two round trip tickets and travel packets for a trip to Paris next September. She squealed.

"Shouldn't I be getting this later on in the year, Daddy?"

"Hey, if you knew you were going to get a trip anyway, what was the point of waiting? You'll get something else for graduation, girl. Now come over here and hug my neck." She threw her arms around him.

Her first thought was going with Garrett. Then it occurred to her that there was no way Garrett was going to be able to go to Paris with her. First, her parents would want to know, of course, who she was taking. Second, she didn't think he would accept the trip, even if indirectly, from her parents without them knowing about their relationship. She would have to take someone else. She thought of Monica. She might go, but she did have three children to take care of. Tracey thought of Angie; Angie would go and they would have fun. But again, how would Tracey explain her to her parents? A friend she met at school? Maybe.

Lucky for Tracey, she didn't have to make that decision right then.

Her mother gave her a new laptop, then promptly told her she expected her to go to church with her on Sunday. Yeah, well, even a Christmas gift from her had its price.

"You are going with me to Colleen's tomorrow, right, Tracey?"

"Yeah, what time?"

"I told her we'd be there around ten."

"Breakfast first?"

"Yeah."

"Well, I'm gonna go to bed now."

"Goodnight, baby." She soothed and stroked Tracey's hair before she left.

Nearing her bedroom, she heard the sounds of Grapple Arena III coming from her room. That was the fighting game she'd gotten with the gaming system. She slipped inside and shook her head as she saw her father in front of her television. The adapter from the handheld game projected the game onto the TV screen. She sat down on the loveseat next to him to watch him play the game.

"Addictive, isn't it?"

"Hush, Tracey, I'm tryin' to do somethin' here," he gritted out between jerks. When he finally lost a match he turned to his daughter and put his arm around her shoulder. "Don't tell your mama you saw me in here doing this. She thinks I'm too old."

"Well, you are."

"Aw, hush, Tracey." He leaned back against the seat. "It's good to have you home, baby girl."

"I'm sorry I haven't been home much this semester. I've been real busy."

"Socially, huh?" Tracey smiled sheepishly. "Well, that's understandable. I'm glad you've made friends this year. You're a young woman with a bright future. You need to make connections."

"Don't talk to me like I'm one of your students, Daddy," she told him.

"Speaking of students, how are things going with Alexander as your faculty advisor?"

"I don't know. That's something I wanted to talk to you about."

"What?"

"What do you really think about him?"

"Well, professionally, I have a lot of respect for him. He's been able to conquer adversity in that he's at a white university in one of the whitest law programs in America and yet he's managed to be successful. He's kept his identity intact and his dignity."

"I guess that answers my question."

"You don't like him?"

Daddy was smirking. He could always read her. "No, it's not that. I do like him. I was just curious."

"Travis!" They both turned towards the door.

"That's my cue. I'm going to bed now, baby girl. I'll see you tomorrow morning." He hugged her with one arm and kissed her on the cheek before he went out of her room, shutting her door.

Her bed looked like a cloud waiting to accept her. Still, she didn't sleep well. When she didn't drift off after an hour or so, she took out her cell phone and sent a text.

—〰—

Tracey sat in a cream leather salon chair wrapped from head to toe in a cream robe. Her wet hair, infused with some sort of deep conditioning lotion, was wrapped in a plastic bag as she sat under a dryer. Breathing deeply, she watched her Aunt Colleen chatting with one patron and another. Tracey watched her move with authority. Aunt Colleen always moved with authority, always knew what she wanted and where she was and who she was. Tracey admired her for that. Tracey had a lot to think about. Once upon a time, she had thought she knew those things, too.

Tracey wondered what Garrett was doing then. Was she as much in his thoughts as he was in hers? What were they going to do? They were both graduating in May. He would go his way and Tracey was going to have to go hers, right? The thought caused her physical pain. She pressed a hand to her stomach. She was hoping like hell Mama wouldn't notice as she came toward her swathed in her own robe. But because she had that mother-type sixth sense, she did.

"What's wrong, Tracey?"

"Nothing." She sniffled, trying to be strong.

Carolyn stared at her and said, "Come on. Let's go to the restroom."

"Ma, I'm fine," Tracey protested. But her mother turned off the dryer and dragged her away, mumbling something barely comprehensible about hormones. If Tracey didn't follow her, she would think her daughter disrespectful.

In the bathroom, Tracey looked under the stall doors. There was no one there. No one to save her. She started to cry even harder. Even as she was pulled into her mother's arms, she knew she couldn't tell her mother what was wrong. Of course, Carolyn would tell Tracey she loved her daughter no matter what, that as long as Tracey was happy, she was happy. She would say everything Tracey needed to hear from her. And she would probably think she meant it. But right after, she would tell Tracey what the rest of the world would think. She would start every sentence by clarifying, "Now, I'm not talking about me, because I love you." She would tear down everything she'd built up. She would tell her father, who wouldn't waste the time with pleasantries.

Mama pulled back from her. She smoothed her hair back and held Tracey's chin up toward her. "Tracey, did you do something?" Her eyes were serious. "I know you said everything was fine at school, but... What I mean to say is that you're my daughter, and I know you. Is it a man? Are you pregnant?"

"No!" Tracey squealed.

"That's good." Mama nodded. "But it is a man?" Not answering was like an admission of guilt for her. "What did he do to you?" Not the best question.

"He didn't exactly do it to me, Ma."

"Then what did you do to him?" Better question. "Tracey what did you do to him?"

"Look," Tracey told her, "I really don't feel like talking to you about this right now." No use searching for an excuse, her mother wouldn't believe any of them anyway. Tracey splashed water on her face.

"Are you sure you're not pregnant?"

"I'll be fine, Ma. Thanks for the concern."

In the end, Tracey decided she would go home, or rather back to school, and not think about it. She just wouldn't think about it.

Chapter 17

"Jesus, lady! Where did you learn to cook like this? Not from your mama, she is not so good in the kitchen."

Mary Margaret Atkins leveled a killing look at her brother.

"Unc Beau, you never met a piece of food you didn't like." Angie grinned at the only member of her mother's extended family she could stomach.

"I met plenty of your mama's food I didn't like!"

"Now Beau, how many times you going to say it?" Mary Margaret's pale green eyes were starting to flash with anger.

"I'm just saying."

"Everybody in here knows what you're saying," Jerry, Mary Margaret's other brother, called from the living room where he was watching television.

"That's enough," Big Atkins said to his brothers-in-law. He was always trying to keep the peace.

"Well," Jess McNealey, Big's sister, started, "as long as we all enjoy the fellowship of the day and celebrate in Jesus' name, everything's all right."

"Do I have to celebrate dry-ass turkey?" Tonya, Beau's wife, spoke up. Her words were a little slurred as she slumped sideways in her chair.

Mary Margaret slammed back from the table and grabbed her plate, taking it over to the sink. She started the disposal.

Big stood up and came to stand behind her. He tried to slip his arms around her waist.

"Leave me alone."

"Aww, Mary Margaret." He swayed forward, trying to hold her.

"Leave me alone, Big," Mary Margaret said again, like she meant it.

Big just grinned.

"Dad," Angie admonished him, "please leave her alone, or she's going to give you hell later. And hell to you means hell to us." She motioned to Rett, who rolled his eyes. He wasn't going to let his family's holiday curse get to him this year. No one had left the house furious and refusing to come back yet, so he figured they were in the lead.

"All you have to do, Angela, darling, is get your mama to give me a little kiss. That'll solve everything."

Angie looked plaintively toward her mother, willing her to do just that. But she wouldn't. Mary Margaret Atkins was as stubborn as the millennium was long. She had always been picked on by her brothers, and that had extended to their no-good wives once they were married. "Please, Mama, give him a kiss so I don't have to watch him slobber all over you."

Rett laughed then, and, when she saw it, so did his mother.

The curse had been averted for a minute.

"Ho! Ho! Ho! Merry Christmas!"

There went the cease-fire.

Nate, Wayne, Trish and her kids were filing in. Rett and Angie exchanged looks.

"I'm not on 9-1-1 duty this year," Angie whispered in his ear. "I'm so out of here." She stood up and fixed the prettiest, most dazzling smile on her face. She didn't bother to greet her cousins, and they certainly didn't open their mouths to her. She mentioned something about meeting friends for drinks. Mary Margaret shot her a glare, but remained quiet. Her brother Jerry did the same.

Rett would stay, of course. He needed to be peace-maker if at all possible. It usually wasn't. As soon as the beer and Tennessee bourbon started to flow, there were going to be problems.

They would sit around talking, watching football, and laughing at jokes that weren't really jokes. Rett would watch his mother try to hold on to her temper. She had an awful one, but she knew that as soon as she let it rise, her brothers would use it as an excuse to argue. One would side with her for the hell of it. The other would side against her for the same reason.

Then Big would try to settle it, and they would turn on him. By that time Rett and his cousins would have gotten in on it, too. There was no longer a door to the den. It had been broken off its hinges twice at past dinners and they'd decided to stop replacing it.

Rett took a beer and stood up so Trish could have his seat. The kitchen was getting too crowded. He eased out into the living room where Jerry reclined in his dad's chair.

"That's what's wrong with everything today." Jerry gestured at the TV with his thumb. Rett looked up and there was a telethon on. *Oh, God.*

"See, them people start having them babies—"

"Jerry—"

"No, no, let me tell you. If you going to be a lawyer you going to be seeing stuff like this all the time, and I don't want you to get fooled. I mean I know for a fact half of them is out there on welfare and they think that for every baby they get, that's just another check. It's like a job to 'em. If they can get something from you—"

"Come on, Jerry," Rett said, swallowing.

"Come on what, boy? I'm trying to make sure you still see the truth. I don't know what school's telling you but—"

Forget being peacemaker. If he stayed he was going to be the one starting the fight this time. Rett took a breath but didn't answer. He just walked out of the house.

Sitting in his car, he reached for his cell phone and dropped his seat back.

"Hello." Her voice was low, but excited. She was happy to hear from him.

"You up, Trace?"

"Yeah, babe." She said it quickly. The little endearment had just slipped out. At one time she would have hesitated over using such an affectionate term for him. Rett's heart soared… and his pants tightened. He sighed, but a grin found its way to his face.

"You want to talk?"

"Yeah."

—⁂—

He and Tracey hadn't planned to see each other before they went back to school, but neither of them could stay away. They'd agreed to meet at a remote hotel just off exit 89. Their time together was intense, and something they both needed, but Rett couldn't help being bothered by her answer when he asked her to stay the night.

She looked up at him and broke his heart. He didn't want the words to come out of her mouth but they did. "I can't stay the night. I know I'm an adult, but my parents will wonder where I am."

Her fear was single-handedly destroying the both of them.

Chapter 18

When Tracey got back from Christmas break, being with Garrett was the only thing on her mind, even though he'd been a bit distant since Christmas. He must have been happy to see her, too, because she was barely inside before he was making love to her, eating her alive. For a while, it seemed like things were back to the way were at the start. But it didn't last.

Two weeks later, on a Friday, Garrett and Trace were together at home, working all day. That night she was going out with Monica and Sabrina for dinner. She hadn't seen Monica since she got back and Sabrina had called that afternoon to talk about their Employee Rights final. Tracey invited her to dinner as well.

"So you're going to be out all night?" he asked as she dressed for dinner.

"No, honey, I'll be back around nine or ten. It's just dinner."

"Where are you going?"

"Rachel's, of course." She kissed him before she grabbed her purse.

"Well, I may go out tonight, too," he called to her as she got ready to go out the front door.

"Good," she yelled back to him, then added, "Just be home at a reasonable hour!"

—∞—

Rett knew Tracey. He knew how she felt. He knew that they lived in the "Heart of Dixie" and, while a lot of things had changed, a lot of them had not. People like him, people like Tracey… She envisioned her father forcing her to watch *Eyes on the Prize* and *Roots* and even *Shaka Zulu* until she came to her senses. He'd seen every one of those miniseries, and would quote them when Tracey was being ungrateful.

As for Garrett's family… From what Tracey could gather from him and Angie, their nuclear family was a pretty standard middle class group of people. Once you started throwing in uncles and aunts and cousins and second cousins, things started to get a bit sketchy. They never came out and said what their family was like, but from what Tracey gathered, family gatherings with the Atkins and Hinsons were very different than those of the McAlpines and Moncriefs.

Beyond their families, Tracey was still holding on to the few friends she'd made in school and was protective of her burgeoning friendship with Moni. Garrett had basically moved into her place, but still kept the majority of his clothing and belongings in his car because she didn't want her mother or father to come to the place and find something of his. Not just because he was white, but because they would never, ever, support her living with a man or even giving the impression of living with a man out of wedlock. He still hung out with Clay quite a bit, but she knew he worked at maintaining his other relationships, using law school as a handy excuse for his general absence. Angie still came over often.

Garrett knew better than to show up with some of his friends at the same place Tracey was having dinner with her friends.

She saw him there and sank back into her seat and tried to look inconspicuous. Nearly impossible, though, with Monica's jokes. She'd started in on their waiter as soon as they sat down, flirting outrageously. The flirting was meant to be a joke, though Tracey could barely breathe with Garrett right there across the dining hall from her. Halfway through dinner he walked towards her. Tracey panicked.

"Tracey." He greeted her with a neutral smile.

"Garrett, hi."

He looked from her to Sabrina, and then to Monica. He stuck out his hand. "Hi, I'm Garrett Atkins, Tracey's—"

"Friend!" Tracey interjected. "He's a friend of mine from class!" Sabrina and Monica shook hands and smiled politely.

He was already angry when he added, "Tracey, I'd like you to come over and meet a few of my friends."

Monica and Sabrina looked at each other, then at Tracey.

"Oh, I know them both from class," she answered, not moving. Tracey waved at the guys at his table and smiled. One of them she recognized as his old roommate, Clay. Garrett looked at her and she had never, ever, seen the condemning, angry expression he wore. He nodded at her curtly and then walked back to his own table. Monica started to snicker and Sabrina followed suit. Tracey pasted on a smile, too, though there was an icy freeze inside her.

He almost broke the hinges off her front door.

"What the hell was that all about?"

"What do you mean?"

"You know what I mean. I was ready, and you knew it. I was *ready* and you made me look like a damn fool. I know it was your decision not to be out in the open about it, but—"

"I was right about that, wasn't I?"

"No, Tracey, you weren't, but I was hoping you'd come around. You promised me you would, but I guess that didn't mean anything to you." Tracey leaned back in her chair and tried to distance herself from what he was saying. "Don't you dare tune me out, Tracey! Don't you dare! We are going to talk about this whether you want to or not."

"People could get the wrong impression."

"What? That we're sleeping together?" The door remained wide open as he stalked over to her. "Tracey, we *live* together."

"Don't. It's not that. It's—"

"What is it?" he yelled. He was so close she could feel his breath on her face. She knew he wasn't going to hit her, but she had also never seen him this angry before. "Are you ashamed? Tracey, is that it? You don't want any of your friends to know you're screwing a white guy?"

She might have hit him; however, she didn't remember hitting him. There was a rancid silence, then the big red spot spreading across his jaw and cheek.

He took a deep breath and took a step away from her. She didn't meet his gaze.

He walked over to close her front door. "You don't even know what I've been going through. It doesn't even occur to you that I have just as many obstacles to overcome as you do. You think it's all about you." He sounded defeated. "You don't know what I have to deal with, what my *dad* and my *sister* have to deal with. It's not as much of a secret as you think it is. I've been handling this for months. *Months*, Tracey."

"I didn't—"

"You didn't know because I didn't want you to know. I didn't want you to get upset. But screw that, Tracey! Your friends don't know, your *father*, the all-powerful Travis McAlpine, J.D., doesn't know a thing. He's not having to defend you to his friends or having to deal with the funny looks from his coworkers. And unlike me, *you* barely go to your church. I go to my church every Sunday morning and I have to smile when people are smiling at me, going through the motions but talking about me behind my back."

As usual, Tracey was swept up in the intensity of the moment and all her words left her. She didn't even know what to feel.

"What's so wrong with it, Tracey? What's so wrong with you and me lovin' each other and not being afraid to show it? I can deal with the BS, but you have to deal with it, too. Why can't you?"

She couldn't answer and she couldn't stop the tears from welling up. It wasn't on purpose. She didn't start to cry because she wanted to distract him or force him to be sympathetic. She cried because he was right. Tracey had believed in their anonymity. Still didn't quite know how it hadn't gotten out. But it hadn't touched her life as apparently it had Garrett's.

"Tracey, don't cry. Please. I don't want to hurt you. It's just that it's making me crazy. You're making me crazy. I'm sick of you acting like I don't exist as soon as you walk out the door." He put his arms around her and massaged her neck. He kissed the tears out of her eyes. "Tracey, you're killing me," he whispered. "I love you, and you're killing me. If it were just sex, that'd be different, but I want more than that, so much more. I want to go to the movies with you, to go dancing with you. I want to go to the grocery store with you and hold hands while we argue over what kind of beer to buy. I can't take things the way that they are. I can't be with you, it hurts too much." He pulled back and away from her. "I'm leavin'. I have to. I'll pick up my things later."

"Where are you going to stay? Garrett, you're not on the lease at Woodland Towers anymore."

"I'll be at Angie's. If you change your mind, you know where to find me."

—⚏—

Tears swam before his eyes on the drive to his sister's house. His nose was running, too, and he swiped at his face with his hand. It didn't help, and the gaping hole in his heart just seemed to widen.

He tried to get himself together before he went into his sister's apartment, but as soon as he walked in, she looked up and smiled. He tried to smile back but knew he failed. He called her name. "Angie."

"What is it?" Her voice was gentle as she motioned for him to join her on the couch. He could tell from her tone, from the warmth and sadness in her eyes, she already knew.

"I don't know what to do."

"Just give it some time, Rett. I promise you it will work itself out."

Rett just shook his head. His throat burned as sobs racked his body.

He needed to go home, even if he had to face Big and the fact that he had been right.

—◊◊◊—

After spending the night at Angie's, Rett went home early in the morning and started pounding beers. When Big came in the kitchen, he took one look at his son before walking with him out to the carport.

"What's going on, son?"

"You said some things were out and some in. Well, I don't have an 'in' anymore, Daddy, and hell, it's putting me out."

"What is that supposed to mean?"

"It means you won't be hearing anything else about me."

Big nodded, but he studied Rett's face anyway.

As the weeks turned to months, Big became more unsettled every time Rett came home. His son was getting drunk, starting fights, and chasing every skirt that crossed his path. Or so he heard. That Charles always had something to say about Rett. Whether it was true or not, Rett barely spent any time at home anymore, and when he did, he didn't have much to say. There was trouble brewing and there was no doubt in Big's mind it all came down to that black gal.

Chapter 19

Tracey had hoped they would be able to talk the next day when Rett came for his clothes, and he would come back to her. Instead, she went to meet with the VP of Human Resources at Rico's company that morning, and by the time she got back home she found every trace of him gone. To say that she was destroyed would be putting it mildly.

The best thing she could do was to avoid him. She even rescheduled her meetings with Alex to other places on campus. She couldn't run the risk of running into him. If she did, Tracey would lose all her resolve and probably be reduced to a blubbering idiot. Once she saw his former roommate, Clay, in one of her classes and he stopped to talk. She didn't mind because she wanted to know how Garrett was. She wanted to know how long it had taken him to get over her. What Tracey found out was that he was sick as a dog and the doctor couldn't find out what was wrong with him. She thought about the fact that she hadn't been feeling too hot, either, and wondered if she was coming down with what he had. She wondered if she should call just to see if he was okay. Instead, she texted him saying she hoped he felt better soon. He didn't text back.

About three weeks later, she was sure she was getting what he had.

Tracey went to the center looking for Monica. The counselor sat at the table with her knees drawn up to her chest and her arms wrapped around them, listening to old Mrs. Walker telling stories about when she was in the military.

Tracey walked in and waved to her. Monica waved back and motioned for Tracey to wait in her office. She turned her attention back to the older woman.

After Mrs. Walker walked away with her brown leather purse tucked beneath her arm like a football, Monica entered the office and leaned against the desk in front of Tracey. "You're off today, aren't you?"

"Yeah, um…can I talk to you?"

"Sure. What's on your mind?"

Tracey smiled brightly at her as she mustered the courage to say it. Moni beamed back at her but her smile faltered when Tracey's did. Tracey's bottom lip started to tremble. She dropped her head into her hands.

"Tracey?" Moni's voice was urgent and worried as she placed a warm hand on her friend's shoulder.

"I think I might be…be…" Tracey couldn't get it out. She just couldn't. She hugged her arms around herself and rocked.

"Oh, my God, Tracey. Who? Alex?"

Tracey looked up, confused for a moment about who she meant. When it dawned on her, she shook her head quickly. "No, of course not."

"Well, who? You haven't mentioned anyone to me all this time. I didn't even know you were, well, you know…in a relationship with anyone."

"I, um, I couldn't tell you."

"Why in heaven's name not?" She squatted in front of Tracey and took her hands.

Like a child, Tracey shook her head and pressed her lips together.

"Tracey, if you think you're pregnant…" She lowered her voice on the last word. "You should—"

"I don't want to talk about it."

"You came here, Tracey. You came to me to talk about it."

True, but this pain had changed that.

"I'm gonna go home, okay?" Tracey stood and started out of the office.

Moni slipped around her and blocked the door.

"Tracey, tell me."

Stubborn silence.

"I hope you know how much I care about you." She stepped closer and threw her arms around Tracey. "You can tell me anything. Anything. Did someone hurt you? Were you—"

Tracey couldn't hold on to it alone anymore. She told Moni everything, from the very first day she and Garrett met to the way he came after her, to that night when he introduced himself at Rachel's.

"Damn, Tracey." She sat at her desk with Tracey slumped like a rebellious teenager across from her.

"Have you talked to your folks?"

Tracey shook her head.

"Have you talked to him?"

Tracey shook her head.

"Are you sure you're…?"

Tracey nodded.

"Didn't you take precautions?"

"Yes, we almost always used something. The couple of times we didn't I figured we'd be okay because I was on the pill."

She processed the information. "You might not have anything to worry about. It might be a false alarm."

"I don't think so. I stopped taking the pill and still no period. Plus, I had the morning sickness before I even thought that was what it was. My clothes don't fit anymore. I know it."

"That would make you at least two months, maybe more. Tracey, you know we have the facilities here, we can find out for sure."

"I don't know what to do."

"I'm *telling* you what to do."

"I'm not ready yet."

"Tracey! How *old* are you? You're a grown-up, thinking, rational woman. You are not like the girls I talk to in this room. You know what you have to do."

"I know. I just can't…I just can't do it here, today."

"Why not?"

"I don't know."

"Well, if I let you out of here, you have to promise me to do it either at home or somewhere before the week is out. I know you probably feel safer not knowing, but things like this don't go away in time. They can't." Tracey just sat there, unable to speak, trying so hard to keep that lump in her throat down. Monica wiped the tears streaming down Tracey's face. "Think about if you are. Would you want to deny the baby proper care just because you didn't want to face it?"

Tracey hadn't thought of that. Wincing, she assured her friend, "I'll do it. I'll do it today."

"Here?"

"No. No, I'd feel more comfortable at home."

"Do you want me to come with you?"

Tracey shook her head.

"Okay, sweetheart, okay. Just give me a call one way or another." She hesitated, scratching one of her forearms. "You know, you have to talk to him. Even if this hadn't come up, you would still have to talk to him 'cause you were wrong for what you did."

"That's easy for you to say. Walk a mile in my shoes and all that."

"That's selfish, Tracey. I swear, I don't even know you."

That hurt. "You do."

"I'm not so sure. You hid this relationship from me when all I've wanted to be was your friend. I don't know what you thought of me, but not enough to know I'd be fine with whoever you chose to be with. It didn't have to be Alex. I just thought you might like him."

Paralyzed again, wanting to say something, to apologize, Tracey remained stony and silent.

Monica sighed. "My feelings about this aren't the issue. *You* got him into this relationship with a promise that you would get over all your hang-ups, but you didn't."

"I thought I would."

"So you thought it. It was still an unrealistic, immature assumption on your part, and very unfair to him."

"I really don't need you to tell me that."

"Apparently you do," she replied. "Especially since he made the effort for you. And you could have at least given me a little credit that night at the restaurant. What did you think I was going to do? I can't speak for Sabrina, but I know that if you have someone that makes you happy, then I'm happy."

"Moni, I'm sorry. I truly, deeply am."

Monica acknowledged her statement but plunged ahead. "You've got to tell him. You have to confront him and have closure on this, no matter what the outcome of the test is."

Then Tracey said what had been on her mind for such a long time: "I don't have to tell him."

Moni's look of horror would have come off as quite comical if the situation weren't so serious. She didn't say anything, but the look she gave Tracey was enough. The following silence in the room was so thick, it inspired claustrophobia.

Monica cut through it, saying, "Tracey, listen. You don't have to tell him, you don't have to tell anyone. Hey, you don't even know yet. But if it's true and you still don't say anything…You don't have to if that's the way you want it, but I don't think it's right. And professionally speaking, you are headed for much more heartbreak than you've had up to this point."

"Yeah," Tracey muttered.

Before Tracey left Monica hugged her hard, expressing her forgiveness in the form of a kiss to the cheek.

Outside, Tracey got in her car. She knew what she had to do.

—m—

That night the phone sat cradled in her lap for three straight hours, pelted by perpetual tears. She had to call him and tell him. If she didn't, Tracey couldn't, wouldn't, forgive herself. But if he knew, what would he do?

She grabbed the phone and tapped out the numbers without even looking at them and pressed the cold plastic to her face.

"Tracey!" His voice washed too much brilliance over her. He was so happy for what she concluded were the wrong reasons. Fool that she was, she couldn't stop her belly from flipping over just from the sound of his voice.

She mustered her courage again and said, "Garrett. I need to talk to you about something."

"Well, what? You want me to come over? I can be there in two seconds."

"No, I don't want you to come over. You probably won't want to after you hear what I have to say."

"What is this, Tracey? If you're calling to tell me what I've already figured out for myself, I don't want to hear it. If you called to tell me—"

"Listen to me, damn it."

"No, you listen to me. You can't expect—"

"Garrett, I've missed my period."

"What?" His voice was so low she could barely hear him.

"I missed my period four weeks ago. I didn't think anything of it. I'm not always regular. But I'm due for another one and it hasn't come, either."

"Oh, God," he breathed and she could imagine him laying his head in his hands.

"I'm not sure, though. I haven't been tested yet." *Why the hell didn't I get tested before I called him?* she thought.

"I'm coming over."

"No, don't!"

"Bye, Tracey," he said and hung up the phone.

—〰—

"Who was that?"

Heart, pounding, Garrett looked over at his sister. Then he looked at her roommate—now his roommate—sitting at the computer desk playing some pointless role-playing game.

He wanted to tell Angie, but it was too soon to say anything to her, and he would never talk in front of Mr. Brain Dead.

"I gotta go."

Angie's brow creased with confusion. "Where?"

"None of your business," he answered and put on his shoes, grabbed his jacket and wallet, and headed out.

"You going to crank the car up with your finger?"

Garrett snatched his car keys from Angie, gave her a quick peck on the cheek, and flew out of there.

He got to the corner pharmacy in what had to be record time. He ran in and went down the aisle of condoms and lubricants and intimate ointments. With shaking hands, he picked up one of the home pregnancy kits and flipped it so he could read the label. His eyes barely focused and, for just a minute, he thought he was going to start hyperventilating. How the hell was he supposed to know which one to pick? And why were they so expensive?

Rett bit down on the inside of his cheek hard enough to draw blood.

Keep it together, man. Keep it together. If she's not pregnant, then there's nothing to worry about. If she is…

An image of Big flashed in his mind. Right behind that one came one of his mother, Mary Margaret, and her side of the family.

He ran a hand over his face. Those thoughts wasted time and energy. All efforts needed to be directed toward getting what he needed, getting to Tracey, and praying to God she was not pregnant.

He grabbed a box of every kind of test he saw, ignoring the money. He'd use his credit card and cross that bridge when he got to it, too.

Careful not to drop his cargo, Rett walked to the counter in the back of the store. No need to purchase them up front where God and country could walk in and see him.

Lucky for him, there was no line. He spilled the boxes onto the counter and forced a smile at the older Middle Eastern fellow behind the counter.

"I'm sorry, sir." The pharmacist held up a placating hand. "I will be with you in one moment."

Rett realized too late that he had brushed past another customer in his haste. He turned slightly and should have received an award for his ability to hide how startled he felt.

"Dr. Burke?" The pharmacist gestured and Burke came forward.

Reflexively, Rett reached for the boxes on the counter.

"No, no." The pharmacist halted him. "You may leave those there. This will take but a moment."

Rett cursed under his breath but stepped back.

"Mr. Atkins," Alexander Burke greeted him.

"Dr. Burke," Rett returned.

The attorney looked down pointedly at the boxes on the counter.

Rett felt all the muscles in his body go rigid. He thought about the first time he'd met Tracey. She had been the absolutely cutest thing he'd ever seen propped up against the wall. Even with her feisty attitude, he'd found himself lost in her big brown eyes and her shy smile. And she was so smart, and she had been everywhere under God's sky and could talk about anything. Rett actually *liked* listening to her talk. But she made him so angry. Furious. And yet, Rett loved her absolutely, with everything he had in him. He thought about watching her have dinner with Burke at Rachel's. She was gorgeous that night, more so than he'd ever seen her and enough to make him take another step toward having her in his life for longer than a semester or two.

Burke might have felt that way about her, too.

But it would never be a reality for the older man. Never.

Rett puffed out his chest and raised his chin with a smile.

Chapter 20

Twenty minutes after she hung up the phone with him, Rett barged into Tracey's house with a grocery bag in hand. He emptied the contents out onto the table in front of her and said, "I didn't know which one to get, so I got them all. You should have seen the cashier." He looked at her as she stood paralyzed staring down at the little red, blue and white boxes. He stood there a minute longer, then came around the table to sit beside her. He took the pillow she was holding from her arms and replaced it with his body. For a long time, he held her and whispered into her ear that everything would be fine, no matter what happened. Tracey couldn't bear the support, the concern. She started a brand new style of wailing and he just held her tighter.

When she felt able to speak again, she asked, "Why are you so good to me?"

"Hell if I know," he replied and stood, taking Tracey with him. He grabbed several of the tests and walked her to the bathroom. He took her in, gave a few encouraging words, then disappeared behind the door. Tracey took down her pants and sat down on the cold stool.

She picked up one cardboard box and read the back of it. It had a five percent chance of being wrong. She wondered if she was in that five percent.

She opened the test and took out the sealed plastic envelope and the instructions. She read and re-read them. They weren't that hard. She opened another and the instructions were pretty much the same. One just peed and held the little stick in the stream. She took two tests at once. She wiped and stood, pulling up her pants with her one free hand. She flushed. Tracey didn't look at the tests and put them in the dry sink without looking at them. She opened the door and Rett stepped in. She looked at him, not the sink. "What does the first one look like?"

"Two stripes in the window," he said. Tracey looked at the test to see if it was true.

"Jesus Christ."

"What's that mean? Is it positive?"

Tracey nodded.

"The other one's blue," he said.

She looked at the other one. She didn't want there to be two lines. She didn't want one stick to turn blue. She didn't want to be pregnant, but she was.

With trembling hands she picked up each test put them back into their boxes and threw them in the trash. She started to wash her hands. She was at a loss for what to do, what to feel. Then the dreaded tears started to flow.

"Tracey." He reached for her.

She jumped away from him and fell into the wall, banging her elbow. It hurt. She turned and rammed her thigh into the corner of the sink. That hurt, too.

Garrett ran a frustrated hand through his hair, but he stayed. He tried again to reach for her, to comfort her. Garrett Atkins. Prince Charming in shining armor on a white horse. Tracey was so angry all of a sudden that she couldn't think. She didn't even know why she was angry. And *that* made her *more* angry. She pushed him away from her and went into the bedroom. She crawled into the bed and rolled up into a ball. He followed her and sat next to her. He put his arm around her curved back and waited for her to open up. She lay there for what seemed like hours until she did open up and let Garrett take her into his arms. He stretched out alongside her. Tracey didn't remember falling asleep, but when she woke up he was in the kitchen cooking. She walked in and leaned against the refrigerator.

"How you feeling?" He placed some onions in the skillet. They gave a fragrant hiss as he pushed them around in the popping oil. He added peppers.

"I'm all right, I guess." Tracey closed her eyes and wrapped her arms around her waist, wondering how big it could get.

"You know, I had morning sickness," Rett said.

"I heard." He looked up at her quizzically. "Well I knew you were sick. I saw your roommate in class.

I thought sympathetic pregnancy was a myth. Who knew?"

"I went to the doctor and he couldn't find anything wrong. Said I was the picture of health. He said I was acting just like a man who was about to have a baby. It was funny at the time. He asked me if it was Kim. I told him that it couldn't be…" His words trailed off and he seemed to have run out of them.

They held each other with their eyes. She began, "I'm sorry."

"It's not just your fault. We both had our share in this."

"That's true, but I took the responsibility of—I don't know how it happened. I mean, I was on the—"

"I know how it happened," he answered, still holding her gaze. "Antibiotics. Antibiotics often render some forms of oral birth control ineffective." Her eyes widened, and he held up his hands and argued, "I didn't think of it then. And to tell you the truth, I wouldn't have known it had I not just finished reviewing a case where the very same thing happened."

Tracey looked away and gave this some thought. She didn't know how she could blame him. It was something she already should have thought of herself. She changed the subject. "How do you feel?"

"Well, oddly enough, I'm okay. I mean, I know other guys in my position would be upset, angry even, but I'm not. We just ended up in that one percent you never really think happens. This doesn't have to be a bad thing if we don't let it be."

"I know," she said, thinking of a doctor Monica had told her about.

"I've gotten extremely lucrative bids from a lot of firms. And we know you're taken care of." Tracey got dizzy, and it didn't have a thing to do with the little growing thing inside of her. His thoughts strayed far from hers. "Well, you couldn't start working just yet." And Tracey could see him counting months in his head. "It'll be due around the end of August, I'm thinking. You could still finish this year, take the summer off and start working when the baby is three or four months old. I'll definitely be able to afford real good childcare by then." He turned to her as if looking for her accord.

Tracey couldn't give it. She could only stand there shaking against the nausea and guilt. She didn't know how she'd persisted in her cowardice for so long.

"You're not thinking about…Tracey, how could you? Could you? Oh, my God." His voice seemed to wilt along with his body, his shoulders curving down. She still didn't say anything. He stepped back as if she repulsed him. He nearly tipped the pan. Tracey reached out to touch his arm, to make him understand. This time he did tip it. Long, tender wisps of onion, almost transparent, flew into the air with hot oil splattering all over. The pan hit the tile and rang out like a bell tone. Tracey stood there staring at it with her hand outstretched. She just watched the pan lie there, not broken, but battered. Battered.

Garrett moved as far away from her as possible, as if she had a disease. He moved into the living room without taking his eyes off her. He moved into his jacket, and then backed into the door. He grabbed his stomach as if he had just been stabbed in the intestines and walked out. Tracey saw him bend over the porch rail and empty the contents of his stomach, even though he hadn't eaten. She watched him swipe his mouth with the back of his hand. He stood straight, but in seconds his shoulders rounded and she watched as he shook there, alone. There was nothing for her to do, so she watched as he walked towards his car, as he opened the door, as he got in. She watched him leave her. Really leave her this time.

—〰—

For three days, Tracey didn't leave her home. She didn't eat, she didn't sleep, she didn't do anything. She didn't even cry anymore. She sat in the darkness she made for herself: shades pulled, the curtains drawn, air stagnant from an unclean kitchen, and silence, silence, silence.

On the first day, she replayed the scene in her head. Only each time she saw it, it changed. It grew more and more elaborate. She saw him yelling and angry. She saw him telling her that she was going to have the baby no matter what. She saw an explosion, Garrett forcing her to change her mind the way he'd forced his way into her life from the very first. Tracey saw everything except him being broken by her. She cried whenever that particular scene tried to force its way through. Jesus, it had happened so fast.

On the second day, she held her stomach and imagined what her baby was like. She wondered if it was a boy or a girl. She wondered who it would look like. What would the baby's skin and hair be like? Would he or she be as neurotic as Tracey or as driven as Garrett?

Her phone rang off the hook. Everybody on earth left her messages. Everybody except her love, who had left her. Tracey wondered what her friends would think about her baby. Her body nearly cracked open at the thought of what her parents would do. But on that, she tried to let those things go and just hold on to herself.

And then, late on that second night, she heard the phone ring. For some unknown reason, for once, she answered it.

"Hello." Her own voice was new to her.

"I'm begging you to have it."

"No, Garrett."

"I will take care of it."

"No, Garrett."

"You won't ever have to worry about it afterwards."

"No, Garrett."

"Please don't do this to me." And that was the end. She hung up the phone and that was the end.

On the third day, Tracey prayed. She prayed over the sound of his voice and the pain she had manacled him with. She knew she couldn't terminate this pregnancy. Tracey was already attached to her — Tracey had begun to think of the baby as "her" — for more reasons than she could count. *She* was a symbol of something beautiful. *She* was something beautiful herself. Tracey prayed then, for the strength to bring her daughter into the world alone. She prayed for the strength to face everyone and everything she had to face for her. She prayed for a future.

She picked herself up then. She showered. She lit her house and cleaned. She opened her windows to brisk air on a sunny January day. Tracey had a plan. She felt alive and optimistic, ready to take on the world.

She heard keys rattling in her front door. Her heart jumped up into her throat because it could only be Garrett. Somehow she wanted it to be Garrett. She also wanted desperately for it *not* to be Garrett. So, when she opened the door, she tried to be relieved to see her mother. Then, the real anxiety set in.

Chapter 21

"Tracey, you should have known I was coming." Her words were quick and her neck curled. "You don't go for days without answering the phone or calling. You didn't even respond to my emails."

Tracey was bawling before she got in the house. Her mother dropped all her belongings in a chair and rushed to her daughter's side. She fussed over Tracey, making it worse. She cooed at her that everything would be all right. Then—as was her way—she angrily demanded that Tracey tell her what was wrong. Tracey worked very hard to get the words out, but couldn't seem to. "Mama, I'm...I'm—"

"Pregnant!" That was so like her. God! That was so like her. There Tracey was struggling to tell her mother something that was so important and her mother had pre-empted her. Another moment stolen by Carolyn McAlpine.

"Couldn't you just let me say it? Could you not just let me get it out on my own?"

Her mother didn't answer that. Instead she jumped up and screeched, "I knew it. I knew it when you were home for Christmas."

"How could you know?" Tracey argued. "I didn't even know."

"Mothers can tell, Tracey. We can smell it." Then, in what seemed like the same breath, she said, "I can't believe this. My baby is pregnant!" Then, "You can't possibly have a baby."

Tracey licked her lips and dug her fingernails into her palms in order to hold her tongue.

"God, Tracey, what are you going to do? Who's the father and why haven't Daddy or I met him? And what about school? I suppose you can finish in May if you're not too far along. Just how pregnant are you? Yes, you can definitely finish school. You couldn't be more than three months. You're not really showing. Then again, I didn't show until I was six months pregnant with you. But you are wearing that big shirt." Up went Tracey's shirt as her mother scrutinized her belly, touching it with cold fingers. Tracey snatched the shirt down. Her mother's eyes snapped to hers. Carolyn's hysteria was gone and her eyebrows drew close. Her mouth pursed. "So, what are you going to do about it? And are you going to explain to me what has happened?"

"I'm going to have the baby."

She pursed her lips even tighter in a look that was equal parts disdain and something Tracey couldn't quite place. "So it's safe to assume that the father is around and supportive, whoever he is, since you haven't introduced us to anybody."

"No, it's not safe to assume that."

"What?" Mama took Tracey's hands in hers. A kind move, though her face was still accusing. "What are you talking about, Tracey?"

"Mama, he knows I'm pregnant. I told him. He—"

"He wanted you to get rid of it?"

Tracey didn't say that. Her mother did. She didn't confirm it, but she didn't deny it, either.

"I couldn't do it. He told me—" And that's when Tracey just couldn't go on. She had let her mother believe the lie, encouraged her even. Luckily, He was merciful with the innocent baby inside of her and He didn't strike her down.

In tears, Tracey was ready to take it all back and come clean. But right then, her mother took her in her arms as she had when Tracey was little. "It's okay, baby. We'll figure everything out together. We will, you'll see."

Shock overcame her. Her mother hadn't scolded. She had yet to recommend a place where she could send Tracey for the next seven months to say she got married and the father of the baby died in a freak ballooning accident. She hadn't said a word about her soul. She hadn't pressed her for the man's name or how she'd met him, how long they'd been in a relationship.

She did none of the things Tracey expected her to do. For the life of her, Tracey didn't know why.

"Have you seen your doctor yet?"

"No," she answered. "I just…just found out."

Carolyn nodded and reached for her cell phone. "We have to get you an appointment right away. I'm trying to find Dr. Singh's number. She's the best person to deliver my grandbaby." Ah. Tracey understood then. Ah.

Her mother kept scrolling but slipped in, "How are we going to tell Daddy?"

Tracey felt sick and tasted the tang of bile in her mouth.

Her mother had apparently found the number, because she was holding the phone to her ear. "I see you haven't thought about that. You do realize he's not going to respect your desire to keep this man a secret. He's going to want to know."

Tracey started to speak but her mother held up a hand as she talked with the operator at Dr. Singh's office.

She put her hand over the mouthpiece. "And he'll find out. Even if you don't tell him, he'll make it his business to find out."

God, Tracey hoped she had been careful enough for that not to happen, but knowing her father she could never be sure. My father had enough legal contacts *internationally* to ruin the life of a young attorney who didn't really *come* from anywhere. If Garrett had connections beyond those he'd garnered during school, maybe he would survive a Travis McAlpine onslaught. But it was unlikely. Daddy knew where too many bodies were buried.

"You know he will," her mother reiterated.

Then she started to talk into the phone again. And for once, Tracey was happy, *ecstatic*, to have her mother organize her life and take care of her whether she deserved it or not.

—m—

Telling her father felt like someone digging into her heart and trying to rip it out. Tracey sat there in his office—a place where he wouldn't scream—looking at him across his desk with her mother standing with arms folded in the corner. She told him the same true but incomplete story she'd told her mother.

"Tracey?"

"Yeah, Daddy."

"You have to tell me the whole truth at some point in time."

"What do you mean, Daddy?"

"You know what I mean, but there are more important things we need to take care of right now."

"Sir?"

"Well, first, you need to move home. Immediately."

"Daddy, I've only got three more months of school."

"That three months and fifty miles from us and Dr. Singh. Anything could happen."

"Mama?" Tracey turned to her, but she said nothing. She only seemed to argue with him when it was something *she* wanted.

"How am I supposed to finish my degree? It's too late for me to try and take comps. It's either/or in this program."

"Maybe you should have thought of that before you got pregnant. This is not a discussion. I'll call Alexander."

"No!"

"I'll call him and arrange everything. You can finish your thesis but you don't have to do it there. You can do it remotely. You can go back and meet with him or do research as needed, but you're moving home."

"I'll be fine at the house until school is over."

"Maybe, but I didn't give you a choice in the matter. Obviously, you haven't been making the best choices for yourself, anyway."

If he had hit her, she would have felt less assaulted.

He didn't care. "We'll talk about your final living arrangements again after you've had the baby."

A shaking hand covered her mouth.

He went on. "If that means you work for my firm after graduation, then—"

"No." Tracey didn't even remember opening her mouth to let out that word. But there it was.

"No?" He didn't yell, but his neck stiffened and his eyebrows clenched. The soft warning in his voice was enough to make her skin ice over in gooseflesh.

Finally, for once in her life, she spoke up for herself. "I can't accept that. This is my responsibility. You can't be expected to take care of it. I'm an adult and—"

"A responsible adult wouldn't have gotten herself pregnant by a man who lacks character and jumps ship. A responsible *unmarried* adult would have been trying to complete the master's program her parents paid for while living in a house her grandmother paid for."

Her mouth dropped open. Her father had never talked to her that way before.

Tracey tried to stay calm. "Daddy, I can understand why you feel that way, but as you've pointed out, it's time I take care of myself."

"Tracey, this is not a negotiation."

"I wasn't negotiating."

"Good, then we understand each other. I will not have my grandchild being raised with any less care and opportunity than you had."

"But…"

He just looked at her. She didn't know what to say.

He leaned across the desk. His black eyes bored into hers. "By the time this baby comes, you will tell me who the father is."

"There's no point in that."

"You don't tell me what 'point' there is in anything, girl."

Tracey shook her head. She couldn't tell him. She couldn't do it.

Suddenly, her father's demeanor changed. "That's fine."

"Huh?"

"I said that's fine, Tracey." He pushed back in his chair.

"What does that mean?"

"It means what you think it means. You don't have to tell me. I'll find out."

—◊◊◊—

"Stop tensing up, Tracey," Monica soothed. "Just rest your forehead against my hand and let me do all the work, okay?" Monica held Tracey's limp head in one hand. She grabbed the water gun with her other and began to rinse the lather from Tracey's hair. "Man, Tracey, you got a big watermelon head."

"Thank you, Moni. Don't ever let it be said that you're not a sensitive woman. And can't you hurry up? The water's hot. You're 'bout to burn my ears off."

"Hush, girl. This won't take a minute. You're more tender-headed than Lena."

"You should talk to my Auntie Colleen. You should've seen her trying to braid my hair when I was little. I cried so hard. That woman will snatch your lungs out through your scalp if you let her. Granted, no matter what she's doing to you, it will still come out looking good. You just have to be willing to suffer."

"Why didn't you have your auntie do this, anyway?"

Tracey paused for a second, reveling in the feel of the cool water against her scalp. Sighing, she responded, "That wouldn't have required that I drive here, would it?"

"What is it with you and this need to run from every problem you have? Your parents already know. I've met them, and neither one of them seems like the bogeyman to me."

"Do we need to go over this again? I'm going to be spending plenty of time at home soon enough."

"Don't get so fussy about it—"

"Just don't start with me."

Monica tapped her shoulder and Tracey sat up while she toweled her hair dry. "What makes you think I'm starting with you, Tracey?"

"You are always starting with me."

"What exactly are you planning to do, girl? How are you planning to pull this off? Tracey, this is a small town. This is a small *state*. What makes you think you won't run into him when you're here? And you said his family doesn't live ten miles from yours. What makes you think you won't run into someone who knows him? Furthermore, there's graduation. You might see him—"

"I'm not going."

"What?"

"I'm not going to graduation. I'll be big as a house by then. Seven months pregnant. Look, Monica, this will work, and if you care about me, you'll just support me."

"I support you, baby girl, I'm just not as optimistic as you, obviously."

"Our paths would never have crossed if it hadn't been for school. Our worlds don't connect."

"Everybody's world connects. There's only one world, Tracey!" Moni was getting frustrated. Tracey had turned out to be more stubborn than Moni ever would have guessed.

"You haven't told Alex, have you?" Tracey looked like she'd swallowed an egg.

"Noooo," Moni drawled. "I didn't have to tell him anything. Tracey, no matter how many jackets you wear, you're still showing."

Tracey cursed. She had seen Alex twice for school and he hadn't said a word.

"And how do you think he found out it was Garrett?" Moni asked.

"What!" If Alex knew, then it wouldn't be long before her father knew.

"Alex told me he put two and two together after he'd heard some things about Garrett and saw him buying like a thousand home pregnancy tests one night."

Tracey covered her face in embarrassment.

"Am I really this stupid?"

"You're not, but I swear you've got me puzzled about how you're managing this pregnancy."

As usual, Tracey ignored her and went back to engaging in magical thinking.

"I just have to play it right, keep a low profile. I really don't have to leave the house as much as I did before. Rett will be gone come summer when I'm showing. Nobody but his roommates would put us together, and I think they're gone in the summer, too."

"I think pregnancy is making your brain shrink," Moni mumbled.

"What?" Tracey shrieked.

"Seriously, you aren't making any sense. But I'm just going to smile and nod and be there by your side no matter how crazy you get. And, *baby*, you have no idea how crazy you're about to get."

—⁓—

Moni asked Tracey only once how she expected to take care of a baby alone. She immediately dropped the issue when Tracey began talking about her trust fund. The trust she got when she was eighteen, the one she got when she was twenty-one, the one she would get when she turned thirty. The job her father had promised her even though she would take it only as a last resort. And the inevitable sale of her grand-mother's house, though it pained her to do it.

The only question Tracey didn't have an answer for—even a half-baked one—was what she was going to tell the child about her father.

Chapter 22

When she should have been manning the phones for a swim team fundraiser, Angie was calling her friends. She tried to get Tracey, who had been distant since she and her brother broke up. When she didn't answer, Angie called her brother.

"Hey, Rett."

"Hey, Angie."

"You sound wiped."

"What time is it?"

"You don't know? God, Rett, what are you doing asleep at the apartment in the middle of the day?"

"What?"

"Wake up!"

"Stop yelling!"

"Listen, I just tried to call Tracey—"

"Who?"

"That perked you up, didn't it? Yeah, I want to know why y'all aren't together anymore."

"Were we ever together?"

"Hey, hey now, bro. Just a month ago you were in love. You were trying to get it in the Sunday paper, you were so in love. So what in God's name changed that?"

"None of your bus—"

"Okay, okay. I see there's no point in asking you anything about it right now. But I tell you what. No matter what either of you says, I know it's complete BS and when I see either of you—"

"Angie, you've got several people on hold. We were hoping you would show some responsibility while we—"

That was Mark, the peppy leader of this failed fundraising effort and Angie's coach.

"Sounds like you gotta go."

"Wait."

"Bye, Ang." Rett hung up.

—∿—

Rett went through graduation in a fog. For months he hadn't seen or heard from Tracey. He knew through Angie that she had left school to finish her thesis from home, which almost guaranteed he wouldn't see her. So he spent his time studying, working, and drinking. If he allowed room for anything else, he allowed room for time to think about Tracey and the baby he would never have.

It hurt. Hell, it hurt *a lot*. So he sought numbness. After graduation, he went back to his parents' house. He'd accepted a job with a firm near them and he thought maybe being home would help him forget.

He went about his daily routine doing what was expected of him, but he was numb.

One morning he went out for his usual run.

Before starting, he squatted and wrapped his arms around his thighs. He straightened his legs. He exhaled and closed his eyes. This stretch hurt. He stood and raised his arms over his head, clasping his hands together. Then he let his arms down and let his whole body go limp. He shook his limbs out.

He breathed deeply two times, then pushed off. He liked to begin with a sprint and end with a sprint even if that wasn't the right way to do it. He started his run, got his weight centered, and pumped hard with his thighs to thrust himself forward. He was running as fast as he could. Running and running until he felt something just... it felt as if something burst inside him. And then it was her face in front of his eyes. Tracey's face right there. And then he lost the ground and let out a grunt. He felt his head, shoulder, and hip scrape across concrete, burning his whole right side.

Garrett had always treated pain by concentrating on the pain, thinking about it, embracing it. He tried to analyze what was so unpleasant about it. And somehow, from the time he was a kid, the process had always worked to make the pain, whatever it was, go away. At least pain on the outside. Rett lay there for a minute making sure no serious damage was done.

He then pulled himself up and began to make his way slowly back to the house.

"Oh, my God, Big. Look at your son!" Rett heard before he saw his mother push open the screen door in the kitchen. She came out and put her shoulder under his arm.

"Momma, I can walk just fine, thank you," Rett groaned, though he let her go ahead and lead him into the house.

"No, you are not fine! You're covered in blood. What happened?"

"Mary Margaret, move out the way now," Big commanded and scooted her to the side. He sat Rett down at the kitchen table.

"You all right, boy?"

"I'm fine, Dad. I just took a tumble when I went jogging this morning. Scraped up my side pretty good, but it's nothing to worry about."

"Hell, son, you haven't seen yourself. Go on, get cleaned up. Make sure that's the case."

"All right," Rett answered and slowly rose. He exited the kitchen listening to his mom talk about how he always had been the most accident-prone boy on the block.

In the bathroom Rett realized why she had been looking at him as if he were from *Night of the Living Dead* or something. The whole right side of his face was covered in blood. He looked at his clothes. His T-shirt was ripped, with gravel still stuck in it, and splattered with blood. His knee was torn open and looked like hamburger meat. Rett chuckled to himself. "You got me good this time, Trace."

He started to fix himself up.

—∾—

"What got hold of you today?"

"None of your business, Angie," Rett answered his sister, who'd just gotten back from her internship. He bent low over the pool table to take a shot. Satisfaction settled over him because he had avoided the wince that came with the stretch. His body still hurt like hell.

"What happened? Did you get into a fight?"

"Yeah, with a stretch of sidewalk. I'll kick its ass if I come 'cross it again."

"I'm serious, Rett."

"I lost my footing when I went runnin' this morning."

"Tracey would die if she saw you like this."

Rett pulled up from the table and looked at her. "You want to not say that name?"

"Why? You don't want to talk about her here, you know, your own personal Cheers?" As if to punctuate that remark, a couple walked by waving and smiling at him. Everybody in that bar knew him from way back.

"Yeah, Angie," he agreed, "that's exactly it. I don't want anyone in here to know anything about her, or me, or me *and* her, so please just keep your mouth shut."

"God, you are such a dick sometimes, Rett. I don't know how Tracey could stand it."

"Oh, she could stand it, all right. That's about the only part of me she could stand."

"Okay, now, I know you guys broke up, but you're being a real jackass about it right now. I don't understand what's wrong with you, but it's obvious you don't feel like sharing, so I'm going to go back next door."

Rett's friends would never set foot in the bar next door. It was reserved pretty much for the freaks, and somehow his sister belonged to that group. Rett decided to have another drink. He beckoned to the waitress. Her name was Julie, and her older brother had played football with Rett back in high school.

"Julie." He poured on the sex appeal, taking his time looking her up and down. "My, how you've grown."

She was probably just now turning twenty-one, but it was a good twenty-one. "Why don't you get me another beer and play a round with me."

"I can't. I'm working." But she wanted to. Rett could tell by the way she touched her hair that she wanted to.

A wave of disgust washed over him, but it wasn't Julie's fault.

Rett considered that none of friends would hang out in the bar Angie frequented, except maybe Clay. It occurred to him that he had never set foot over there, either, so he went to find his sister.

—∽∾—

His window open to the breeze, Rett lay back in his bed listening to the wind in the trees outside. His thoughts drifted to Angie. His sister had a big mouth. Too bad she had a heart that big to go with it. Cheers. Everybody in Nick's did know him. Or at least they thought they knew him. Hell, Tracey thought she knew him, too. The only person who really did was Angie. Well, Angie and Big. Tracey didn't want to know him.

And there it was. He was thinking about her. Again. Tracey was in his head, and he couldn't get her out. What he wanted to think about was that last time he had seen her and she had decided to hurt him more than anybody ever had. He wanted to think about the way she let him go on and on about how he was going to take care of her and their baby. He wanted to think about the rejection, but it wasn't in him to do it. Every time he psyched himself up with everything she had done to him, he started to see images of her smiling, of her being the woman that all the future women in his life were going to hate. He ran his fingers over the scratches at his temple. He couldn't sleep.

He got up and stretched. Then he walked quietly across the hall.

"Are you awake, Angie?"

"Yeah."

"I just wanted to tell you I'm sorry for the way I acted at Nick's. I'm just sore from this morning and it's giving me a nasty attitude."

"If that's the reason you want to give me."

"It is."

"Okay, I can accept it's got nothing to do with your breakup with that person whose name I'm not supposed to say." She smiled wryly, then scooted over in her bed. "Come on in. Don't just stand there."

Rett came in and sat beside her.

"You can't sleep?"

"No," he admitted. "It's already hot outside."

"Yeah, it is kind of warm, but I'm thinking that's not what's the matter. Come on, talk to me. You never took a breakup like this. Even Kim, and y'all were together a long time. Hell, I barely noticed she was out of the picture. I know you had real strong feelings for Tracey."

"You could say that."

"Right, but it's been months now."

"How is she?" he asked slowly, quietly.

"Guilt by association," Angie mumbled. "She won't talk to me, either. I miss her, too."

Rett nodded.

"What happened with Tracey?"

"I don't really want to talk about it. Just understand that what happened between us cannot be fixed. I know you think I'm the jackass here, but I promise you that what she did goes far, far beyond anything I have ever done."

"Well, tell me."

He couldn't. "Even without what happened, Ang, it still comes down to the fact that I don't know how to be with her and she doesn't want to know how to be with me."

―⁓―

Studying for the bar at his new firm, Rett was surprised by laughing voices outside his office door. His boss's nasal guffaw was unmistakable even though Rett rarely heard him laugh. The man never seemed to be amused by much of anything. He was a slim, pale, immaculate man who wore thousand-dollar suits and looked as though he were born into his profession. And he practiced as though he were born into this profession. It was one of the reasons this was a successful firm and Rett had accepted its offer.

Simmons poked his head in the door. "Come here, Rett. There's someone I'd like you to meet."

Rett took a deep breath and smoothed his hand over the front of his suit.

Rett swallowed. He knew right off who this guy was: Travis James McAlpine. Even if he hadn't seen all those pictures Tracey had of them together at the house, they favored each other too much for it to be denied. Rett swallowed again. McAlpine wasn't as big as his own dad, but he was imposing nonetheless. And Rett knew his track record. Though he didn't practice anymore, McAlpine was a legal legend.

"Mr. McAlpine." His voice didn't feel like his own. It sounded like him, but Rett didn't even feel as if he had said anything. What was even more irrational was that he wanted to impress the man as if he were his future son-in-law.

"Mr. Atkins." They squeezed hands. "I've been hearing great things about your career."

"Oh, thank you, sir, but I haven't gotten started yet," Rett answered cordially. He thought he saw McAlpine's eyes narrow as Tracey's did when she was suspicious. He was imagining things. If he knew Tracey, no one from her camp knew about their relationship.

"Rett, have a sit-down with Mr. McAlpine. I guarantee you just a talk with this man is going to positively impact your career," Simmons declared and ushered them both into Rett's office. He excused himself shortly after closing the door behind him.

"Well, sir. I don't know what Mr. Simmons told you, but—"

"Patrick told me you graduated number four in your class. He said that you had offers from all over but you chose to stay close to home. That's understandable. You'll do well here, where you're from. That's the way the legal network goes, down here, anyway. He told me you plan to specialize in trial law. That's profanity around here, but lucrative as hell if you can take it. He told me you go to church regularly and that my old firm wanted you as well.

"I *did not* tell him that my old firm might have wanted you, but they were instructed that if they pursued you, they would—partners and all—need to start looking for alternative means of supporting their families."

"What?" The shock was out before Rett had time to check it.

"Yes. I didn't think it would be wise to have you anywhere near my firm. You see, my family has a good deal of interaction with the team there. You know how that goes. And any interaction between you and my family would be detrimental to all our interests."

Rett closed his eyes and took a deep breath. "What is this? I haven't seen Tracey in more than three months. It's over. She made that clear. There was no reason for her to send you here—"

"She didn't send me here. I came on my own. While you think three months is a long time after the way you've behaved, I've got more experience with time, and it's not. I don't know what it was between the two of you, and, frankly, I don't care to know. All I care about is my baby's well-being. I knew that you were 'out of the picture,' so to speak. I just want to make sure it stays that way."

"What if I don't want it to stay that way?" What the hell was *wrong* with him? Why couldn't he just shut up, let McAlpine say his piece, and be done with it?

"Walk away from it, young man. Walk away from it."

"Too late, sir." Rett shook his head with a rueful smile. "You don't have anything to worry about. Tracey has already done that for me."

"That's not my sense. My sense is that even though you're angry now, you're already getting over it. And what I'm telling you is to walk away from it. For good."

"Your 'sense' is telling you wrong. I'll *never* get over what happened between me and Tracey. Never."

"Good," McAlpine returned with ice in his voice.

Then something occurred to Rett. "So Tracey doesn't know you're here."

"She doesn't."

"I'm surprised you didn't offer me a bribe."

"For what?" Travis McAlpine scoffed. "I don't need to offer you money to ensure that you do exactly as I say. Is that what you wanted? Money? You want to pay off that eighty thousand you've got left in student loans?" His voice dripped with disgust.

Rett felt the hairs on the back of his neck rise and his cheeks and throat grew hot. He didn't know what to say. There would be no reasoning with this man.

"Why are you here? What do you want?"

"I want you to walk away from it. Live a nice happy life with a nice All-American girl, preferably white, and don't look back as far as my daughter's concerned." Then he just got up and left… or started to.

"What if I don't?"

Travis McAlpine turned faster than a man of his age and size should have been able to. Rett had no idea why he'd said what he said, but he had the feeling he'd pulled the tail of a bobcat.

"You will."

Then he just walked out of the office and started shaking hands and laughing as if everything were fine. He was out there just as arrogant as all get-out. His overconfidence said he had accomplished what he had wanted to come there and accomplish.

Now all Rett wanted to do was find Tracey and tell her she had no right to take his child from him.

—✕—

Two weeks after his run-in with Travis McAlpine, on a hot Saturday morning in June, Rett was driving back to school to gather the last of his things from Angie's house. He planned to put everything in storage temporarily until he moved into his own place closer to work. The cosmic joke wasn't lost on him that his new job was only a twenty-minute drive from Tracey's parents' place. If she stayed there, there was the possibility they would run into each other. The very idea scared him to death. He didn't know what he would do, how he would feel, if he ever saw her again. He just didn't know.

And he was thinking about her again.

Rett didn't plan to drive over there. But he couldn't seem to turn around.

He slowed as he approached the house where he had all but lived with Tracey for a couple of turbulent months. He craned his neck to see past the trees. In the drive he saw a sleek, silver luxury SUV with boxes in back. In the passenger side, he could barely make out Tracey. He couldn't really see any features or defining characteristics, but he knew it was her.

His heart started to bang so hard in his chest he thought it was trying to get out. His hands gripping the steering wheel as he made a loop around the block and approached again.

Approaching the driver's side was a willowy woman with long, straight, jet black hair. Seeing her in profile, he caught the high cheekbones and the straight nose. That was Tracey's mom. Had to be. Even in the pictures she had been a beautiful lady, and now, in the flesh, she was even more so.

She swept her hair back and slid into the driver's seat.

Just walk away from it, young man. Rett thought about those words every day. Every day it had him wondering just what the hell he was doing. What the hell did he want? He wanted to be a lawyer. He knew that much. He wanted to be successful, he knew that much. He wanted that family McAlpine had talked about. He wanted to go to church with that family and to do all the things normal families did. He wanted something easy, manageable.

He doubled back around the block in time to see their direction, and he followed them a couple of cars back, watching as best he could their interaction with each other. He watched the older woman lean over and stroke Tracey's hair. It made him think of a time when Tracey told him that because her mother had seemed to stop aging at forty she continued to treat Tracey as though she were twelve.

About five minutes later, they pulled into the west parking lot of the Galleria. Rett thought two seconds about the insanity of actually following her in there. Then he thought about finding somewhere else to park so that when she ran into him in the mall, she would think it was coincidence. He went around to the main entrance and found a parking spot. He jumped out of the car and checked his shorts and shirt to see if they were hanging right. He leaned down to arrange his socks. He put his shades on and dropped his wallet and cell phone in his pocket. He headed inside. Once inside it occurred to him that it might be stupid-looking to wear shades inside the mall so he took them off and hooked them on his shirt. Then, realizing that looked stupid, he put them in his other pocket. He ran a hand over his face, trying to figure out why the hell she had him acting like this even when it was all over. Maybe he was trying to remind her of what she was missing. Damn, he was always reminded of what *he* was missing.

He walked through the food court slowly, allowing them time to get into the place. He tried to be smooth, to look nonchalant. He tried to—there she was. He saw her walking away from her mother. She walked slowly into a dream that hurt so much now that he knew it existed. He wanted her. With everything in him, he wanted her. He didn't care about what she had done. He had been just as bad. He wanted her in his heart, in his bed, in his life. No matter how hard he tried, he could not stop loving her.

Then he saw it all. She had turned to the side some and he saw it all. His mouth went dry, he couldn't swallow and he could barely breathe. Screw nonchalant. His body took him to her of its own accord. He felt his eyes burning and, as unfamiliar as that was, he knew what was happening. He got to her and grabbed her and glared at her, not trusting himself to speak as his whole body shook with warring emotions. There she was, standing there with his baby still inside her, growing inside her. His baby. His baby. His baby. Trapped between miracle and travesty, he started to shake.

When she saw him her step faltered, and her mother rushed toward her. She fell into his arms saying something about dying and that she was sorry.

"Thank you, thank you," her mother breathed. "Oh, my God."

A crowd began to gather. Rett didn't know what to do. A lady dropped beside him saying that she was a nurse and prompted him to call an ambulance.

"Sir, you need to let her go now."

Rett did not immediately comply. He couldn't let her or his baby go. Not again.

Chapter 23

Carolyn was trying to get into the back of the ambulance. Problem was, so was this white boy whom she'd heard her daughter call Garrett. Carolyn wanted to hit him. She really did, because he was holding up progress.

The paramedic turned around and leaned out the back. "Hey, I'm sorry, but only one of you can come in the ambulance."

"Well, I'm going!" they both yelped. Carolyn glared at Rett, who was glaring at the paramedic.

"I'm going." Carolyn pointed at the intruder. "I don't know who you are, but I'm going. That's my baby in there."

"No, ma'am, I'm sorry," Garrett replied with a ludicrously respectful tone. "I'm going, because that's *my* baby in there!"

Carolyn's eyes widened and for a moment she didn't think about the ambulance or the paramedic. "That's impossible!"

"No, ma'am, it's not."

"But you… you're—"

"Lily White at your service." Garrett dipped his head in greeting.

"But—"

"Tracey is pregnant with *my* baby."

The paramedic raised his eyebrows.

Carolyn hesitated, then her eyes widened. "Oh, I see now. Now I understand everything. Sure as the world turns you're not going anywhere near my baby, especially not in this ambulance. I can't believe this!"

"Look, people, I have to get this girl to the hospital now. So, goodbye." The paramedic started to close the door. Before he did, he added, "I suggest you get it together, find your respective cars, and follow us to the hospital." With that, he closed the door and the ambulance started away.

Carolyn glared venomously at Rett. With a fixed frown, he looked back at her. Then without a word, they started away and found their cars.

—◈—

"I'm sorry. The doctor is with her right now. When she's done we'll let you go back."

Carolyn threw her hands up in frustration. Her baby was in there and there wasn't anything she could do. She couldn't even so much as go back and see her. She placed a hand over her eyes. Then she reached into her purse and pulled out her phone. She dialed her husband. He didn't answer. She left a message for him to call her back. She paced back and forth, back and forth. She barely saw the people who sat in the sterile waiting room. She was not a woman accustomed to waiting. Carolyn hadn't smoked in twelve years, but, Lord have mercy, she wanted a cigarette right then! She took her phone out again and called her sister Colleen. Colleen wasn't home either. Carolyn then called on God. She prayed her daughter was all right. She prayed her granddaughter was all right. She prayed that the son of a bitch that had left Tracey was suffering somewhere—

Then she saw Rett.

"You know what?" She pointed her finger as she turned on him. "I didn't believe for one minute that my daughter could fall in love with someone who could get her pregnant and just leave her. But after seeing you, wooh, I can see exactly how it went! You know, I've been waiting for so long, praying to God up in Heaven that I would meet you one day and—"

"And what?" Rett, who had been sitting in a chair with his hands clasped before him, jumped out of his seat. "Apologize for Tracey?"

"Apolo—are you crazy? Why in God's name would I apologize for her after what *you* did?"

"After what I did? After what *she* did!"

"White people!"

"White people? What is that supposed to mean?"

"It's supposed to mean that after five hundred years, y'all still think you got property in the black community. Well, my daughter is not property. And it's so obvious what's happened here that a blind man could paint a picture of it! She wasn't good enough for you because she was black!"

By this time, Carolyn realized she was screeching. She turned from him and took a breath as she pressed fingers to her throbbing temples. She scanned the room, and sure enough, they had an audience. She turned back to him. He still stood there as if he himself were trying to get a grip. Carolyn went on in a more controlled and quiet voice. "Let me tell you that after seeing you I already know the answer to this, but I want to hear it from you. I want to ask you, young man… Well, it's like this: I wondered for a long time what kind of man would tell the girl he got pregnant that he didn't want anything to do with the baby. What kind of man would feel that my daughter was good enough for sex but not good enough to have his child? What kind of man would treat her like a dirty little secret? Tell me? How could you do it?"

"What…are…you…talking about?" Rett questioned slowly. His voice was thick and shaking.

"You told Traccy you didn't want to—"

"Is that what she said?" he interrupted. Something in the way he was talking, the way he was looking, gave Carolyn pause. "Why don't you ask Tracey who was not good enough for whom before you go and get high and mighty about it? I was never the one who tried to hide her. I was never the one who denied that I even knew her in public. I told my friends about her. I told my sister about her. I was prepared to tell my *parents* about her before she decided she didn't want me in her life anymore. You talk to Tracey. You talk to her, and if you get the truth out of her, boy, you'll learn real fast that I'm not the one keeping dirty little secrets."

Carolyn went quiet, digesting his words. Carolyn knew her daughter. She remembered Christmas vacation when her daughter had cried like a baby in the bathroom. She saw flashes of Tracey on the way to unconsciousness staring up at this young man and looking as guilty as sin. Carolyn knew Tracey. Maybe she didn't know this young man, but his words were the truest ones she'd probably heard in months. In a quiet voice she asked, "Didn't you tell Tracey you didn't want anything to do with the baby?"

"I didn't tell her that. I wanted to have the baby. She didn't. I told her I wanted her to have the baby. She told me that she wouldn't. I told her I wanted a life with the woman I loved and the child I created with her. She said no. I told her I would take care of the baby if she would just have it and she would never even have to see us again. She said no. I begged her, do you hear me, *begged* her. She wouldn't listen. God, she wouldn't listen. Then I went on my hands and knees and prayed about it."

Carolyn could find no words. She sank down in the seat nearest her. Garrett came to sit beside her. They were silent.

Then he asked, "What's wrong with her?"

"Hypertension. Tracey's never been so tense and wired in her life. It's caused her to have high blood pressure. I didn't know what was doing it to her. I do now."

"Has that hurt the baby?"

"No." Carolyn actually smiled. "Little Nathalie's actually very resilient. But if Tracey doesn't—"

"Nathalie?"

"Yes, that's what she's going to name her. N-A-T-H-A-L-I-E. French spelling, Tracey says."

"Her?"

Carolyn felt a twinge in her stomach at the way he said that. Still, he seemed excited about this baby that he didn't even really know about until an hour before.

"Yes, it's a girl and she's due in two months."

"And she's named after me."

"How's that?"

"Garrett Nathaniel Atkins."

His skin flushed a little. And, for a minute, he was happy. Carolyn could see it. She could also see… "Atkins? You're Angie Atkins' brother?"

"Yes," Garrett answered, glancing at her. "Do you know her?"

"Actually I do. She's coming to intern in the summer for an architectural firm I use. I've seen her portfolio, and yes, I've met her. But I thought she was just a friend of Tracey's. I didn't know there was more to it…. How did Tracey think no one would find out? How would she hide it from Angie? How would she continue to hide it from you? And for that matter, how would she even possibly be able to hide that the baby was mixed after she was born?"

"Honestly, I don't think she was thinking. She doesn't always. She just kind of panics and goes from there."

"That's true." Carolyn sighed. "So what will you do now?"

"You mean about Tracey?"

"Tracey and the baby."

"I'm going to do what I wanted to do from the beginning: take care of them. Be a part of their lives. At least, I will be a part of the baby's life. You'll understand if I don't have any desire to be near Tracey ever again in my life. I am relieved that she is having this baby. I thank God that she is having this baby, but I can't forget that she almost took her from me."

"I understand that, but if you want to be a father to Nathalie, you don't have a choice but to come to terms with it."

"I'll find a way," he answered. Then they were silent once more.

—᙭—

Finally, a nurse came out and called Carolyn back. Garrett was quick to ask if he could go back as well, but the nurse looked at him quizzically and said that only immediate family could go back. He answered that he was immediate family. Again, she seemed confused. He then told her that he was the father of the child. The nurse looked him up and down. She obviously didn't like what she was seeing or hearing. She asked if he was married to Tracey. When Garrett said no, she told him he still couldn't go back. And Carolyn, who had somewhat bonded with him, said nothing. She continued back to meet with Tracey's doctor.

Carolyn was surprised to see him when she went back out to move her car out of emergency parking. Garrett Atkins was still there. Three hours later, he was still there. And when he saw her he stood and came over to her.

"How is she?"

"She seems to be out of the woods for right now, but she is physically exhausted. Her pressure is still up, and the baby is restless."

"What are they going to do?"

"Try and keep her pressure down and keep her here for observation. They're moving her up to a private room on the fifth floor."

"Is she awake?"

"No, but that's a result of the exhaustion. The doctor says she'll probably go ahead and sleep through the night."

"What room?"

Carolyn paused for a moment. "I don't know that you will help the situation by seeing her. We all need to handle what's happened here, but not until Tracey's well and that baby is here."

"I understand that. And I'll go if I add to the trouble. But please, I just need to see her. Please."

"Room 563."

Chapter 24

Her dreams at the hospital were vivid and accusing. Garrett was always there, he was always in love with her, and Tracey was always pushing him away. Whenever she awakened, her dreams were still in her head, and the anxiety and grief overwhelmed her.

Later, she envisioned Garrett sitting there next to her bed. He would cradle his head in his hands as he sat in the chair beside her bed. One time he cried for Tracey and called her his love. It got to where she always saw him there. Sometimes he would tell her things, silly, inane things. Sometimes, she felt so happy she cried. Those times, this vision would crawl into bed with her and hold her and she would hold onto him so tight that sometimes he disappeared. She asked her vision sometimes if her baby would be okay. He would always tell her that their baby would be fine. He would kiss her sometimes, and Tracey could feel that he still loved her. Never mind that Rett didn't, wherever he was. Tracey knew that this apparition did.

Later, she saw him as a satellite, an orbiting guardian angel, when the doctor told Mama the baby's vitals were fine. Her loved ones ignored her satellite as they filed out but he came to her when they were gone and he held her tight. He promised her that their baby would be happy and healthy; he promised her a house; he promised Tracey understanding for every stupid thing she did; he promised to always love her.

—⁓—

Tracey remembered very little about the first two days in the hospital. Everything clouded together and she couldn't tell reality from dream. Her first vivid memory was of waking up feeling the baby kick. Tracey held her tummy trying to quiet her as she took in the room filled with flowers. The flowers were from her mother and father, she knew. But her first instinct was to think they were from Rett. She divested herself of that particular wish right away. There was no way he would send her anything even if he knew where she was.

"I'm ashamed to even bring these in." Though gentle, Monica's voice startled Tracey when she swept into the room. Moni carried a coffee mug filled with a soft lilac and saffron colored flower arrangement.

"Oh, come on in, girl," Tracey replied, grinning, or trying to grin. Her throat was dry and her face felt as if she had been wearing a mud mask too long. She searched for a glass of water. Always anticipating another's needs, Moni tipped a cool stream of water from a pitcher into a glass. She handed it to Tracey and helped her sit up. Sitting up was no easy feat with the heavy baby girl curled up inside her.

Moni sat in the chair beside the bed. "How ya feeling?"

"Oh, as if I've been in the hospital for three months and I'm not sure why."

"You don't remember?"

"Nope, the last thing I remember was going to the mall with Mama."

"Well, you were at the mall with your mom and your pressure went up and you fainted. The paramedics were called. That was the day before yesterday."

"The day before yesterday only?"

"Yep."

"Are you sure my baby is all right?" Tracey clutched her belly. They had told her Nathalie was fine, and the baby seemed active and healthy, but what did Tracey know?

"Yes, she's fine. At least as long as you don't keep stressing yourself out. But if you want your doctor, she's around here somewhere. I can get her."

"No, not yet. Where's Mama? I'm surprised she's not here having a fit."

"Oh, Tracey, honey baby, you're up. How are you feeling? Oh, God, you scared me half to death!" her mother said softly, rushing into the room.

"Speak of the devil," Tracey quipped dryly. Her mother came right over and let down the side rail on her bed and sat down next to her, holding her hand.

"Not the best ever, but I'm okay."

A nurse came then to take her blood pressure and draw some blood. She also examined Tracey's belly.

—m—

"We need to talk to her." Sharp and authoritative, Carolyn's voice commanded the doctor's attention. Tracey had been conscious for a day with perfectly good vitals. It was time.

"I understand you need to talk to her, but as you well know, her condition is delicate right now. We don't want her to experience a lot of stress," Dr. Singh stated plainly.

"But you said she was stabilized." Rett's brow furrowed.

"She has stabilized," Dr. Singh allowed. "Her blood pressure and all the vitals look good, but she's dilated more than she should be. We don't want her going into labor early."

"I love her, I would never want to jeopardize her and the baby, but there are some things we have to settle."

The doctor seemed to contemplate their words and finally nodded reluctantly.

"Tracey," Carolyn called in a voice that feigned calm and civility as she swept into the room. Her mother was a bit dramatic. Her voice was never calm, civil, or smooth. She didn't look at her and Tracey felt the way she did when she was eight and drove the car into the pool.

Then Garrett Atkins stepped into the room with the doctor right behind him. Tracey's heart monitor went haywire. Her doctor freaked out, which of course made things worse. It was actually almost comical later. Out of the corner of her eye, Tracey saw Rett leave the room. She had to get a grip on herself. "I'm fine. I'm fine. I was just a little surprised. That's all." She tried to take deep breaths and calm herself. Her monitor slowed its beeping and she insisted to her doctor that she was fine.

"He can come back."

The damn doctor looked at her mother, not Tracey.

"Stay." Carolyn told the doctor. And she did.

Mama went out into the hall then, and was followed back by a more timid Garrett Atkins than Tracey had ever seen before.

The heart monitor sped up a little, but Tracey was steady. The doctor assured herself that Tracy was fine before she left the room.

"We have to talk," her mother said.

The pit of Tracey's stomach felt as though it were on a plane descending too fast. "About what?"

GRAYSON COLE

"About you."

"What about me?"

"Let's hear what you have to say, and don't you dare lie to me. You've already done enough of that."

"I don't know if I can explain," Tracey choked out, feeling the pregnant tears begin to well up inside her. "I just wanted to avoid any problems. I didn't want you or Daddy to be angry with me. I just... I wanted..." And she couldn't get the rest out because she was overtaken by the kind of sobs one always saw in the death scene of a movie, only her feelings were real. What was even more mortifying was the fact that Garrett was holding her and trying to calm her down. And what was even more ridiculous was that he was telling her that stress was bad for the baby. Her mother was looking at him as if he were crazy.

"Tracey, I don't know what to say about this. I just don't know what to say. I thought I raised you better. And—just a question—how long were you intending to keep this from your daddy and me? You had to know we'd find out when she was born. It's the kind of thing you can tell just from looking at a child. What were you going to do when she looked just like him?"

"You think she'll look like me?" Rett asked. It seemed like a ridiculous question to ask at the time. Why the hell did he sound so happy?

"All the babies in our family come out looking like their daddies," Carolyn replied off-handedly.

"My baby girl, Nathalie," he said in awe. He pressed his hand to Tracey's inflated stomach. Garrett smiled, stroking her stomach as if he had been doing it all along, as if it were the most natural thing in the world. "Angie will be glad to know she's going to have a little niece to corrupt."

Carolyn turned her attention back to him. "The baby's already big as a house, as you can see." *Thanks, Mama.* "They may have to do a Caesarean. But I hope that's not necessary."

"That's the way my sister and I were delivered," he said, nodding his head. "We were both nearly ten pounds."

If Tracey were white, she was certain she would have gone pale. She already knew the baby was big, but the very idea!

"Listen, Garrett," Carolyn spoke with a gentle voice. Tracey recognized contrition in it. "You'll have to forgive me for what I said in the waiting room that day."

"What did you say?" Tracey asked.

She didn't pay Tracey any mind.

"I believed that you had abandoned Tracey and the baby. When I saw you I thought…"

"I understand," he said. He *always* understood. "You didn't expect it to be the other way around. Listen, I was in love with Tracey." *Was* in love with her? "I would never have done anything to hurt her. Then again, I didn't think she would ever do something like this. I guess she knew that the only way to keep me from this baby was for me not to know it existed."

"But you said you knew she was pregnant. You asked her to have the baby."

"Yeah, well, I knew she was pregnant, but Tracey led me to believe that she was going to abort the baby. I had no idea she was going to carry her to term."

That was not altogether true. Tracey never actually said she was going to abort the baby.

Her mother's eyes found her. Her chin had dropped and her mouth was open. Tracey closed her eyes; she couldn't stand much more of this. Her head began to hurt and, as if she felt it, too, Nathalie started to move within her. Garrett's hands were still pressed to her abdomen so he felt the movement, too. Tracey felt him kneel down beside her. She heard his laughter, heard the amazement that made his voice crack as he yelled, "She's moving! She really is moving in there! She really is in there!"

If they were any other couple Tracey would have shared this joy with him, but they were not any other couple and there would be no sharing between them.

He turned to her mother, whom he barely knew, and beckoned her. "Come feel her move." And her mother came, the both of them touching Tracey, but not touching her at all. She opened her eyes to see them smiling at each other, kneeling there in an intimate moment that still managed to make Tracey feel like an outsider.

She did what she could to stop the tears burning in her eyes from falling.

—∽—

"Baby!" Travis McAlpine came into the room bearing even more flowers. "If I hadn't been halfway around the world, I would have been back sooner."

Garrett jumped up then. Tracey's mother stood as well.

Then Tracey's father uttered a very, very rare and unrepeatable curse.

"Go ahead, tell your daddy what you've done," her mother said, waving her soft hand with its long, pink-tipped nails in the air. Tracey stroked her belly, thinking of what the world had in store for her baby.

"Tracey?" His deep, stern, preacher-man voice started her to trembling. Her daddy was not going to like this.

She didn't say anything right away. She only looked toward the window, watching the fan her mother had brought chop up the world beyond it.

"Tracey, I am not going to keep asking you this. You've had enough surprises for us this year already. I'm not going to pull your teeth to hear another one."

Tracey swallowed and opened her mouth, willing the words to just come out. They didn't, and she wished it could be easier. She wished for once she could speak out clearly, assertively. "Well…"

Her mother crossed her arms in front of her, waiting for the precise moment when her father understood what Tracey was about to say so she could jump in and either help demolish or help save her daughter. Tracey wasn't sure which.

Tracey watched her father, but he wasn't paying her any attention. For the first time since he'd come in, he was noticing Garrett. And staring daggers into him.

"I don't guess you're going to have to tell him after all." Her mother gave Garrett a firm, supportive pat on the back before going to stand beside her husband. Tracey absolutely thought of her mother as a traitor then.

Garrett stood, still watching her father, who was always intimidating. But Garrett didn't seem intimidated. Garrett seemed furious. "You bastard, you didn't tell me. You didn't tell me she was pregnant. You didn't say a word. You fu—"

"Watch it," Carolyn warned.

"Did you know he came to see me, Carolyn?"

"She didn't know, and if you insult one more person in my family, you are going to have problems."

"Yessir," Garrett nodded. Sarcastically, he added, "When you're done, remember to tell your wife what you've done. I've already told her what Tracey's done. Like father like—"

"I don't need to explain a damn thing to anybody!" Travis roared at him.

"Oh really?" Garrett turned to Carolyn. "Ask him about it."

From the look on her face, she would do just that, but not there, not then, not in front of them.

"Before you start throwing stones," Travis bit out, "let's look at you and what you've done. To start, my wife tells me that you begged Tracey to have the baby so you could raise it."

"I did."

"Well, why did you take no for an answer? It was your child."

"I didn't."

"You did. You let Tracey just tell you 'no' and you were through with it."

"I didn't. Tracey led me to believe that she was going to abort the baby."

"She led you to believe? And you accepted that?"

"I had no choice."

"So you accepted it. A legal 'prodigy' couldn't think of a way to stop her from doing it? You didn't check on her to see if she'd done it. You never checked to find out if she really went through with it because deep down you were kind of hoping she would, weren't you?"

"No, sir."

"Oh, I think so. I think since you had already broken up with her, had already decided that she wasn't going to come around to your way of thinking, had already decided that she was going to burden your plans for the future, you wanted her to get rid of that baby. You wanted an excuse not to ever see Tracey again!"

"Daddy, stop it! It wasn't like that. I'm to blame here."

"Oh, Tracey, you have proven your naiveté. What you did was just convenient for him!"

"Oh, that's beautiful. It really is beautiful. *You* told me to stay away from her!"

"Get out." The voice wasn't loud, nor was it soft. "Get out," it repeated. "Even if she is partly to blame, my daughter can't take this right now. It's not the time, and it's not the place. So both of you get out." Tracey's mother wet a towel and put it to her brow. Tracey was already losing focus again as her once love and her father had it out.

"I am going to make sure you can't hurt my daughter or my granddaughter!" her father roared as soon as they were out in the hall.

Tracey could still hear them, at least until she passed out.

Chapter 25

"You look like hell."

"I feel like hell." Garrett tried to smile at his sister. "How's she doing?"

"Stable. At least she was when I left the hospital."

"What did her parents say?"

"A whole hell of a lot. It started out ugly. Real ugly. But after we all simmered down, we reasoned through it. I told them I wasn't going anywhere. The baby's mine and they can't keep her from me."

"And…"

"And we came to a truce. They may not like me, but I think they respect the fact that I'm the baby's father."

Angie squealed and balled up her fists, knocking them together. Her face was bright and happy. "Oh, my God, Rett, you're gonna be a daddy! And I'm gonna be an auntie!"

Rett allowed himself a moment to jump up and down with her. Every time he thought about it, he felt so many emotions—warmth, love, apprehension, and most overwhelmingly, excitement.

After a moment, he and his sister took deep, steadying breaths.

"You ready?" Angie asked Rett as she put her arms around his shoulders.

"No." He squeezed her. She probably felt the chill that washed over his body. Then he popped away from her. "Thank you for coming home early."

"No problem, honey. I love you." She kissed his cheek. Then she held his hand as they went in the living room.

"I need to talk to y'all about something." Rett pushed out a heavy sigh standing across from his parents. He looked at his mother, who sat very still on the couch. He looked at his father, who was pitching forward in his seat, trying to un-recline his chair.

When Big looked up at him he seemed to recognize something. He began to shake his head. "What have you gone and done, Rett? I told you—"

"I know what you told me, Dad. But that didn't change anything," Rett snapped sarcastically. He raked his hands through his hair. He felt Angie's hand on the small of his back, reinforcing his backbone.

"What's going on here, Big?" Mary Margaret asked as she came to perch on the arm of his chair next to him, across from her daughter and son.

Big turned to his wife with a look of dread that made everything worse for Rett. Already, without him saying anything, his father knew. And already they both knew how Mary Margaret was going to react.

"Looks like your son has gone and got himself into a little trouble. Or, should I say, your son's gone and got some*one* into a little trouble."

"What?" Mary Margaret asked, stretching the word out to show she really didn't understand.

"Looks like there's a little'un on the way."

"A what? A—" And everybody heard it before she could stop it. Mary Margaret sounded as if she were halfway to ecstatic already. She tried to calm down. "What, Rett, honey? Is Kim pregnant?"

"No."

"Then who?" Mary Margaret turned to Big, who didn't say a word. "Who, Rett?"

"This girl from school. Her name's Tracey." He swallowed.

"Well, Rett, hon, you know you gotta do the right thing. I mean, we're Christian people. You have got to look inside yourself and do the right thing."

"And, Momma, I plan to," Rett said, but still didn't go any further.

"Tell her, Rett. Go on." Big was staring Rett right in the eye. They all knew what was about to come, all except Mary Margaret. Still, Rett didn't say anything.

Then, as was her way, Angie decided to get it all out. "What they're neglecting to tell you is that Tracey's a black girl."

"No," Mary Margaret said immediately and shook her head. Somehow, it was as if she thought that was all she had to do to make it go away.

Angie leaned forward and countered, "Yeah."

Mary Margaret's stood slowly and her body began to quiver. "Give him a check, Big," she said, her voice deceptively soft.

"What?" Rett snapped hotly.

"Give him a check, Big."

"We have to talk about—" Angie started.

"We don't have to talk about a damn thing! Give him a check, Big!"

"I don't think he's going to take a check, Mary Margaret."

"Oh, he won't? Well, where the hell is she? *She'll* take it. She'll love to get her welfare-loving hands on it. Give him a check, Big!"

"That was uncalled for, Mother," Rett returned with tight lips.

"I *said*, give him a check, Big."

"Momma!" That was Angie.

"Give him a check, Big! Give him a check, Big! Give him a check, Big!" Her face was mottled with red splotches and her eyes were fixed on Rett's. She was shaking and shrieking it by then. And her fingers had stretched and frozen into vulture talons. "My son's not going to have no nigger baby by no nigger whore!" She ground her teeth together, "Give…him…a damn check, Big!" She spun on her heel and stormed out of the room.

The three left stood staring at each other. "You going to go, too?" Rett swallowed deep. His throat was hot and dry. His ears and face burned hot as lava.

"No." Big shook his head. "Won't do any good anyhow. You tell me now, what it was you planned to say."

"I don't see what the point is."

"You heard me."

"I came here to tell you that Tracey is pregnant. It's a long story, but she's going to deliver in a month's time. You're going to be a granddaddy, whether you want to be or not."

"Well," Big said and reclined in his seat again. And that was all there was to be said.

—m—

"Does that word bother you?"

"What word?" Angie asked as she sipped lemonade across the table.

"*That* word," Rett said.

"Oh. Yes, it bothers me."

"Has it always bothered you?"

"Since I was old enough to know what it meant," Angie told him. "Why?"

"Just wondering."

"Does it bother you?"

"It didn't used to bother me. In fact, it didn't bother me that much even when I was with Tracey. I mean, there was this one time when she was over at the apartment, and Charles, being who he is, said it under his breath. I threatened to kick his ass, but that was only 'cause I knew Tracey was offended."

Angie just sighed into her glass. Her disapproval was not disguised.

"You know, it really didn't bother me until today, 'til Momma said it, especially the way she said it."

"Well, why do you think it's bothering you now all of a sudden?"

"It was so horrible when Momma said it 'cause when she said it, she wasn't just talking about Tracey. She was talking about my baby, and that's like talking about me. I mean, it's like she was saying it to me about me."

"Nothing ever fazes you until it's about you, right?"

"Shut up, Angie."

"I'm just saying."

—∽∾—

"Wake up!"

Rett nearly jumped through the ceiling.

"What the—"

"You heard me. Wake up!" Big told him again. Rett put a hand to his head, hoping to clear it. Rett could smell the liquor on his father's breath.

271

"I'm up," Rett grunted, looking around for his clock. He could have sworn he'd just laid down. He was disoriented. "What you want?"

"I want you to get up and put some clothes on. We're going shooting."

"What time is it?"

"Time to get up. I got the truck running. I'll meet you outside in ten minutes. Count 'em, ten minutes."

This was not the first time Big had awakened his son in the middle of the night drunk as a skunk and wanting to go shoot. Hell, it had happened fairly frequently when Rett lived at home. But he was already uneasy. He and Angie had sat in the kitchen listening to Big and Mary Margaret yell all night long. Well, no, his momma had yelled all night long, but Big had been in there with her. Then she'd stormed out of the house and left. Rett didn't figure she'd be back that night. She was probably going to her cousin Betty's. But after she'd left, Big had come into the kitchen with them. They'd watched him get as drunk as drunk could get — which was easy for him — and now, here he was. Well, actually, there he had been, 'cause he was out of the room on the way to his truck by then.

"Damn," Rett hissed and got dressed. He was pulling sneakers on as he made it outside. Sure enough, there was Big sitting in the truck. He slipped in on the other side. When he noticed that Big's head was lolling around, he slammed the door.

Big jumped, then snapped his head around every which way, confused. Rett tapped him on the shoulder. Big turned to look him solemnly in the eye. Rett wanted to laugh so bad at this immediate desire to sober. Especially when Big announced gravely, "You're my son, son."

"Yep," Rett agreed, nodding.

"You're my blood."

"Uh-huh," Rett agreed, putting his hand over his heart.

"And you can't do anything to change blood, no matter what your momma says."

"Yep." This time Rett couldn't mock his father, because, as usual, Big was trying to tell him something important. This just happened to be the way he did it. Even with Angie, when she won her first medal and Big wanted to congratulate her, this was what he did. Rett turned to face forward, thinking about what his father was telling him.

"And you know what else, son?"

"What?" Rett asked, humbled.

"I'm not giving you a damn check!" And after saying that, Big Atkins slumped over in the driver's seat, passed out.

"Damn," Rett hissed for the second time that night. He was sorely tempted to just leave Big there in the car. Let him sleep it off. But he couldn't do it. So he gritted his teeth and got out of the car. As he always had done in this situation, he spent a moment looking at his father and wondering how in the hell he was going to move a near three-hundred-pound man back into the house. But, hey, Rett actually smiled to himself, he'd been doing it since he was a skinny fourteen-year-old. Somehow, he'd managed it then.

Chapter 26

Her eyes felt dry and gritty when Tracey woke up. She walked into the bathroom, where she ran a face cloth beneath warm water even though she had turned on the cold. That was how hot it was outside. She ran the towel over her face, feeling her pores stretch and yawn. They woke late. Back in her room, she changed out of her hospital gown into a purple maternity sundress Mama had brought her from home. When she walked out of the bathroom, there was Garrett staring straight at her, with his face as expressionless as that of a Buckingham Palace guard.

She tried to ignore him as she struggled to get back into bed. Humiliated that she had to rely on him to help her back up she settled and swiped the wild hair out of her face. The pregnancy had made it really grow. Tracey didn't know what to do with it. She reached for the pitcher to refill her cup when, suddenly, she felt Garrett's hand on her wrist. His eyes met hers. The sentiment she saw in them was highly unexpected.

"I'm sorry about the mall. I didn't mean to startle you that way. I didn't want to upset you to the point the baby could be in danger." His voice was hoarse.

"It's okay. I was already feeling overheated."

Garrett ran a gentle finger over the palm of her hand, shaking his head slowly. The grief she saw on his face knifed into her, carving itself forever in her mind. She wanted to ask what had happened, but didn't dare. "I was in shock when I saw you."

"I understand."

"But I don't. Why didn't you tell me? How could you keep something like this from me?"

"I don't know what to say. There's no excuse. I just thought it would be better if—"

"If I never knew my child?" He placed his hand on her belly.

Garrett had always been the compromising one, and Tracey the unyielding. Guilt weighed on her like those big, black plates that balance precariously on the ends of dumbbells. His hand still rested on her wrist. Tracey looked down at it. He was touching her, not the baby.

Garrett Atkins was touching Tracey McAlpine.

Then, as if he had realized it, too, he recoiled.

"I don't think I can ever forgive you for this. I thank the Lord He saw fit to step in." His accent had thickened and he held her with blazing yellow eyes until his words had been understood, until, she guessed, he felt he had made his point.

Tracey turned away from him as soon as she could. Deep breaths helped control trembling that didn't want to be denied.

Garrett returned to his chair. He didn't look at her. Instead, he ran his fingers through his hair, which she noticed had grown down his neck in soft brown and amber waves strung with copper. Dark auburn stubble was beginning to shadow his jaw.

He'd changed, really changed. Already handsome, this tanned, scruffy look combined with his always mesmerizing eyes had made him haltingly so. On impulse she started to reach out and touch the hair he'd stopped cutting. Hardly advisable at right that moment. Tracey tried to shake the sensation.

"Tracey, there's something I need to ask you. I didn't want to bring it up in front of your parents, so I didn't say anything last night. And I truly, truly don't want to put any more undue stress on the baby, but I need to know. I have to know, Tracey. Do you want this baby?"

"What?"

"I need to know if you want her, because if you don't, I do. Nothing has changed. I want to take care of her."

"And what makes you think I don't?"

He leaned his head back against the chair, took a breath, let it out slowly, then faced her again. "I know how you feel about me, and I don't want my baby to have to go through that, too."

Her mouth dropped open. "You mean to tell me you think I could mistreat my own baby because she's...she's...because you're—"

"Look at you, Tracey, You still can't even say it."

"Garrett, listen to me. She's my baby and I love her. I love her so much already I couldn't possibly do anything to hurt her. And that means I love her too much to just let her go."

"So you already love her more than you ever loved me. You let *me* go," he concluded with a voice steady but foreign, not like any he'd ever used with her before. It sounded sad. She twisted her hands in the material of her dress just beneath her belly. "Did you ever love me, Tracey? Did you?"

"Yes, Garrett."

Then, as if that wasn't the answer he wanted, he hissed, "How could you have loved me and let things end up this way?" He rose and stormed out.

She covered her eyes with her hands, willing the tremors away.

She just wanted to be alone and not think. She didn't want to think about any of it.

"She's in here," she heard her mother announce.

The next minute, her mother and her aunts, Colleen and Charlotte, helped Tracey understand the meaning of claustrophobia.

—◆—

A week after she got out of the hospital, Tracey heard the knock at the door of her parents' guesthouse. She immediately assumed it was Monica since no one else seemed to knock anymore. Plus, Moni had planned to come up for a visit and keep her company. However, when she opened the door to the guesthouse, all she saw was long, wispy, sun-streaked blonde hair. "Angie," she breathed, almost unable to get it out.

Just like her brother, she barely looked at Tracey. Instead, her small hands with their silver rings and nibbled nails came out to touch her belly. Tracey didn't expect that and so only stood there, stunned and ashamed. Suddenly her hazel eyes, darker than her brother's and much less fierce, came to meet Tracey's.

"I'm sorry." The hollow sound was all she could manage.

"I know," Angie whispered and smiled. She smiled even though her hands were still resting on Tracey's stomach and her eyelids were struggling to hold up two precarious pools of water. Tracey's death toll seemed to be going up by the day.

"When you stopped calling," Angie said as she finally moved into the house, "I told Garrett something had to be wrong with you. Either that or he'd done something to you. He never told me about the baby... or that you were ever pregnant."

Tracy smiled as best she could. She had attempted to correct with speech what couldn't be corrected. He

279

never knew there would be a baby. "What *did* he tell you?"

"Honestly?"

"Yeah. I'll brace myself."

"That you were an evil, conniving bitch. I think he said you were the devil trying to steal his seed. That was one hell of a fun night drinking."

"Did he really say that?"

"No." Angie grinned, though she didn't sound as if she found it funny. She gave an exasperated sigh. "He said you broke up with him and made me drop the subject. I couldn't get a word out of him beyond that. I will say this though…"

She knew already that she wasn't going to like whatever Angie was going to say, but she couldn't stop herself from listening.

"After you guys broke up, he went around getting drunk and flirting with everything in a skirt. I'm not saying he did anything. I'm just saying it wasn't pretty."

When Angie said that, it was as if Tracey's ribs started to shrink around her lungs and heart and everything. Her windpipe closed right up and she felt light-headed. Her forearm went protectively over her stomach and she bit down on her lip. She had known he was probably with other women. She had told herself time and time again that was probably the case, so why did it hurt her so much?

"I'm sorry, Tracey. But I thought you should probably know. He's changed a lot since you split up. One of the more weird things is that he won't let anyone call him Garrett. It's always got to be Rett. I mean, we've always called him by either name, but not anymore. I don't know, I think he lost his damn mind after y'all broke up."

Tracey was trapped between sickly flattered and just plain old sick.

"Anyway, he drinks all the time, he won't cut his hair, and he snaps at any and everyone that comes near him. It's weirding me out, man. He's worse than me. Tracey?"

"I'm listening," Tracey replied, though she didn't know how her lips formed those words. She found herself leaning against the sofa staring intently at the display on the stereo.

"I'm sorry. I know you guys have stuff to work out, so take this as a warning. I guess all I'm telling you is that he's changed a lot since you were last with him. Take care."

She nodded. "You hungry? I'm starved, like always. You want something to eat?"

"Yeah. You want to order something?"

"I was having a friend come by with some food and videos tonight. I can call and tell her to bring enough for us all."

"She won't mind?"

"I doubt it. Besides, I'd really like you two to meet." Tracey started towards the phone but, even before she could move towards it, her door opened and Monica was coming in carrying a huge brown paper bag with a heavenly aroma spilling out of its top.

"Hi." She smiled curiously at Angie.

"Um, Monica, this is Angie Atkins."

"The sister?" Then, "I'm sorry to sound that way. I'm just a little surprised. I'm Monica Johnson, nice to meet you." They shook hands.

"I hope you have enough food in there for me." Angie rubbed her stomach.

"Girl, I could feed a whole troop. So that means we might have to stretch it if Tracey eats." Tracey threw a cushion at her and all three women laughed. Ice broken.

―――

Later, Angie and Tracey both laughed deep and long as Monica regaled them with the series of unfortunate, incredible, and hilarious events that had led her and Maurice to each other.

They laughed and they bonded and Tracey felt blessed to have friends like them.

She started to cry. "What's wrong with you now?" Monica asked, coming to sit beside her. She added as an aside to Angie, "She does this all the time."

"Nothing," Tracey answered, shaking her head. "It's just seems like it was so easy for you and Rico."

"What?"

"I—I don't know."

"Tracey, no." Monica put an arm around Tracey back, "Tracey, it is never easy to love someone and make it work. Never. I don't care who you are or how alike you think you are."

"I guess not," Tracey answered, but she felt the tears coming in earnest then.

"Jeez, I wish you could drink!" Angie said, coming to sit on the other side of her. "Does this happen all the time?"

Monica had the nerve to snicker. "Pretty frequently."

"Okay, I'm gonna fix this," Angie chirped. "Listen to me…listen. What happened to the canary that had unprotected sex?"

"What?" Tracey asked, confused.

"It's a joke," Angie answered. "What happened to the canary that had unprotected sex?"

"What?"

"It got twirpies and I hear it's untweetable!" she replied with relish.

Tracey felt the laughter come from deep inside her. It just bubbled out and Monica was there laughing with her.

"That was the dumbest joke I've ever heard," Monica said, shaking with humor.

"It's not the dumbest joke I know, though." Angie waggled her eyebrows.

Tracey hugged her best friends close. She and Moni listened to Angie tell the most horrible jokes ever the rest of the afternoon, the next always funnier than the last.

—∽∾—

"You're a damn vagrant, dude," Angie remarked as she helped Garrett pack some boxes.

"What do you mean?"

"I mean you don't have an *address*, Rett."

"I do have an address. That's the whole point of you helping me pack."

"But it's a *sublease*."

"What's wrong with that? I go to work early and stay late, really late. The place is close by. What's wrong with that?"

Angie held her hand out for the packing tape. "You're the one who said you wanted a house, aren't you?"

"So what?" he asked, handing her the tape. "I still plan to buy one. I just need some time to get situated. I would have waited, but I don't feel right staying here anymore, no matter what Dad says."

"I know what you mean."

Rett knew that she did.

"You'd better not be taking any girls there."

"What business is it of yours if I do?" he fairly yelled.

"You have been getting around a little too much lately, if you ask me."

"Just 'cause you see me flirt with a chick doesn't mean I'm doing her. You know me better than that."

"I thought I did." She shrugged guiltily.

"I haven't done it since—" He cut off his words.

"Since Tracey?"

Rett didn't want to answer, but he nodded anyway.

A deep scarlet flush heated his sister's face.

"What is it?"

"You really haven't been sleeping with a different girl every night?"

"No!" Rett yelped. "I don't have *time* for that."

"Oh."

Rett cocked his head to the side. "What?"

Angie squeezed her eyes shut.

"Tell me."

"I might have told Tracey that you've been out with a different girl every night."

"Why in God's name would you do that?" Rett shouted.

"Because you *have* been on dates."

Rett's chest rose and fell rapidly, and he looked as though he were about ready to strangle his sister.

"I'm so sorry."

"Why would you do that? I'm your brother."

"If it had been anybody but Tracey, I swear before God I wouldn't have said a thing."

"Why does it matter that it was Tracey and not some other girl?"

"Because it's *Tracey*." As if that was any kind of answer.

Rett rubbed his eyes. "Doesn't matter."

"Garrett, I'm so sorry."

"Doesn't matter, Angie. I'm not hers, she's not mine. It doesn't matter."

"But I'll make it right. I'll tell her that nothing was—"

"Doesn't matter, Angie. She can think whatever she wants. It doesn't change anything."

"I think she was jealous."

Rett's head snapped up. "Really?"

Chapter 27

Tracey's friends, her mother, and her aunts tried to keep her cheered up, they really did, but Tracey was the most morose pregnant woman that ever existed. Times alone, times when she was left to think about the past year, really did her in.

That's when thoughts of the short but beautiful period with Garrett before the pregnancy crowded in. Those made Tracey smile, but were always followed by memories of their fragile relationship cracking, of Garrett getting angry with her, of the horrible deception that could have led to him believing she was heartless enough to get rid of their child. Then it was usually topped off with a searing pain associated with the idea that he might be out falling in love with someone else.

Tracey tried to occupy herself with baby books and real estate magazines. The time had come to get rid of the house that had been her sanctuary for years but had turned into a place with too many haunting memories. She had already exchanged it for life in her parents' guesthouse. But she wanted to move out on her own, which she could afford if she sold her grandma's house. She had already landed a job that would support her and the baby.

Tracey had a fight on her hands with her parents, though. Neither of them supported her moving out so soon after the baby was born. So she busied herself with trying to convince them that having an independent mother was best for the baby.

But Tracey still had time to think.

The only thing worse than time on her own to think was when Garrett came to check on her and the baby.

He came faithfully two or three times during the week, sometimes Saturday, usually Sunday after church. Tracey knew his church was nearby, but he never talked about it. Instead, he just showed up with armloads and armloads of baby stuff. A crib. Baby bottles. He bought disposable diapers and a car seat for his car. He bought a car seat for *her* car. He bought bags upon bags of undershirts, booties, diaper rash medicine, blankets, etc. He bought toys the baby wouldn't even be able to play with for at least two years. He would spend five minutes unloading, then take off. It was awful.

And there was something there. Something big and terrible and waiting. Something hanging in the air around them waiting to be acknowledged. Part of it was his anger. Garrett hated her because of what she had done. Nearly done. Part of it was her anxiety. They hadn't worked out visitation or what things would be like once the baby came. She knew Garrett was going to have demands, but had no clue as to what they would be. There were so many questions and so many feelings that they just let lie fallow, expecting resolution to flower nonetheless.

He spent more time with her when he showed up to take her to doctor's appointments. He and her mother scheduled the dates between them, never including her in the scheduling. He did not interact with her. Tracey accepted this, his presence and attitude, purely out of guilt because she had erased his smile.

The few times they did talk, he barked orders at her or demanded answers. He asked her for an accounting of her eating and exercise habits. He wanted to know when she planned to move into her own place. He wanted to know where. It needed to be somewhere in the city so if something happened to Nathalie, they could get her help quickly. He wanted to know if Tracey could afford to move into her own place on her salary. Then he dismissed that question. He knew she could afford her own place regardless of what the job paid. And that was another thing that seemed to bother him.

Garrett did buy excessively for the baby, no matter how much Tracey told him it wasn't necessary or to wait until she came. He didn't listen and got indignant when she went out and bought things for herself. The first time Garrett came over to the house, she watched for him from her window. She saw him coming up the winding half-mile-long drive and went into the living room to wait for him. When Tracey didn't see him drive up through the window there, she went outside and saw him reentering the drive. He must have turned around and come back. She turned to take stock of the only home she'd ever really known. Somehow, it transformed right then and there. She saw it as something other than her home. She saw it as maybe Garrett saw it. She thought of her mother's office virtually wallpapered in magazine spreads of the house. She thought of the first time Moni had come over and had gushed about how nice the place was. She remembered talking to Angie and hearing a catch in her voice after something she said about the house.

Angie had breathed, "You have staff?"

"*One* staff," Tracey grumbled.

When he stopped in front, Tracey knew Garrett felt uncomfortable. He'd known her family was wealthy. But she could hear him saying, not *that* damn wealthy.

"Drive around back and park on the right side of me in the garage." He paled and Tracey tried to figure out what was weird about what she'd said. Then she thought of the garage. She put a hand to her face and went back into the house. It wouldn't help that her father's cars and truck were already parked back there, too. Never before had she felt that her family lived to excess. Never had she thought her surroundings ostentatious. And never had she been as embarrassed of the way she lived as she was at that moment.

Then it started, the checking, the questioning, the *buying*. Was Tracey all right? Did the baby need anything? Did she need anything? Was she doing exactly as the doctor had instructed? Garrett was driving her crazy. He really was. Mainly, because with his obsession to show her and her parents he was worthy, he never really treated her as anything other than a vessel carrying his child. Whenever he looked at her as a person independent of the baby, it was with an undercurrent of anger and that damn hovering, awful *something* that waited in the background. Since he knew she had to stay calm, he tried valiantly instead to make sure he didn't see her as anything but a human incubator. Morbidly, she thought of him worshipping next to a shrine of test tubes, wishing his baby was in one of them. All this care he took was so intimate and yet so thoroughly impersonal at the same time. He never said anything to Tracey that didn't have direct relation to the baby. That conjured an image of him trying to accomplish something by talking into her navel. It was probably his next step.

She had to find out from Angie when he passed the bar. She had to find out from Angie that he'd had some sort of accident while exercising a month or so ago and had to get stitches on his leg and arm. Tracey had noticed the fading scratches on the side of his face, but they didn't talk about it. That's the way it was.

Only once, very, very late in the pregnancy, did he show her anything other than that cold impersonal side or that stunted, angry side. It had been so hot Tracey had been sweating like a pig. Just that morning, the air conditioning in the guesthouse had gone out. Her father was having someone come out to fix it, but it wouldn't be until the next day. She could have gone back to the main house, but she didn't want to be in the presence of her worrying parents any more than was necessary. As she stared at the window fan chopping up the world beyond, she was burning. She needed something to cool herself down. Unfortunately, the pool was off limits. She wasn't sure why but her mother had a fear of mixing pregnancy and pools. Tracey didn't think there was any scientific basis, but still she respected her mother's wishes and relied on cool showers.

She turned on the water that day and went to get a change of clothes. She massaged the aching muscles at the base of her back. The bigger she got the more she could barely walk, the pain was so persistent. She forced herself to continue, though, because if she was going to manage a shower, she was going to have to at least be able to walk.

In the bathroom, she sank down on the toilet with her head in her hands. She was miserable. The bathtub looked so inviting. She listened to the water stream in the large, glassed-in shower across from her. She needed to adjust the plastic stool. Tears, ever-present, always plentiful, started in her eyes. The sobs welled up from deep inside, caught somewhere between her heart, her throat, and her backbone. She tried to cut them off but this hormone tantrum was not to be denied. She sat there bawling with water splashing onto her floor from the shower.

That's how Garrett found her.

"What's wrong, Tracey? Is it the baby?"

She hiccupped, trying to stop crying in front of him. "Th-the baby's fine."

"So what's wrong?"

Tracey shook her head.

"What were you doing?"

"Shower. I was going to take a shower."

He squatted in front of her so they were eye to eye. He watched her with a gentle expression. "Your back isn't still hurting, is it?"

Like crazy. "No."

"Are you gonna go ahead and take your shower?" The tears were rolling again as Tracey considered this question. "Tracey?"

"I'm too big, Garrett! I can barely stand and with that stool, it's too awkward and I can't reach everything and—I can't take a bath 'cause God knows it'll be centuries before I can get out again and I can't even reach my knees, let alone anything else."

He contemplated her in silence for a moment. She turned her attention to a loose spot in the bath mat. His hand entwined with hers as he helped her stand. When she stood, he kneeled in front of her.

"Put your hands on my shoulders so you don't lose your balance."

Tracey complied.

He pulled down her big white shorts and huge, unappealing cotton bloomers. When they reached her ankles, she stepped out of them. Garrett stood and turned her around to unsnap her bra. She gave a silent prayer he wouldn't notice how ugly the big white cotton harness was. He turned his back to her to adjust the water and the stool.

She stood there waiting on him, completely naked and more than a little self-conscious. For a minute when he turned back to her, he stared at her body. She wondered what he saw: big, fat Tracey with stretch marks? Or did he just see the beach ball attached to her middle? Did he just see his baby? She got her answer when he rested his hand on her bloated stomach.

Damned if that child wasn't already in love with her daddy. Nathalie started moving beneath his touch and he started to smile big. She kicked and he laughed as if it was the greatest thing that had ever happened to him. It didn't occur to Tracey at the time that it probably *was* the greatest thing that had ever happened to him.

Then, with a much more sober expression, Garrett reached out his hand again and she allowed him to help her into the shower and onto the stool. She puzzled briefly over how he was going to accomplish this without getting wet himself. Would he take his clothes off, too? The very thought made her shiver.

"You need warmer water?"

Tracey shook her head. Hot water would have suffocated her for sure in the summer heat. Even at night it was stifling. He took off his shirt and she was surprised with a full view of his broad shoulders and lean chest with its light sprinkle of sandy-colored hair. The familiarity of his strong arms assailed her senses. For a moment, she was beset by a memory of those very muscles beneath her fingers when they strained above her to give them both pleasure. Her whole body heated and she couldn't wait for him to touch her.

He took off his jeans, but left on the long shorts he wore underneath and stood beside the shower.

As one hand cleansed, the other massaged tight muscles strung between her shoulder blades. He helped her stand a little and moved the towel down and over her bottom until she barely felt the towel anymore, but soft, slippery, warm hands. Then he moved to her thighs and she felt his arms encircle her as he washed the fronts of them. She twisted until he was in front of her again and he moved the towel up, soaping her belly. The hand with the towel slipped down beneath her stomach to slide between her legs. The feeling made her jerk and he quickly moved his hand up again whispering, "Shhhhhh." His hand traveled up to her sensitive breasts. The towel made a loud splat as it hit the ground, forgotten. His hands on her breasts were soon joined by his lips when he stepped into the shower and leaned over her. Her arms moved to circle his neck, to never let him go again. Finally, his eyes, opaque amber and green by then, came to meet hers before he laid a devastating kiss on her lips.

Completely drenched, he kissed her senseless. When he stopped, they were in her bedroom, kept cool by a few fans.

"Can we?" he asked.

"Normally, I think it would be okay, but I'm not supposed to."

He nodded slowly. Still, he laid her damp body down on the bed. He slipped his shorts off and settled next to her, nuzzling her breasts. His tongue slid softly over her moist skin and his hands touched gently because he knew how sensitive she was. He made love to her in all the ways he could.

—∽∽—

In her sleep, Tracey shifted and the moisture between her legs startled her fully awake. Garrett's arm, cupped around her tummy as he curled up behind her, tightened. She was lying there trying to figure out how to get up without waking him when she heard a soft hiss.

Reluctantly, she looked toward the bedroom doorway. Quickly, she stifled the adolescent urge to jump up when she saw her mother standing there. Instead, Tracey silently shooed her away with her hand. Tracey slid out of bed slowly, trying to worm her way from Garrett's protective arm, not an easy task for a pregnant woman. She donned a robe, a huge purple piece of terrycloth, and went into the living room. Her mother was sitting on the sofa with her arms crossed.

"I knew I should have had the locks changed when I moved out here," Tracey mumbled, rubbing her eyes.

"Tracey," her mother started but stopped. She must have been in mild shock. "Tracey," she tried again. "What did I just see?"

"I should hope you'd know, Ma," Tracey griped, in a sour mood because she was having serious cramping. "Honestly, how do you think I got this way?"

"Don't get smart with me. This is still *my* house. I don't care what you did before, you know better than to do it here. Besides, I thought you and he were—"

"If it makes you feel better, we didn't do tha—" Tracey stopped speaking. Her hands dove beneath her belly to support it as the pain and pressure shot

297

straight into her back and all the way down her legs. Tears prickled her eyes as she stumbled from the pain.

"Ohmigod! I'm miscarrying!" she screamed to her mother through tears.

"You are not miscarrying!" she yelled back, though her eyes were as big as shortbread cookies.

"I am! I am! I'll die if I do!"

"Stop it, Tracey, you're going to be fine and so is your baby."

"But it hurts!" Tracey howled. "God, it hurts! It's like there's so much pressure I can't stand it. Mama, you've got to call the doctor! I can't lose my baby!"

"Tracey." Her mother used excessive calm to compensate against her excessive histrionics. "Tracey, you are not going to lose your baby. You're just going to have it. Baby, remember, you're already dilated. You knew this w—"

"No!" Tracey yelled even as she felt the contraction subsiding, but still relatively hysterical. "I can't have it now."

"Well, honey, you've had this scheduled for almost nine months now. You may want to change it, but little Nathalie's not having it."

Tracey looked down at her huge belly. "My Caesarian isn't scheduled until next week. She can't come out that way! She's too big! All of that can't come out of me!"

"Your doctor will be the judge of that."

Tracey was certain horror was written in red script on her forehead.

"Tracey, baby, try and calm down. Remember what you learned in your classes. The main thing here is not to panic. Besides, you were already quite dilated at your last visit. You can have this baby."

"The hell I can!"

Even in that situation, her mother scowled at her language.

"Just try and calm down, baby! And don't sit. It's best if you try and walk around for a while. I'm going to go and wake up Garrett."

"No," Tracey squealed, desperately grabbing for her arm. "No, you can't tell him!"

"Don't be ridiculous, Tracey," was her answer to that. It didn't matter anyway. He was already walking in the room in his jeans, pulling on a shirt.

"What's wrong with her?"

"You don't have to be so damned matter of fact, and you can ask *me*, you know!"

"All right, Tracey, what's wrong with you?"

"I'm in labor!" It shouldn't have been so satisfying to watch him freeze with only one arm in his shirt.

Just like that he walked over and put his arms around Tracey. He squeezed a little and kissed her on the cheek. Somehow, the hysteria left her for a moment and she took a deep breath.

The hysteria came right back.

"Carolyn, could you please call Dr. Singh. I'll get her things together and we'll take my truck."

"Okay, let's go."

Chapter 28

Rett felt as if he were the one giving birth. His breathing was uneven and his heart pounded. His whole body was rigid with tension. And Tracey wasn't helping any. Every time he looked at her in the rearview mirror, he felt himself pale, sickened by the fact that there was nothing he could do. That he had, in fact, done this to her. He gripped the steering wheel until his knuckles turned white.

"I'm so sorry about the pain, baby," her mother crooned, stroking her face and belly.

"I'm sorry, too," Rett added lamely.

"Oh, it's way too late for that," Tracey snarled.

Rett winced.

"Shh, Tracey," Carolyn soothed. "Just think, you're going to have your sweet little baby here in just a minute. A little beautiful baby girl. Nathalie."

Tracey seemed to quiet.

"Rett," Carolyn called.

"Yes, ma'am?"

"I left my phone at the house. Can you call my husband?"

No, Rett thought. *No, I cannot.*

He took out his cell phone and tossed it to his… his what? His baby mama's mama?

—✺—

Somehow, Travis managed to beat them to the hospital and led them to Tracey's private room. Rett followed impotently as Travis wheeled his daughter around with the nursing staff and his wife flanking him.

Angie and Monica showed up then, as well as a couple of Tracey's aunts. Then more people came and everyone wanted to see her. The staff, as Tracey got close, began to usher everyone away.

Rett had been a bystander that entire day, but no more. He'd been at a loss as to what to do when Tracey went through the contractions. He'd been grateful when the doctors gave her drugs to help with the pain. He'd watched her mother make the appropriate contacts and direct people in an organized fashion. But now, he couldn't stand on the sidelines anymore.

It was time for the baby to come.

Carolyn didn't want to leave, but even if she was Tracey's mother, she couldn't stay. Only one person could be in the delivery room at a time, and Rett—for once—had something that trumped the McAlpine clan.

"I'm the baby's father," he announced. "I'm coming into the delivery room."

The nurse looked to Tracey and she nodded her sweating brow.

—∾—

After violent pain, heavy drugs, a natural birth that Tracey was completely unprepared for, and Garrett acting as Dr. Singh's enforcer, there was her little Nathalie in her arms. Right away, Tracey could tell the baby had Garrett's beautiful light hazel eyes. She also had a full head of sandy, nearly blonde hair. It was thick and curled softly. Her skin was almost the same as Garrett's, with his bronze tan, but kissed a little longer by the sun. She was perfectly beautiful. Beautiful. Tracey wept silently as she counted Nathalie's little fingers and toes and marveled that anything could be so tiny and so wonderful. Garrett crowded at the head of the bed with Tracey and cried openly, too.

The nurse came forward to take the baby.

"Mama needs to get some rest now," she told Tracey.

Tracey was a mama.

A mama! She reached for her baby even as she was being lifted from her arms.

"I'll bring her back when it's time for feeding," the nurse reassured her.

Tracey didn't know why she couldn't just keep Nathalie in the room with her. She was tempted to ask her father to make them bring her back, but she checked the impulse. She was a mother. She had to stop the urges to have her father fix everything for her.

—∾—

The next day, Tracey woke to see Angie standing over her looking a little flushed. It was the first indication that something serious was going on. She leaned over, kissed Tracey on the forehead, and sat down in the chair beside the bed. She held Tracey's hand. Tracey looked around the room and there was her mother sitting in another chair, also wearing a strange look.

"Where's Garrett?"

"Down in the nursery with the baby," she answered. Then in hushed tones, "Tracey, there's someone here to see you."

"Do I look bad?"

Angie winced.

"That good, huh?"

Tracey looked over at her mother. "I'll help you. Angie, give us a minute."

Angie nodded and stepped out.

As her mother wiped her face and combed her hair, Tracey opted to question her about the visitor instead of arguing that she wasn't an invalid. However, Carolyn offered no information. All she did was smile tightly. When done, she planted herself on the windowsill with her arms crossed. Angie returned with a man Tracey had never seen before.

He was a tall white man with hair that had maybe once been dark red, but had faded to a brassy color. He was a thick fellow with what looked like a permanent smile in his familiar hazel eyes. He wore a short-sleeved mustard golf shirt and khaki shorts with a woven leather belt. He was very handsome, very fit, and looked to be around fifty years old. He wore a plain gold band on his left ring finger. In his hands was a bouquet of fresh-cut white daisies that were so pristine they didn't even look real. Tentatively, he moved towards her, then seemed to think better of it. Instead, he turned and placed the flowers on a table and turned back, tucking his hands in his pockets. Tracey swallowed, thinking she knew exactly who he was.

"Hello," Garrett's father finally said, his voice sounding very much like his son's.

"Hello," Tracey replied clumsily, trying to sit up. The pain in the entire lower half of her body was not about to let her do it gracefully. Her mother and Angie both rushed to her side.

"Oh, no, you don't have to sit up on my account. I know what it's like. Both Rett and Angie were big babies. And back in those days, they just kicked everybody out of the room and strapped you down. My wife was not happy with that at all." He gave an awkward but familiar smile, then gestured toward the flowers. "I brought these for you. I hope you like them. I didn't think...I didn't know what kind you liked."

"They're beautiful."

"Well," he breathed and looked around, everywhere but at Tracey. "You know who I am?"

"Yes, Mr. Atkins."

"Big," he corrected. "You know, he didn't tell us until, well, until a few weeks ago. He also told me about your difficulties otherwise..." His voice faltered and he squinted a little. She remained silent. "Rett's mother couldn't be here. I know she's sorry about that." This man, with his warm, encouraging smiles and Southern gentleman's accent, could not make the lie believable. And Tracey, even though she knew he wanted her to, could not help him. She couldn't make this meeting easy for him, because it wasn't easy for her. "Well, I guess you're wondering why I'm here."

She made herself speak. "No, you have every right to be here. You're Nathalie's grandfather." The relief she saw in his eyes made him look decades younger. He really was a handsome man. Angie looked just like him, but Garrett shared only his coloring and smile. "Have you seen her yet?"

He grinned big just like Tracey did whenever she thought of her beautiful baby. Her heart grew with every thought of Nathalie, and this man who had very nearly missed out on being a part of her life seemed to feel the same. "Yes. She's beautiful, isn't she? I never would have thought—" Big cut off his words with a hand to his mouth.

"Listen," Tracey said, tired of this dancing around. "The more we walk on eggshells the more uncomfortable it's going to be. Say what you feel." Some of the tension went out of the room.

"I just want you to know," he began, "I've always wanted grandchildren, and I love my grandbaby. I do, she's my first. When Rett told us, it was hard to imagine. I have to be honest and say I wasn't… well… he had another girlfriend, y'know. And I had always thought… I'm really putting my foot in it now, aren't I?"

"No." She managed to smile at him. "I understand. I know about Kim. I also know what kind of shock this must have been for you because I know what my own parents' reaction was."

He scratched his chin. "You do intend to allow us to see her, don't you? All of us already love the heck out of her. You wouldn't—"

Tracey cut him short, realizing his discomfort because she was growing hot with her own. Back on eggshells. Everyone thought she was heartless, and Tracey guessed she had been. "Garrett can see her. He signed the birth certificate, even. At first I thought it was best for everyone if he didn't know. But now that he does…"

"I see," Big responded. "I think I can tell you that when I found out, at first I did wish that you had gotten away with keeping it from him. I agreed wholeheartedly with your decision to hide this from him. I told Rett as much."

"Really?" Tracey tried to keep the anger beneath her ribs. "And what did he say?"

"Something best not repeated. I only felt that way because I knew there would be some…tension in the house for a while. But I adjusted. Angie's told me a lot about you." His voice cracked with the slightest indication of pain. "Well, I'm sorry, but I've got to run. It was good meeting you, finally. I hope we can get to know each other better."

Tracey wanted to believe him, and when he came over to hug her quickly, she did believe him. Angie walked him out. Tracey exhaled finally.

"What did he say to you?" That was Garrett's voice. His face was creased with concern.

"Nothing, Garrett."

"Because if he said something to upset you, especially at a time like this, I think I'll—"

"What did he say to you?" That was Auntie Colleen coming in with her hands on her hips.

"What did he say to you, Tracey?" That was her father storming in with Monica in his wake.

"It's good to know you're all so concerned," Tracey offered dryly. "He didn't say anything upsetting. Just ask Mama. He wanted to know if he could see the baby. If Garrett could see the baby."

"And what did you tell him?" Garrett asked.

"I told him that was fine. That we'd work out visitation and everything. What's wrong with all of you? If you were so worried he was going to come in and do something to me, then why on earth did you let him in here at all?"

"That wasn't my idea," Carolyn said.

"I didn't know he was coming, Tracey," Garrett answered, middle finger and thumb massaging his temples.

"Well, all of you can stop looking like I've just been held hostage. We talked, he was pleasant, everything's fine."

Rett and her father both seemed to breathe a sigh of relief.

Then her parents took off. They told her that they were going home to get the room prepared for her and the baby and that they would be back to get Tracey. She and her healthy baby were being released. Tracey's aunts and Moni left shortly after. As soon as they were out the door Angie turned to her.

"Did Rett tell you what happened when we told them?"

Garrett was silent but didn't make a move to stop her.

She began to walk around the room, seeming to gather her thoughts. "Well," Angie began, "Rett asked me to do it with him, I guess for support."

Tracey looked over at him and he crossed his arms over his chest.

"He told them that he had gotten someone pregnant. My mother was okay at first and then, ah, she demanded that my father get out his checkbook."

Tracey's reaction had to be written on her face because Angie said, "Save your shock, Tracey. You're going to need it for later. Well, Rett told them right away that the baby was almost born anyway. My mother asked Rett how long he'd known. He told her and explained that you had planned to raise the baby by yourself because you didn't want to burden him with it."

"That was kind," Tracey muttered, turning to stare out the window that didn't show her anything but clear blue sky.

"Well, my mom wanted to know if he'd told Kim, if they were still together. He told her that they had broken up a long time ago. That's a whole different story right there. Whatever."

Garrett shrugged.

"But what's more important, I guess, is the way the rest of the conversation went. Well, Garrett told them, you know, about you." She gulped. "Or, rather, I did.

"My mother didn't take it so well. That's where the check came in, and she…uh…said some things. She's not as open as the rest of us, so to speak. She said some things and told Garrett Nathaniel Hinson Atkins to take the check and get rid of you."

Tracey breathed slowly. Mary Margaret Hinson Atkins didn't want her lily-white son having a baby with a black woman. Though she had expected that kind of reaction from people, she didn't expect it to come from so close to home, nor did she expect it to hurt so badly, although Tracey's hurt was more for Garrett than herself. He loved his mother.

Angie cleared her throat and went on, "Dad refused to write the check and Rett would have refused to take it if he had. Rett told him that he was going to be a…a…" Tracey saw the tears but barely believed they were coming from one of the strongest women she knew. Angie sank into the chair against the wall with her head in her hands and her hair covering her reddened face.

"I told him," Garrett continued for her, a stoic expression on his face, "that I was going to be a father. Momma went on about no son of hers, and I guess I am no longer a son of hers. But my daddy has, obviously, accepted things as they are."

"What do you mean 'no son of hers'?" Tracey asked.

"She wanted me to choose, and I did. That's that."

Tracey glanced over at Angie, who sat silently, a guarded look on her face. She glanced back at Garrett, whose lips were pressed together and whose stance was rigid. She scooted over in the bed a little and patted the seat next to her. He looked a little perplexed then, as if he wouldn't sit beside her. But, finally, he did. She leaned up and hugged him close to her. Tracey felt him shudder as he pulled her tight. She stroked his hair as the sob broke free. Angie slipped out of the room, a hand covering her face. He whispered something to Tracey about never having cried until he met her. She squeezed him and couldn't stop crying, either, even when she heard him say, "You didn't tell me, Tracey. I wish to God you would have told me."

After everything they had gone through, Garrett had remained unbroken, unshaken, and now the weight of the world which he had so superbly balanced was too much. Tracey didn't grieve for herself then. She had done enough of that.

There was a tap at the door, and she wiped his tears with her hands.

Chapter 29

After Tracey and Baby Nathalie came home from the hospital, her mother insisted she stay in her old room for the first couple of weeks with the baby. She'd been foolish a time or two, but she made the wise choice this time and snapped up all the help and coddling she could get. Her parents were great; her friends were great; even Garrett was great. Still visibly uncomfortable in the presence of her parents, the new, doting father braved it anyway. He also braved the tension between them to be there for his daughter who looked more and more like him every day.

Six weeks later, Tracey moved back out into the guesthouse. True enough, she still lived at her parents' but she felt more independent. She sorely needed to feel independent, capable, not at all foolish. How could she expect herself to raise a daughter, to have her daughter depend on her, if she was always depending on others?

Garrett came more frequently then, if that was at all possible. Nearly every day, for hours on end when he wasn't working, he watched the baby while Tracey caught up on sleep. The situation was tense and awkward, but he didn't care. As long as his baby was there, he told her once, he was going to be there. And he was so good with her. From the start, even her aunts commented on how well he fared with little Nathalie. They never said he seemed more naturally inclined to child care than Tracey, but she knew for sure it was implied. Tracey actually didn't mind. In fact, she was ecstatic that Nathalie had a father who loved her and cared for her. Whether he loved and cared for her mother was another story altogether.

He still barely looked at her. He talked to her when he had to and with a civil tongue. Even after what they had shared in the hospital, his tone lacked warmth. He avoided her touch, even when she gave him something for the baby or took her from him. Lepers probably had it better than Tracey did.

One afternoon after Nathalie turned ten weeks old, Tracey sat in the kitchen while Angie washed her clothes in the small-sized washer and dryer unit. She didn't say why she needed to wash at Tracey's place and it didn't occur to Tracey to ask. That's how close they had grown. Both she and Moni had started to feel like sisters to her; Moni, the older, wiser guide and Angie, the younger, louder rebel. Only Angie had begun to spend more and more time with Tracey at the house, much like her brother.

She was grateful Angie came by so frequently. She liked the company, the help with the baby, and the distraction from the dark, dark cloud that never seemed to be too far away. Tracey did whatever she could to keep the cloud at bay. Depression was not going to interfere with her ability to be a good mother, and Angie was always good for a laugh or a lightened mood.

Tracey brought up Garrett's attitude toward her.

"He hates me," she declared.

That Angie didn't say anything to contradict Tracey served as confirmation.

"I get that I did something horrible. I get it. But it's been months."

"Yeah?" Angie continued to fold her clothes. Her response seemed distant, or maybe preoccupied.

"It's been months. Garrett did get to see his daughter born. He sees her all the time and gets to do full daddy-duty. I can understand him not forgiving me. But he's still so angry. It hasn't lessened at all."

Not a word from the laundry quarter.

"I mean, did he change?"

"Might've done." Angie placed a towel in her laundry basket and started on a pair of jeans.

Tracey chewed her bottom lip, then huffed out an exasperated sigh.

"Do *you* think he's changed?"

Angie put the jeans down and looked at her for the first time. Her expression was easy to read: irritation.

A cold apprehension washed over Tracey. She had never seen that look before.

"Actually, Tracey, I thank the good Lord he hasn't changed. If you don't like what you're seeing, sorry. I hate to be the one to break it to you and all, but that's Rett. Maybe you need to get to know my brother."

That got Tracey's hackles up. "I do know your brother, Angie."

"No, Tracey, you know the person he wants you to know, you know the facts he wants you to know. Staying in the house all the time may have made you close, but in the end it limited the things you could know about him. Think about it. You've barely seen him with his friends or family. You don't know the first thing about the way he acts with other people. And my brother is not the talkative type. He's not going to tell you everything that's on his mind. He's not going to—"

"But we did talk."

"Has Garrett ever been arrested?"

"What?"

"Has Garrett ever been arrested?" Angie repeated the question that had taken Tracey by surprise.

"I don't think he has," Tracey answered stupidly.

"Two times in juvenile court for the same thing."

"For what?" she whispered, nearly choking.

Angie didn't say. "Tracey, you like to dance, right? Does Garrett? Have you ever seen him dance?"

"Now hold on a minute. Granted there are some things I don't know about him, but he and I used to

316

talk all the time. He told me about what was going on with Kim and everything."

"For you to be so damned jaded, you're the most naïve person I know."

Tracey raised an eyebrow.

"Garrett is a wonderful man, but he is just that, a man. When you're trying to get someone into bed the first thing you do is make it clear that you're free and, if you're not free, that the relationship you're in is so bad it cancels any obligation on your part."

"But he—"

"Is a man."

Tracey was crushed.

"I'm not saying he wasn't or isn't in love with you. All I'm saying is that sometimes you are insensitive and unrealistic. You don't see outside yourself. No, my brother hasn't changed. He's done his level best to adjust, to stay who he is, but everyone has their break-ing point. He can't just stay happy go lucky and call it all water under the bridge if it affects him every day." Angie swallowed and her eyes went glassy. "Everyone has a breaking point. Everyone."

"Is this about Rett?"

"You don't know anything," she lashed out, as if she hadn't heard the question. "You haven't had to lift a finger. You haven't had to face a soul you didn't want to face. No one's said so much as an unkind word to you. You're spoiled. You're just spoiled, and because my brother doesn't dance to your tune like everybody else, you want to sit here and whine to me about it."

"Angie! That's uncalled for."

"Some of us have real problems, Tracey! Some of us don't live in a multi-million-dollar house with parents that can get us jobs and give us a house to stay in. I can't believe you were so scared to let anybody see you and my brother together. In the end you haven't suffered one single, solitary second for it! Who cares if somebody stares at you at the grocery store? Who cares about that? That's *nothing*, Tracey. Nothing."

Wow.

The dryer dinged to indicate it was finished. Angie stormed into the laundry closet to check it. Tracey didn't know what made her follow, but she did. Black mascara tracked down Angie's pretty face before she wiped it away.

"What is this about?"

"Nothin' for you to worry about. You don't have to worry about *anything!*"

Tracey shut the dryer before she could take anything else out and stood in front of it, forcing Angie to face her.

Tracey knew Angie lashed out when she was emotional, but this was hitting below the belt and Tracey was losing patience. "Angie, don't tell me what problems I *don't* have. Tell me what's wrong with *you*."

"I can't stay there anymore," she finally bit out.

"At your parents'?"

Angie nodded. "Daddy's fine and he'll take up for me, but it's hell there now. I never f-fit in in the first place, but now… She's so angry all the time, Tracey. And she still tries to be civil to Rett, but she hates me. She *hates* me, like I'm to blame for everything. All I wanted to do was to get her to see reason b-but…oh, God!"

Tracey grabbed her and held her. Tracey loved her like the sister she'd never had, and she couldn't stand to see her like that.

"I'm so sorry." Tracey held her until her cell phone rang.

Angie looked at the screen, then answered it. "Yeah?… I know. I know. But she can't talk to me like that. She shouldn't talk to Dad like that. And she shouldn't talk to you like that."

Garrett.

"I can't stay there. I just can't… Maybe it will pass, maybe it won't. I'm not going to be disrespectful to her, but I'm not going to listen to her poison, either. I had to leave… I don't know. I don't know, Rett! I don't care if you don't approve of my friends but—"

"You can stay here," Tracey mouthed to her.

She looked up and squinted incredulously.

"You can stay here," Tracey repeated.

"Are you sure?" she whispered back. "Your parents won't care?"

"My parents like you better than me," Tracey insisted, only half kidding. "There's an empty bedroom in this house and three empty ones in the big house if you include mine. We've got plenty of room. You can stay here until the fall semester starts."

"Hold on, Rett," Angie said into the phone. "I'll pay rent."

"We don't need your rent, Ang. Just stay here. I don't want to see you cry again."

"Are you just saying this because I was a bitch to you?"

"Mainly." Tracey tried to make her smile with her answer and was pleased when she did.

"You have to make sure it's okay with your parents," Angie insisted. Tracey nodded, knowing full well that it would be. Really, they loved her, and Angie seemed to *like* being on her best behavior around them.

"You would have to get your own place first, wouldn't you?" she spoke into the phone again. "Rett... I told you, I can't stay there anymore. I can't do it. If Tracey's parents don't mind, then what's the problem?"

Tracey didn't hear his answer, but Angie got off the phone shortly after.

"He wants me to stay with him."

"He's on a three-month *sublease*."

"He thinks I need to be with family."

Angie *felt* like family. "What do you want?"

"I could live with Rett."

"But you don't want to."

She shook her head. "I'm comfortable here."

"What does your dad say?"

"He's not saying much of anything, but I know it's putting a strain on him. He loves little Nathalie and sees her at Rett's when he can. He loves me and Rett, too. He loves our mother, but she won't change. It's lose-lose no matter what for him."

They went to talk to Tracey's parents, who had grown accustomed to Angie, who seemed to always be on her best behavior around them, potentially due to how much esteem she held for Carolyn. Tracey could tell Angie felt awkward talking to them about her parents, but she wanted them to have the whole story. She wanted to reassure them that she wasn't trying to take advantage. She didn't have to say much before her parents agreed to the temporary arrangement.

That evening, Angie, Mama, and Tracey discussed Tracey's plans to get her grandmother's house ready to sell. Afterward, Garrett went with Angie to get her things.

—✵—

While they were gone, Tracey took inventory. She wrote a handwritten list.

- My parents accept that I had a child out of wedlock. They don't like it, but they accept it. Their friends might have something to say about it, but so far not to either Mama or Daddy's face, and they continue to be pleasant to me.

- Only a few members of my extended family look at me sideways, though that look speaks volumes: "I always knew she was going to end up with a white boy."
- My closest friends, new and old, don't care one way or another.
- I have a beautiful daughter that I love more than anything.
- Nathalie's father not only contributes financially but participates in her care and rearing.
- I have a roof over my head.
- I have food in my belly. My baby has food in her belly.
- I am getting ready to start a great new job.
- I want for little.
- My daughter wants for nothing.

Even the strained circumstances surrounding Tracey's pregnancy were nothing in comparison to what some of the girls she used to work with at the center went through. In short, Angie was right.

Maybe it was time Tracey changed her attitude.

Chapter 30

"You're on my bad list, Rett," Clay told him. "You just up and disappeared for a couple of months."

"I tell you what: if you come do this with me, I'll explain everything *and* won't kill you for messing around with my sister."

Clay really looked like he was going to fade away. He got pale even under his perpetual tan. "I haven't done anything with Angie. Honest, Rett, nothing."

"God, Clay," Rett answered, immediately taking back what he'd said. "I know that. I was just making a joke. It took me a little while to notice, but I can tell you like her."

"Just so you know, I would never try anything with your sister."

"Angie can take care of herself. Besides, I can't think of anybody better for her."

"You mean that?"

"Yeah, man."

"And you're not just saying that 'cause you want me to go and vandalize somebody's front yard."

"This is not an act of vandalism. This is a catharsis."

"A what?"

"I'm just letting off some steam."

"You don't let off steam by messing up somebody's front yard," Clay remarked. Rett raised his eyebrow at his friend. Then he shook his head. "Unless they're my friend Rett, obviously."

"Obviously," Rett answered, throwing a second chainsaw into the back of his SUV.

"You going to tell me why?"

"Because it's not safe to have all those trees in the front yard blocking the view from the road. Anything could happen just on the front porch and no one would be the wiser until it was too late." Rett did not add that this was the house that had made him succumb to stupid Tracey. It was the place that promised something they could never really have, a secret world untouched by anything beyond it.

"When are you going to tell me the whole thing?"

"The whole thing about what?"

"Well, Rett, I'm not stupid. I know somethin' big is going on with you. If my ears were serving me right this morning, there's something about a baby. And I know for damn sure that Kim isn't pregnant. In fact, Charles says she can't get pregnant." The irony of that was not lost on Garrett. Kim was going to hate him more than she already did when she found out he was getting the child she had been trying to "give" him for more than a year. Yeah, she was going to be out for blood.

324

They pulled up in front of Tracey's grandmother's house forty-five minutes later.

"This neighborhood's really…really…"

"Really what?" Rett tensed up.

"Why are we doing this?"

"I told you."

"Well, you haven't told me who lives here."

"The mother of my child used to live here. This is still her house."

"Here?"

"Yeah."

"Tracey McAlpine lived here?"

Rett didn't look at his friend, proud he hadn't even flinched. He was surprised that Clay knew. In the end he should have been relieved; he no longer had to figure out how to break the news. "Yep. You should see the inside of the house. It's gorgeous. Anyway, let's get to it."

"So you have a baby?" Awe peppered Clay's voice.

Rett couldn't help the grin. He had a bee-you-tiful baby. He reached into his wallet and pulled out three pictures. He paged through more on his cell.

"Would you look at that?" Clay breathed.

"Yeah." Rett's chest puffed out proudly.

"Isn't she just a precious little thing?"

Rett beamed nodding. "Her name's Nathalie."

Clay handed the pictures back and clasped Rett on the shoulder in affection.

"When it happens to you, man…" Rett mused. "I mean, I can't describe the way I feel when I look at her and hold her. I keep wanting to cry like a little bitch."

Clay laughed. "Rett, you still haven't answered my question. Why are we doing this?"

"Because I've always hated these trees."

"Yeah, but do you have permission to do this?"

"Look, are you goin' to help me or not?"

Clay shook his head. He then started to unload the truck.

Rett climbed the first tree to start trimming branches. Clay made his way up with him.

"How did you know?" Rett asked. "Did Angie tell you?"

"Naw, man." Clay shook his head. "After that night at the apartment, I knew something was up. You made sure of that. Then, I don't know why, it never came up again, but you stopped seeing Kim and I just knew."

Rett didn't say anything. He just nodded.

"Rett," Clay continued.

"Yeah."

"I think she was good for you."

"What makes you say that?" Rett's chest got tight all of a sudden.

"Because I know you, man. You were happy. You were half the jackass you normally are. It was easy to see. And when y'all broke it off, it was clear as day what had happened. You had that 'screw everybody' attitude you get when things don't go your way."

"Really?"

"Hell yeah."

Rett digested this for a moment, then questioned, "What's my attitude saying to you now?"

He asked this question because he really wanted to know. His brain and heart had been at war since that day in the mall. He'd thought that with the birth of his daughter, he'd be able to forget Tracey and focus on this new and important part of his life. He'd thought that with his new job and being a daddy, he wouldn't have time to stew over the mess that was his relationship with Nathalie's mother. He'd been wrong. His feelings for Tracey continued to be a puzzle for him.

"Why are you cutting down her trees?"

"Because she's planning on selling this place and I'm doing my part to help."

"Without her knowing anything about it?"

"I've told her twelve times that it needed to be done."

"So you're helpin' her, whether she likes it or not. And you're cutting down trees that you felt hid the house from the road."

"Shut up and help me take this branch down."

Hours later, they sat on the ground, dripping with sweat, wondering at the general mess they'd made of the yard and drinking beer.

"Maybe this was a two-day project," Rett offered.

Clay laughed so hard he kicked at the trunk of the nearest tree. Then his eyes went wide and he scrambled to his feet.

"What are you doing?" Rett asked, too sore, hot, and fuzzy to follow... until he witnessed Clay snap a picture of the yard with his camera phone and start to type on the keypad.

"You jackass!" he yelled. He caught up with his friend just after he hit the send button. The message was sent directly to Angie.

Well, that was a way to get Tracey to call him.

Sure as he breathed, "The Devil Went Down to Georgia" sounded on his cell.

"Yeah?" he answered.

"What the hell are you doing at my grandmother's house?"

"Helping you sell it," he answered, knowing full well it would piss her off.

"You have no right, Garrett. No right."

"So?"

He held the phone away from his ears to protect his eardrums from loud and intense yelling on the other end.

Garrett and Clay finished clearing the yard on Sunday.

The house was sold in a week.

Tracey didn't expect the house to sell so fast. She figured she'd have at least three months, especially with the exorbitant price she put on it. But it was obvious it wasn't going to happen that way now. She'd gotten an offer, not from a nice family but from a convenience store chain. Rett got perverse pleasure out of the fact that the place where it had all begun was going to be torn down to make way for something new.

Chapter 31

A few months after the house sold, Nathalie was finally sleeping through the night for the most part and though Tracey loved being a mother, she felt a constant pressure and strain. The girls had noticed and had orchestrated a girls' night out. Garrett was going to take Nathalie for the night.

She glanced at her reflection again. She wore a casual white button-down over a safari-style skirt that fell just above mid-thigh, showing lots of leg. Probably too much leg for a woman who was still five pounds away from pre-pregnancy weight. Probably too much leg for a mommy, period. But Nathalie's daddy did love her legs. And Tracey wanted to unnerve him. She really did. All this cold distance between them was also a drain on her. She thought that maybe a good fight would help her get the tension out of her system. No matter what had happened between them in the past, flashing that much leg was *bound* to get something started.

"Do you think Daddy will like this, Nathalie?" she asked when she realized the baby was awake and trying to roll herself over on the bed. Tracey scooped her up before she could and put her in the pack and play with her teething ring.

Tracey expected Garrett any minute to pick her up for the weekend. Though he saw her nearly every day, Garrett attempted to take Nathalie every weekend. Attempted because sometimes Tracey just didn't feel she could let her go. Sometimes the baby was colicky or running a fever or just cranky, and she didn't want to let her out of her sight.

Garrett fought Tracey every time. It amazed Tracey that two people with law backgrounds never once thought to go to court over the baby. Tracey's parents tried to force her daily. They just *fought*. Usually he gave in after twelve rounds, but about two months before, he'd just threatened to stay over for the weekend if she wouldn't let him have the baby. And he'd done so. He'd done it a couple of weekends in a row, and even though the tension was still there between them, Tracey started to believe that there was more. God help her, she started to want more. But then, for the last couple of weeks, he hadn't tried to stay. He'd even relented when she told him that Nathalie had a bit of a temperature and she didn't want her out in the air. He'd held her, kissed her, played with her, then gone.

Tracey didn't know what to expect this evening, but Nathalie was up and playful, and Tracey was prepared to let her go when Garrett asked, especially since the girls were coming over.

The doorbell rang. She grinned at the baby and opened the door. In walked both Monica and Angie. Angie was *twitching*, and Moni looked as if her patience had run completely out.

"Oh, God, what is it?"

"Is your computer booted up? Oh, my God, is it booted up?" Angie asked.

"Yeah." Tracey questioned Moni with a glance. She shrugged.

"Look at it. He *just* put these pics up on his profile." Angie pointed to the screen.

Tracey leaned down to see. Breathing just stopped happening. Garrett Nathaniel Hinson Atkins was laughing with his arm around someone. Then he was holding *someone's* hand. Tracey gaped at them. Her bottom lip started to quiver and she clamped down on it with her teeth.

"According to *her* profile, she's a divorce attorney," Angie announced.

Tracey couldn't take her eyes off the woman in the photo. She was taller than Tracey, slimmer than her, with bigger breasts than hers, even with the breast feeding. And, oh, most importantly, she was darker than Tracey. She wore a hot pink, baby doll dress that fell to just above her knees. She wore high, skinny-heeled stilettos. A long ponytail fell over her shoulder. She looked like an underwear model, and not the classy kind.

And Garrett looked different. Gone were his golf shirt and khakis. He was wearing a designer t-shirt, stylish jeans and sneakers. He looked a bit more *urban* than Tracey had ever seen him, and she was at a loss as to what to say.

Angie turned around and looked at her friend and saw something in Tracey's expression that made her say, "It's not as serious as it looks. They've only been on like *two* dates. I don't think anything has happened."

"Her picture is next to my *daughter's*," Tracey growled.

"That's just because they're in chronological order and…" Angie trailed off before she chirped, "Legs much? Damn, Tracey. You're a hot mama!"

Monica still didn't say anything.

Tracey wasn't paying attention. The caption beneath Nathalie's picture read, "This is the real lady in my life right here."

The doorbell rang again. Then the door opened, and Rett came through it. Immediately, he lifted Nathalie from the pack-and-play. He hugged her too tight, as usual, but she only giggled and sucked on his chin—the traitor. She gurgled and got a grip on his hair. All Tracey could think was that if he were to take her baby around that woman, they would look like a family. Nathalie looked like she could be theirs. Behind Tracey, she heard Angie click off the monitor.

333

"Do you have her things together?" His eyes flicked down to her legs for only a fraction of a second. If she'd blinked, she would have missed it. But his reaction no longer seemed to matter.

"I'll get them," Tracey said and moved into the bedroom. Her mind worked at a fevered pace as she tried to figure out what was going on. Garrett and a black woman that wasn't Tracey. Did they sleep together? Where did they go together? Garrett and Tracey never went anywhere. What did they *do*?

She finished packing Nathalie's bag and found that she couldn't bring herself to go back into that room just yet. She didn't understand it, she honestly didn't. If the woman had been white, maybe she could have understood it, but not this. Her stomach churned. She went into her bathroom and closed the door. She leaned against it and tried to come to her senses. Why did it matter that she was black?

Tracey heard a knock.

"Tracey, what are you doing in here?" Moni.

"Getting the baby's things together." Tracey opened the door.

"So he's seeing someone. So it's a black someone." As usual, she got to the heart of things. Tracey nodded and closed her eyes as she leaned against the doorjamb. "He wasn't going to stay single for the rest of his life, Tracey. And for that matter, neither should you."

"I didn't expect him to."

"Or is this about the fact that you're not the only fly in the milk anymore?"

"Moni," Tracey gritted through her teeth.

"That girl is just as black as you are, and it seems to me like you have a problem with that." Tracey squeezed her eyes shut even tighter, to the brink of giving herself a headache. "I'm just stating facts."

"What's goin' on in here?" Angie asked, coming up behind Moni.

"I hear, 'once you go black, you don't ever go back.' " Angie's eyes crinkled at the sides as she giggled.

Monica burst out laughing; Tracey did not. She stepped out of the bathroom.

"I don't think she's his girlfriend," Angie said.

A thought occurred to Tracey. "He better not be bringing her around my daughter. He can't just bring women in and out of Nathalie's life."

"Has he ever brought another woman around her before that you know of?" Moni asked.

She wasn't even asking Tracey. She was asking Angie, who thankfully said no.

"Okay then. Trace, this is a girls' night. Let's just get out of here and have some drinks and not think about it."

"Yeah, girl, and can I tell you, you look hot? legs." Then Angie added, "Rett's always going to do what's best for Nathalie, so don't worry about it," Angie added.

She knew it was true. There was obviously no point in waiting around for him anymore. But until that point, no one could have told Tracey that she *was* waiting around for him.

She realized then what was at the heart of her problem with this new chick being black. Tracey knew for a fact that he had never felt about any of the white girls he'd dated as he did about her — that is, when he felt that way about her. Tracey figured that being who she was, she had something they never could, something special that made Garrett want only her. She didn't put herself and those girls in the same category at all, even though she knew in her head she should have. Then here came this veritable black siren, and she felt that any grip she might have had on him was loosening. Garrett was slipping through her fingers.

How stupid was that?

Speak of the devil. He darkened the doorway. "Is Nathalie's stuff ready?" He looked over at Tracey as if *she* had done something.

None of them looked at him.

He gritted his teeth.

"Is this it?" he asked, pointing at the bag on the bed. She nodded. He took the bag and inspected its contents. "Where's her bobo?"

"She had it in the living room. It's probably in the pack-and-play."

He gave a curt nod, then surveyed all three friends with a glare and went back into the living room. They all automatically moved to the door and watched him buckle Nathalie into her car seat.

Then they all went into the living room. And Angie, well, she pulled an Angie.

"I saw you updated your online profile with new pics this afternoon," she said.

Garrett looked up, not at her, at Tracey. His lion eyes skewered her where she stood and she could have sworn he could read her mind.

"Karen is just a friend from the firm, Angie," he said, but he was *looking* at Tracey.

"She doesn't *look* like a lawyer." Angie raised one eyebrow.

"She's not a lawyer. She's studying to be a divorce attorney. Currently, she's the office manager, as if that makes a difference."

Then he left.

And then the three girlfriends left.

—∾—

When the ladies got back to the house, they were all finally relaxed and feeling no pain. But when Tracey saw Rett's car outside, she panicked. She rushed into the house ahead of the girls in search of her baby...

who turned out to be sleeping like an angel in her crib in her room. After checking her over to make sure she was okay, Tracey went in search of Rett.

He was in her bedroom, in her bed.

"What's going on? Is the baby okay?" Monica asked as she came to stand beside her.

"My darling baby has a sniffle, but she is perfect," Rett responded with a lazy smile.

Angie came in behind Monica. "Are you nekkid?"

Showing his maturity, Garrett stuck his tongue out at her.

"I was waiting for Tracey," Rett slurred as he struggled to sit up in Tracey's bed.

"Are you drunk, Rett?" Monica asked the question that was on all their minds.

"Yes, yes, I am," he replied as he gave up the struggle to sit up and lay back on the pillows. Monica rolled her eyes and Angie expelled a labored expletive.

Garrett's eyes snapped to her, then to Tracey as a twisted—but sexy as hell—smile lit his face and he said, "Precisely."

Tracey's eyes bucked when she heard that.

"Would you like to, Tracey? I know you would. So call off the attack dogs and we'll get down to it." Tracey bit down harshly on her bottom lip, feeling the pain shoot clear through her chin. Monica was about to say something in her defense but Tracey couldn't let her. Shamefully, she already felt moisture starting between her thighs. Mortification for the guilty was only worse when he or she was being championed.

"He's drunk," Tracey said steadily, even though inside she wasn't anywhere near steady. "You guys go ahead. Petey got the guest room ready earlier, so go on up to the house. I'll make sure Rett gets home okay."

"You have got to be out your mind." That from Monica.

"If you're worried about him driving, I can take him home," Angie offered.

"You've been drinking, too."

"No," Garrett drawled. "Y'all run along now, me and Tracey got something to do."

If she were white, Tracey's hot face would have surpassed red. Instead, she—hopefully—maintained her deceptive calm.

"Tracey, we can kick him out," Monica said. She still had never seen Garrett at his best.

"You are more than welcome to try," he warned. "But Tracey and I are going to have consenting sexual intercourse before I leave this house no matter what you do. Remember exit 89, baby?"

Oh, dear God, help me! Tracey thought. He said it, and she did remember, and she wanted it so bad, so *suddenly*, her body started to throb.

"Go ahead, guys," she urged them again. "Don't aggravate him anymore. You see he's itching for a fight."

"Are you sure?" both Angie and Monica asked.

"Yeah."

"Can I take the baby up to the house with me at least?" Angie asked. Angie had stayed over a few times by then. Tracey was amazed it had worked out so well. Never once had she heard her friend curse in her parents' presence, and she had even started attending church with her mother and aunts, even without Tracey.

Tracey shook her head. "I've hardly had anything to drink and she's sleeping. She'll be fine in her room." *Besides, he won't do anything crazy with her here.*

Reluctantly, they left her standing in the doorway of her bedroom wondering what she was going to do with him. "Garrett…" she started tentatively.

"Tracey," he answered with a half-smile.

"What do you want? It's obvious you don't want anything to do with me anymore, so what's this?"

"Tracey," he replied tiredly. "If you remember, I told you once that I would always want you, that I loved your body. That hasn't changed."

"Not like this. You're drunk."

"Tracey, please don't fight me." His expression changed and something about it let her know, maybe because she knew him so well by then, that he wasn't nearly as drunk as he would have her believe. He was serious. "You need this, and God knows I need this."

"What about Karen?"

"Nothing happened between us."

"Didn't look like that on your profile."

"What's it matter?" His tone grew gruff and his eyes were accusing "I tried. Damn, I tried."

Please stop.

"She's very good with her tongue, you know. And those hands! She could get paid for what she does with 'em. I imagined what it would be like for her to wrap those long, fantastic legs around me."

Why can't you just shut up? she wanted to ask him.

"I mean, she is luscious. Her bottom would probably fit right into my hands!" Tracey was opening her mouth to cuss him out when he pinned her with a savage look, "But… she's not you." He dropped his gaze to his lap with an exaggerated shake of his head. "So that's what I'm doing here. Just driving back over here and parking my car out there got me hard as a rock. I'm good enough for that, aren't I? Hmm? It'll be just like old times."

"Garrett, don't do this," she pleaded, even though that treacherous moisture crept down onto her thighs. Hell, she couldn't control it. He started to rise and she backed towards the doorway, sucking in all of her breath. He really wasn't wearing a stitch of clothing and his body was as perfect as it had ever been, with its smooth planes, curving muscles, and inviting lines. She could see the pale hair barely noticeable as it sprinkled across his chest. It made a thin line down the center of his stomach between the hard muscles all the way down to circle him. She swallowed, barely able to take his beauty.

Garrett stalked toward her and Tracey was frozen in anticipation, maybe in fright. He started to nuzzle, nip, and suck at her neck, going for the jugular in every sense of the expression. She twisted and twisted from the tingling sensations coursing through her. In soft, gently spoken words he whispered, "I'm good enough to fuck, aren't I, Tracey?"

She felt fire, pure fire, cut through her chest and burn the pit of her stomach. She wanted to crumple right there under the pressure of his hateful words. Then she wanted to fight. She wanted to do something, anything, to stop his cruelty, to stop this near-painful arousal she still felt. But before she could act, his lips started a fresh attack, rendering her impotent all over again. She felt his hands go into her hair, his fist closing around the bulk of it. Then she felt him pull downward, forcing her to look up at him. She resisted without even the slightest whimper to show her strength. Garrett tugged even harder. She remained silent, her natural reaction arrested by pride.

Tracey simply stared back at him, waiting. He smiled. Finally, he pressed his lips to hers and kissed her hard. There was nothing nice or pleasant about the kiss he bestowed upon her, nothing at all, and her traitorous body adored every bit of it.

He pressed a hand beneath her thigh until her leg was lifted and propped up on his. She felt one of his hands snaking under her skirt and past the elastic of her panties until his fingers pressed inside her and she could barely breathe. There was no way to stop what was about to happen, and yet Tracey was foolish enough to try. "Garrett," she murmured, knowing no control over her voice, her own reactions. Even as she made her protest, she slid herself against his fingers.

"Rett," he said, correcting her though she could barely make sense of anything. He kissed her deeper, then pulled up short, leaving her bereft. "Rett."

She knew what he was waiting for, and she knew there would be no relief for her if she didn't give it to him. He wanted her to surrender, place her pride on a platter, and sacrifice the control she had held on to so firmly from the very start. His fingers plunged deeper, moving rhythmically between her legs. She was thankful for him holding her there because there was no way she could have remained standing on her own. She twisted her head from side to side, hoping to deter his kisses. She twisted her body also to either evade or aid—she wasn't sure which—his magician's hand. Then it came out on the wings of an exhaled breath: "Rett, Rett, please." And then as if following suit, her body surrendered itself and she was wracked with the most powerful pulses of electricity and bliss she'd had since the first time they were together. Hot embarrass-

343

ment coursed through her, mingling with each passionate wave of fulfillment. It was impossible to feel one without the other. Still, he did not free her.

Instead, he let soft, tender kisses fall on her pinched eyebrows and stroked her tensed arm and thigh with his hands. Then, as her breathing returned to normal and her muscles started to relax, he started all over again. Realizing that it would be useless to resist him, Tracey tried to relax and be still, show him no emotion. She was under the impression that if she did this, he would just give up the fight and leave her alone. There were so many things wrong with that logic. It hadn't worked that first time they were together. It hadn't worked just moments before. Tracey thought maybe since it had been such a long time, she had just forgotten how effective his ministrations were. Still, he couldn't have *possibly* been this good before. Already he'd brought her to the precipice, her body was still moist, and nipples that were already hard grew painfully taut at his slightest movement. And, as if he knew that, as if her body were talking to him, he pulled down the front of her shirt and her new bra along with it. His lips hovered over her breast and Tracey tried to get him to stop, self-conscious about her milk. Rett ignored her protests and his mouth clamped over her breast. It hurt and aroused her all at once. Tracey bit down hard on the inside of her jaw to keep her pleasure silent.

"Delicious," he whispered.

Her breath wouldn't come out right and all she could think of was what was coming next.

Finally her acquiescence came in the form of grabbing his hair as he had hers, and dragging him back up. Her lips instantly found his with greedy desperation. He kissed her back hard, then tore away. He dropped to one knee and slipped her panties down and off. Still kneeling, he grabbed her hips, angling them towards him and she was lost as his tongue sought a brand new attack. He pulled one thigh up onto his shoulder and lay open his way.

"God, Garrett, I can't do this," she moaned, even though she had already gone too far to turn back.

"Rett," he ground out against her. As she felt his teeth sink into her sensitive flesh she groaned that name because she couldn't help herself. She had to give him what he wanted in order to get what she wanted. She felt his hot tongue lapping at her and his lips sucking her into him and she knew she was going to die. But just as she felt the vibrations start, he stopped, rising to bite into her shoulder and wrap his arms around her. He was breathing hard and seemed to be trying to calm himself. As he took a saving breath, Tracey slid her hands low between their bodies to press his length into her.

Immediately, she felt his hands slip beneath her knees to lift them around him. He pressed her into the wall and pushed hard inside her. It had been over a year and she faltered as she tried to catch her breath, gasping to fill her lungs. He pressed harder and faster and faster each moment and he was killing her. Her hand caressed his hips, his ass, his thighs so she could feel him pump against her body. She urged him on and slipped her other hand around his back to pull him closer, closer to her. He finished his onslaught, and Tracey stifled a scream, not wanting to wake the baby. The sob was wrenched from deep inside her and she was nearly blinded with the pleasure of it. She felt him shuddering and heard the loud, ragged battles for breath that let her know he had died, too.

For a moment, he stood pinning her against the wall, his arms stretched out flat on either side of her. Without notice, he carried her to the bed. They lay there side by side, not touching. Tracey pulled her shirt up over her breasts, pulled her skirt down over her thighs, and shifted her legs to see how much discomfort she felt. It *had* been more than a year, and she had had Nathalie.

"Are you sore?" he asked, reading her mind. Tracey nodded, unable to speak to him after what they'd done. "You should have stopped me."

She didn't know how long they lay there not speaking before they drifted off. What she did remember was waking up to check on Nathalie, then coming back to bed to find Garrett sleepy, rubbing his eyes and reaching for her. She lowered her body on top of

346

his and took her time exploring him, tenderly taking her fill of him all over again. She was ready in minutes as she rose on her knees over his body. Beneath her, he urged, "Yes, baby. Like that. Jeez." Then he quaked to another release, grabbed her and hugged her to him, holding her still, letting go as she followed him into bliss again.

Nathalie woke them in the wee hours of the morning. She was hungry. Tracey got up to feed her. Garrett joined them. He'd never said so, but Tracey knew he enjoyed watching her feed the baby. And it was something, even with the animosity between them, she'd never denied him.

After Tracey fed her, he took her and prepared to put her down again. Then he got dressed. She started to realize—as if she didn't already know—that nothing had changed. Nothing at all. Inside, her body was rent and she ached for him, yet here he was, dressing and giving her his back, silent and barely acknowledging that he, too, had lost control only hours before.

Slowly, Tracey eased the covers up over her and turned her head into the pillow. She waited for the tears, but this time they didn't come. She looked for the feeling that bored a hole in her chest whenever she remembered she couldn't have Garrett, no matter what. It wasn't there. All she felt was the dying pleasure, slick-pressed between her thighs, and numbness all over the rest of her body. She couldn't even muster the nerve to hate him for what he'd done to her. To her? Who was she kidding? Done *with* her.

He turned toward her after his clothes were back on. He stood staring for a long while. "Tracey, what I did tonight was wrong." She didn't know if she agreed or not. Oh, it was wrong all right, but he didn't get all the blame for it. "It's just that I've been fighting it for so long." He ran fingers through his hair in frustration. "And I can't bring myself to be with anyone else." He said this with his head bowed as if he were ashamed to admit it. He didn't want to want her.

"I see," she managed through numb lips and a throat she couldn't feel either.

"No, Tracey, I don't think you do. What I'm trying to tell you is that I couldn't help myself, and even after everything, after everything, I don't want to hurt you."

"I'm just a little sore."

"That's not what I mean, and you know it. I used you, and I'm sorry. I guess I could try and tell you I didn't want to hurt you tonight, but it would be a lie. I thought I wanted to hurt you. I thought I wanted to punish you for everything. But even though that's what I thought, I didn't mean to, if you can understand that. I didn't mean to hurt you."

"You didn't," she insisted, mustering up the words from God knows where. In truth, he hadn't hurt her through sex. He was hurting her with his cold distance. She didn't want to go back to distance. She wanted that night to be cathartic and maybe the beginning of something new.

But it was just sex. They were just releasing the sexual tension always polluting the air and their brains when they were around each other.

He opened his mouth to say something, probably to peg her for the liar she was. But he didn't complete the action. He turned in the doorway and walked out. He was leaving. In minutes, Tracey heard Nathalie's door open and close. Then the front door opened and snapped shut.

—◊◊◊—

Monica came back early. Tracey was lying awake as she had since Rett left, in the same clothes, but without her panties, curled into the fetal position. Monica took one look and dropped to the bed next to her. She tried to smile.

"Think of the bright side, you didn't sleep with him."

Tracey coughed then and turned away from her. What could she possibly say? She could only twist her hands in one of Nathalie's blankets. She had lain with it since Garrett had gone. Monica knew it then.

"Tracey, why? Why did you let him do it? I know how you feel about him, but, God, the way he went about it. He didn't have to go out like that."

"I know," she responded, pressing her nose into the blanket smelling her baby.

She hadn't made a peep since he left. Which had given Tracey plenty of time to replay the night. Time to remember how right it felt to be with him, no matter that a mountain rested between them. Maybe Garrett didn't love her anymore, and he really had taken pleasure from her body against both their wills and given it back to her against both their wills. But she still loved him and she still wanted him. But Tracey didn't know what to do. She didn't know how they could possibly circumnavigate that mountain. "He was angry," was all she could think of to say.

"How long can he stay angry, Tracey?" Monica demanded. "And even if he is hot with you, he doesn't have any business acting like he did last night."

"I'm an adult, Moni," she countered through her shield. "He didn't do anything to me I didn't let him do."

"Look at you, Tracey. And listen to yourself. This is no longer a black-white thing. It hasn't been for a long time. Now, I don't know what the real deal is between the two of you, but it's time to get over it. You hurt him, you hurt him badly. You tried to keep the one person he loves most in the world out of his life. That was you, you did it. But it is time now to get past that. He can't punish you, hurt you, for the rest of your life. And you can't let him. I don't understand how you guys function. You're civil and caring to each other one minute, pissed and fighting the next minute, then the next time I turn around you're in bed together. This doesn't make any sense, and it's destructive. It's time to heal, to move on."

"I don't know how," Tracey answered, barely able to choke the words out.

"That's why you have me," Monica offered. She hugged her friend close in the same way Tracey had seen her hold her own daughter. "We'll get through this together."

"You don't understand," Tracey said to her finally.

"Then tell me."

"I love him."

Then Nathalie stirred. Monica held up a hand and went to get her. Tracey felt the edge of the bed give way and looked up to see Monica handing her her gurgling, happy baby. Nathalie grabbed a fistful of her hair, which she promptly put in her mouth. The baby smiled and it was as if Tracey's whole face crackled. She giggled back and Tracey gave her a kiss and hugged her too tight. She didn't know if it would change, but just looking at her baby took so much hurt away. That's what people really meant when they said babies were miracles.

Monica left to use the phone.

—m—

"Listen, Monica, with all due respect, this isn't your business. It isn't your place."

"I'm not denying that, Rett," Monica returned softly. "Still, you have to know how your behavior is affecting her."

"But do you have any idea how her behavior has affected *me*?" Rett returned.

"I do. *Everybody* does because you make sure not to ever let anyone forget it. She never put forth the effort to be with you, we get it. She lied to you, we get it. She was on a course to keep Nathalie from you, we get it. But you're just acting childish now."

"I don't think my maturity is any of your business."

"We've established that none of this is my business, but—"

"Let it go, Moni. What happened, happened."

"But you don't love her—"

"Don't you ever say that!" Rett growled with so much anger in his voice that Monica gasped on the other end. "Look, Monica. I have no problem with you. I'm asking you to stay out of this."

Then he hung up, feeling that he was about to explode.

What the hell was he supposed to do now?

Rett had never stopped wanting Tracey. He felt like a fool every time he thought about it, but it was the God's honest truth. There was no getting past it. The all-consuming love for his daughter that he knew would never, ever go away, was understandable. But that feeling should not have extended to her mother. Rett had prayed for relief from this gnawing hunger for Tracey, and yet no relief had come.

His cell phone started to ring again and he glanced down at it. Karen. Or as Angie had put it, using her jackass way with words, "Tracey's stunt double." Rett shook his head, cursing himself even more. He should answer, but he wouldn't. That woman was sexy as all get out, and boy, was she willing, but he hadn't been able to do it. In fact, this was probably going to end the same way his relationships with the last three women he'd tried to date had ended. He was going to just stop answering the phone. After a few angry or hurt messages, she would give up and move on. That was for the best.

God, last night had been, for sure, the best sex he'd ever had. Ever. Ever in life. Raw, hard, honest, passionate. Rett would relive it in fantasies when he was ninety-nine years old. Always amazing between them, this time he'd gone so long wanting her, he'd gone so long without sex—since he'd seen Tracey that day in the mall carrying his child—and it was the first time all of their emotions, ugly and good, had been bared to each other. Amazing.

And he wanted more.

More of that and more of the feeling he got when he sat next to her while she fed his baby and they sat together and talked like a family.

He wanted everything.

He could turn his car around and go back and get right back in bed with her, staying there until she begged him to be with her for good.

Monica was wrong. He loved Tracey McAlpine with everything he had in him.

Chapter 32

Maybe time was what it took.

Garrett and Tracey didn't talk about the events of that night. Instead, they went back to the way they had been before he made love to her. Sort of. Things did change a bit. Tracey started her job as an employee relations specialist covering the southeastern region of the country, which allowed her to work from home as long as she had her handy laptop and headset. Rett had been doing well at his firm, but started putting in much longer hours. As a result, he still spent the same amount of time with the baby, but usually it was at Tracey's house, late into the night and he brought work with him. It felt—dangerously so—the way it had when they first met, only now it felt more real. Nathalie was proof every day of how real.

And Tracey could actually feel his anger starting to ebb, as was her fear, even though they didn't broach any difficult subjects.

Instead, they started taking little tests with each other. One such test was taking the baby out with the both of them. Before, they only did that when she'd had to go for either routine doctor's visits or when the baby had her series of ear infections that kept them both up for weeks.

This time, Rett made mention of the fact that he needed things for his new place. Tracey hadn't seen it yet but, but the house was all he talked about and it enhanced her embarrassment at continuing to live in her parents' pool house. When he recommended that they go shopping together, she was quite appalled. There was no reason for it… Okay, maybe no *good* reason for it, and her first instinct was to panic.

She didn't think it showed. In fact, she plastered on a bright smile and said "sure" before going to her bedroom and taking huge gulps of air as her heart pounded like a jackhammer. It was a test. She knew it. And if she wanted him to trust her, she had to pass it. Reminding herself that he was her daughter's father and they would be tied to each other *forever* helped a bit.

She pulled herself together because she had made a vow to be brave for her daughter, and for him.

They didn't show any bravado. They got out of the car and started towards the supercenter without really speaking to each other, with Tracey carrying Nathalie. Instead of holding hands like people who sleep together did, they walked at what could only be termed "a safe distance" apart from each other. On this walk that took an eternity, Rett glanced at her and she at him but without so much as a smile. In the store, an old man working the front pushed a buggy out in front of them with a warm Southern smile. Tracey smiled back but did not look at Garrett as she buckled Nathalie in. She looked everywhere but at Garrett.

They split up inside. Tracey went for the groceries. Garrett went for household goods like a new ironing board and light bulbs. They would meet in center aisles, coordinate their finds, then split up again. Once or twice, when they stood together, Rett was approached by someone—usually white—that he knew. He always introduced his baby first, then introduced Tracey as her mother. Conversations were nice, civil, but ended quickly and caused the skin on Tracey's face to heat and tighten.

Before long she was exhausted and unhappy, but she was thankful that this still hadn't been as horrible an experience as she had expected.

After she was done, Garrett ushered her and the baby to the front of the store. When they went to stand in the checkout line, he turned and was greeted by yet another person he knew.

The compact blond fellow with ruddy cheeks grinned at Garrett and exchanged a half-hug with him. He reached out to shake Tracey's hand as Garrett re-introduced them. She didn't recognize him, but she had heard of him. Kelly Banks had been one of Garrett's closest friends in high school.

That's when Tracey noticed her cute as a button baby with her arms up and hands out, making a grabbing motion and baby-talking with the most adorable little smile. That meant she wanted to be picked up, but she wasn't reaching for Tracey or her daddy. Instead, she was reaching for this guy that Tracey had never met before.

And he was reaching back with a huge, huge, hummungous grin. He picked her up and smooched her loudly over and over on the cheek until she laughed and squealed. "You are the best girl," he cooed. "The best girl. You know I'm going to marry you in about eighteen years."

"Stop saying that!" Rett punched him in the arm, but he was laughing, too.

And her baby was tickled pink.

The confusion must have registered on her face.

"Me and my best girlfriend used to see each other every weekend when I played football at Rett's."

Kelly hugged her close again and pressed kisses all over her face. Tracey tried to resist the urge to take the baby from him. Not just anybody should be kissing her baby, but Garrett obviously thought this was okay. "I miss my little girlfriend."

Garrett loved playing his latest football video game. He talked about it all the time. Tracey didn't know why she had never connected him playing the game on the weekends with his time with Nathalie. She had never thought Nathalie had been introduced to his friends or that she spent time with anyone other than him. It was stupid, naïve, but it just had never occurred to her.

Tracey was stunned. She was stunned even when they packed the bags and the baby into the car and left with promises that Rett would bring Nathalie by from time to time to see Kelly.

That evening, they chatted about Kelly. They planned a time for Tracey to see the house Rett had settled on. Then, they made love. Slowly, gently.

Chapter 33

When he arrived, Rett felt like the fish in his cooler were swimming around in his belly. He was at Tracey's house, and her family was having a reunion.

"Where can I put this?" Rett asked Carolyn as he eased into the kitchen holding a large red and white cooler. He held on firmly even though Petey came over to relieve him of his burden.

"Are the fish cleaned already?"

"Oh!" Rett gulped. "Naw, not yet."

"I got it," Petey insisted and took the cooler back outside. He popped in for a moment to get a chair, a wicked-looking knife, a bowl and a bucket.

"I can clean my own fish," Garrett insisted.

"He likes doing it," Carolyn answered. "Listen, Petey's been with us a long time. He came from some very hard times. Let the man do his honest work and everything will be all right."

Rett nodded.

"Um, where's… uh…"

"Tracey and the baby are outside. So's your sister."

Rett didn't know what to do. He didn't know if he just wanted to go out back there without Carolyn to help ease his way. Was he supposed to speak to people before he saw Tracey? Was her overbearing father out there? He didn't know what to do.

"Go on, now," Carolyn insisted. "Back by the pool."

Rett went then, wondering why he had been invited. He wondered even more why he'd come.

He wound his way through people, saying 'hello' and 'excuse me,' and making a beeline for his baby. Once there, he waved at his sister, who was in the pool with at least ten kids and said hello to Moni and her husband Rico. After he kissed his baby and handed her back to Colleen, her great aunt, he led Tracey back to the guesthouse.

"What's up?" Tracey asked when they got inside.

"I don't know what I'm doing here," he confessed.

"Me, either," Tracey offered with a snort of laughter.

It was not lost on him that he was seeing that sunny smile and hearing that easy laugh more and more these days. More and more.

"You have a daughter here, it makes you family."

"I bet your dad wouldn't agree with that."

"Neither would your mom," she quipped with an easy smile.

"Is it sex?" he blurted.

"What?"

"I don't know why I just blurted *that* out."

"Is what sex?"

He ran a hand over his face. "Are we getting along just because of great sex?"

She crooked her head to the side and considered him. "No."

That's all she said.

"Kiss me, babe," he said to her, and just like that she leaned into him and did that. Every single time they kissed, he felt as if a car was revving up inside him without a muffler.

He didn't know what had changed, but something had. Something between them had turned good again, and he was damned if he knew why. Shortly after Angie moved in at Tracey's—which he had not thought was a good idea—and he had taken down the trees that day with Clay, things had just gotten…better. And, of course, there was that night she'd opened for him. Now he was at Tracey's family get-together feeling awkward but not particularly interested in leaving.

"If we don't go out and hang with my people in the next five minutes, my mother is bringing the party in here."

Garrett kissed her again quickly, and then stepped away. "When are you moving again?" He followed Tracey out of the house.

"As soon as I find something I like and I can convince Travis and Carolyn McAlpine it makes sense for me to be independent. Why?"

"I think you should move in with me. You know, like roommates."

She started to say something, but he stopped her. "Don't get mad. Please, don't get mad. I only ask because I remember everything you said before Nathalie came about how you didn't want to live off your parents—"

"I don't. I have a job."

"*And* you would feel better in your own house. Our house. I want you and Nathalie to move in."

Tracey's mouth worked but no sound came out.

"You don't have to answer now. Give it a little bit to digest."

"But we... we aren't—"

"Tracey, I'm not asking you to marry me. I'm not asking anything to change. There are three bedrooms in this house. One for you, one for me, one for Nathalie. You're working, I'm working, we'll split bills down the middle."

"Wha—"

"Look, Tracey, we're getting along now."

She remained mute with her mouth open. Not a good sign.

"We both want to spend our time with Nathalie. We only just stopped arguing about that. We can obviously get along together. I know what it's like to live with you. You know what it's like to live with me."

"Yeah," she said slowly. "I'm going back to the party."

—〰—

"You can't just ask the mother of your child, 'Hey, you wanna be roomies, buddy?' "

"I know. I am truly a new kind of stupid."

"You'll get no argument from me on that, brother dear," Angie agreed.

"Why the hell didn't I just tell her I wanted her to move in with me?"

"Why the hell didn't you just ask her to marry you?"

Garrett was appalled. He probably looked appalled.

"You know, Rett, you and Tracey are the two dumbest smart people I know. You want to marry her, don't deny it."

"We haven't worked everything out."

"What's left to work out? You and she and Nathalie are a *family*. Say it with me. Not like a divorced family or a broken family. Not like family on Mama's side. You operate like a *family*. 'Garrett and Tracey sitting in a tree. K-I-S-S-I-N-G. First comes love, next comes marriage…' Wait, in your case next comes baby in a baby carriage."

Angie was fast enough to prevent him from tackling her and body slamming her on the ugly green sofa Tracey hated. She didn't say she hated it, but he could tell.

Chapter 34

She moved in.

I know. I know. I know, Tracey thought every time she considered it. But things were obviously better between Garrett and her. They went out frequently together as a family and Tracey no longer cringed at the thought. They were both convinced Nathalie was a genius from the way she had seemed to be reaching for words one day and talking full speed ahead the next. Rett no longer seemed to be holding on to the rocky situation surrounding Nathalie's birth.

And Nathalie was growing so fast. She was eight months old and already trying to walk. And she was gorgeous. And both her mother and her father loved her very much.

And they were living together. The three of them were a family. Only… not. Garrett had his room, Tracey had hers. Which Tracey tried to explain to her parents was not technically living in sin. Well, maybe it was. She ended up in Rett's bed once or twice a week. He ended up in hers the rest of the days.

It wasn't the sex. Or, well, it wasn't just the sex. Garrett had guessed that maybe that was what had eroded the barrier that had lived so long between them. In all honesty, Tracey was certain it was Nathalie. They were a family. There was no denying anything anymore. And when they stopped denying, they started living… and loving.

It was so odd. Something just beyond her reach still created a division between them, like a glass wall. She didn't know what it was or why she felt it, but it was there. Maybe she was asking too much. Maybe she was taking for granted that things were good, finally good… but…

—⁓—

One Saturday, Tracey sat down on the sofa, bringing with her the big plastic bear full of ribbons and barrettes. Then she reached for her little tyrant. Tracey was impressed that Nathalie had learned to say four words already: Mama, Dada, baba, and *no*. The baby sat in her lap, but when Tracey picked up her comb, she shook her head mutinously. "Nathalie, baby, you have to get your hair combed."

"No."

"Yes, little girl. Yes."

Slowly, reluctantly, Nathalie peered up at Tracey and touched her face with her silky soft fingers. She let her long curling lashes fall over her father's eyes. She'd only been outside for ten minutes without sun block but Tracey worried over the fine tiny cinnamon freckles on her cheeks and nose. Tracey's heart softened.

"Oooh, child, you ought to be ashamed of yourself. Yes, I am going to comb your hair and there is nothing you can do to stop me." She steeled herself against the eyes that were tearing up, the soft pink lips that were trembling, and the redness staining her golden cheeks. She did not like getting her hair combed. She ran her fingers through Nathalie's wild, tight curls. Then she picked up the wide-toothed comb she had bought for this particular purpose. As soon as Tracey started running it through Nathalie's tangles, her little girl started to cry. Tracey would never get used to this ritual. That child was so tender-headed and so upset by the process that Tracey could barely do it to her. Tracey prayed she would fall asleep soon so they could continue without the tears, but that was more than she could ask. Obliviously rebellious, Nathalie sniffled loudly and let out a brand new wail as she saw her father walk through the door.

"What are you doing to her?" Rett demanded, sailing in. Tracey sent him a look she hoped froze him where he stood. He dropped his briefcase on the desk in the foyer and walked over towards them. It was Saturday, but he'd gone into the office for a little while anyway.

"I was trying to comb her hair," Tracey answered through her teeth, not wanting to let on how relieved she was to see him. "You know she's staying over at Kelly and Marne's tonight with little Leslie."

He knelt and plucked her from Tracey's lap. Nathalie threw her skinny little arms around his neck, burying her face into it. He walked over to the sofa, holding her and taking off his jacket at the same time. After sitting down, he rocked her gently while cooing that she was his special little girl. Tracey sat there impotently, holding the comb in her hand. He kissed Nathalie's forehead and asked if she wanted him to brush her hair. Tracey's daughter, the traitor, nodded her head as she wiped away the tears in her eyes with the back of her hand.

Rett looked over at Tracey.

"Go ahead," she answered, relenting.

Rett leaned over and took up the brush lying beside him on the couch then began to stroke it through the baby's hair, without even combing the tangles out first. And she let him, she let him do it. Tracey watched, shaking her head, as slowly, lovingly, he brushed Nathalie's hair out and put a braid on each side of her head. She didn't say a word. She didn't shed a tear. *I taught him how to braid her hair!* Tracey thought. When he was done, he cuddled her up into his arms and Tracey could see that she was on her way to sleep.

It made her smile. "Daddy's little girl."

"And Mama's." He chuckled. "She won't eat anything I give her."

"Well, *that's* true."

—᠁—

Rett stood close to Tracey on the balcony off the master bedroom, his bedroom, if they were talking to her parents. His chin rested on her shoulder and his arms around her waist. "I love this," she said.

"Me, too," he replied softly, giving her the gentlest of kisses on the side of her neck. That touch wrung another little yelp out of her and she turned as Garrett circled her with his arms.

The kiss was everything. Beauty. Sweetness. Passion.

He kissed her deeper and his hand crept up beneath her shirt.

Tracey's response to him was immediate and without regret. She put her own hands beneath his shirt and pushed him back against the wall. She followed close and tried to consume him with her lips, tongue, and fingertips. She wanted this contact desperately and everything that came with it.

He dragged her inside and stripped her of her shirt. He cupped her breasts as she leaned into him and stole another kiss, letting her tongue tangle briefly with his. He pulled his own shirt over his head.

Tracey pressed her hand to his chest and began to run her fingers through the silken hair covering it lightly. She watched her hand move over his flesh in fascination. Each time she actually touched him was like something altogether new because she had spent so much time only imagining touching him. It was like receiving a gift every time. Her eyes widened when she saw those chill bumps prickle his skin. "Are you cold?" she asked seductively.

"No," he answered with a rasping voice, putting them both down on the bed. His hand captured hers and he kissed her palm, his warm tongue snaking over her sensitive flesh. Abruptly, she pulled her hand away and rolled over on top of him. She brought her lips hard against his while running her nails up his sides. With strong hands he drew her even closer, the startled wildness in his amber eyes melting her. His eyes fell to her lips and he brought her down to kiss him again.

—∽—

Garrett stood and walked over to the bathroom, closing the door behind him. Every time she saw his naked body, she knew he was absolutely perfect. She ran her hands over her moist skin, taking care against the heightened sensitivity that always overtook her after making love with Garrett. The slightest brush was too much sometimes. When he opened the door again, he halted to watch her run hands over her breasts and over her stomach. She didn't think to stop because they had never supported any inhibitions between them, at least not in bed. His eyes heated her, making her bolder. Her gaze still locked with his, she arched her back and let her legs slip apart. She touched her warm thighs and he leaned against the door frame. When she slipped a hand down into the moist area he had so artfully brought to convulsion, he strode over and put his hand over hers. Instead of stilling it, though, he moved his hand with hers, causing desire to blossom in between them again.

"Do you know how beautiful you are? And when you do this…" He moved her hands over her body. "When you do this, you look like Circe."

"Wow, you really do get poetic," Tracey retorted breathlessly.

"A country boy still has to read from time to time. You know my undergrad work was in English."

"I thought it was poly-sci."

"That, too." He grinned." Baby, I'm sorry," he said and Tracey turned to face him.

"What?"

"I'm sorry I asked you to move in here and be my roommate."

"What?"

"It was stupid."

"I'm here. I moved in. Life is good."

"Your parents are not happy about it."

"Your mother isn't happy I'm alive."

He laughed.

Slowly but surely, it had gotten easier for them to communicate. They were less and less likely to get angry or hurt when together.

"Tracey, you and I both have done and said a lot of stupid things."

"You certainly have," she retorted.

"Baby, I'm serious." He stroked her arm. "Through the whole time, though, I still loved you."

Her heart started to race.

"I was angry for those three months, but even then I missed you and I couldn't get over you."

"I never got over you, either," she told him, although it was hard the way her throat suddenly started to close up.

"And you love me?"

Her lips were dry. She licked them. She nodded.

"Say it. Please."

"I love you, Garrett." But she didn't look at him when she complied. All of a sudden she felt so exposed.

He turned her face to him and kissed her senseless.

"Tracey, I have loved you from the day I saw you leaning against the wall in those overalls and that ratty windbreaker. Your hair was all over your head and you looked like you'd been in bed all day. And it was then and there, that day, when I started to think of my future as your future. The first time I saw this house was about two months after we broke up. I saw it and I said that when you came to your senses, I was going to buy it for you. When I saw you at the mall that day—"

"Do we have to talk about that?" Embarrassment made her cheeks hot.

"Tracey, don't be embarrassed. I was angry; I won't deny it. Angry enough to want to kill you for a good ten or fifteen minutes—" She grimaced. He went on, "But it was probably the best day of my life, outside of today." He paused and rolled out of bed. "I need shorts for this." After he put on shorts, he came back to the bed. Tracey frowned, trying to understand.

He went on, "I think if we can make it through everything we've been through and still love each other, still want to be around each other day in and day out… then that means something."

And then he was kneeling in front of her and her eyes went round. He produced a black box and opened it.

"Oh, my God. Oh, my God. Oh, my God."

This was it. This was the strangeness, the subtle tension, the waiting game. This was why she had felt they were a family, and *not* a family. This was it.

"I hope you're saying 'Oh, my God' because you're happy." He chuckled, but the sound was nervous.

"Yes, yes, yes. I'm happy."

"That's a yes?"

"Yes."

"Yes, you'll marry me?"

"Yes!" she squealed. Then he slipped the diamond solitaire onto her finger.

When he stood and pulled her up and hugged her, she couldn't help jumping up and down.

—⁓—

"He's been asking everybody on earth if they thought you would say yes," Angie supplied the next night. So many of Tracey and Rett's friends and family had showed up that evening that it had become an unofficial engagement party.

Her eyes found Garrett's, and she hoped he got their message. She could never have said anything other than yes. She squeezed him with one arm and gave him a quick kiss.

"Yeah, he even asked me," Moni said.

Tracey lifted her glass of champagne to her and Rico. They were standing next to her parents. Angie and Clay stood with their arms around each other, even though Big had done his level best to intimidate the boy he'd known since he was in short pants.

Some of their other friends were there, too, and the occasion was truly joyous. Tracey didn't know how she got so lucky, but her heart was filled to bursting with emotion for everyone there who loved her little family and wished them the very best.

Later that night, after the small get-together and after Big had taken Nathalie for the night, Tracey and

Rett sat next to each other on the screened-in balcony holding hands in the cool dark and rocking in the swing. Tracey barely felt the air. There was too much warmth within her holding back the brisk spring night.

She turned her gaze away from him and stroked his hand with her thumb.

"What are you thinking?" he asked gently.

"Just that I don't deserve you."

"Hell, I don't deserve you, either, Tracey, or Nathalie, for that matter. Maybe with some work we can try to deserve each other. I've already got some ideas about how you can get started."

"Oh, really?"

"If you come inside with me, I'll show you."

"This sounds like it could take all night," Tracey answered, putting her arms around his waist and letting her hands travel up over his chest as she followed him into the warm house.

"I'm counting on it taking a lifetime."

―ᴍ― ―ᴍ―

About the Author

Grayson Cole loves language, romance, and the fantastic. She is intrigued by the relationships people build and what makes them work. Grayson hopes to bring intense and engaging characters to life for her readers along with well-developed, interesting characters.

Currently residing in Florida, where she writes, cooks and paints, Grayson has always called the South her home though she also has a longstanding love affair with travel and enjoys sharing stories of her adventures. She dabbles in lots of languages: a fair amount of French, travel Spanish, German, and Tagalog.

Come meet Grayson at her home on the web: www.grayson-cole.com

2011 Mass Market Titles

January

From This Moment
Sean Young
ISBN-13: 978-1-58571-383-7
ISBN-10: 1-58571-383-X
$6.99

Nihon Nights
Trisha/Monica Haddad
ISBN-13: 978-1-58571-382-0
ISBN-10: 1-58571-382-1
$6.99

February

The Davis Years
Nicole Green
ISBN-13: 978-1-58571-390-5
ISBN-10: 1-58571-390-2
$6.99

Allegro
Adora Bennett
ISBN-13: 978-158571-391-2
ISBN-10: 1-58571-391-0
$6.99

March

Lies in Disguise
Bernice Layton
ISBN-13: 978-1-58571-392-9
ISBN-10: 1-58571-392-9
$6.99

Steady
Ruthie Robinson
ISBN-13: 978-1-58571-393-6
ISBN-10: 1-58571-393-7
$6.99

April

The Right Maneuver
LaShell Stratton-Childers
ISBN-13: 978-1-58571-394-3
ISBN-10: 1-58571-394-5
$6.99

Riding the Corporate Ladder
Keith Walker
ISBN-13: 978-1-58571-395-0
ISBN-10: 1-58571-395-3
$6.99

May

Separate Dreams
Joan Early
ISBN-13: 978-1-58571-434-6
ISBN-10: 1-58571-434-8
$6.99

I Take This Woman
Chamein Canton
ISBN-13: 978-1-58571-435-3
ISBN-10: 1-58571-435-6
$6.99

June

Inside Out
Grayson Cole
ISBN-13: 978-1-58571-437-7
ISBN-10: 1-58571-437-2
$6.99

2011 Mass Market Titles (continued)
July

The Other Side of the
Mountain
Janice Angelique
ISBN-13: 978-1-58571-442-1
ISBN-10: 1-58571-442-9
$6.99

Holding Her Breath
Nicole Green
ISBN-13: 978-1-58571-439-1
ISBN-10: 1-58571-439-9
$6.99

August

The Sea of Aaron
Kymberly Hunt
ISBN-13: 978-1-58571-440-7
ISBN-10: 1-58571-440-2
$6.99

The Finley Sisters' Oath of
Romance
Keith Thomas Walker
ISBN-13: 978-1-58571-441-4
ISBN-10: 1-58571-441-0
$6.99

September

Except on Sunday
Regena Bryant
ISBN-13: 978-1-58571-443-8
ISBN-10: 1-58571-443-7
$6.99

Light's Out
Ruthie Robinson
ISBN-13: 978-1-58571-445-2
ISBN-10: 1-58571-445-3
$6.99

October

The Heart Knows
Renee Wynn
ISBN-13: 978-1-58571-444-5
ISBN-10: 1-58571-444-5
$6.99

Best Friends; Better Lovers
Celya Bowers
ISBN-13: 978-1-58571-455-1
ISBN-10: 1-58571-455-0
$6.99

November

Caress
Grayson Cole
ISBN-13: 978-1-58571-454-4
ISBN-10: 1-58571-454-2
$6.99

A Love Built to Last
L. S. Childers
ISBN-13: 978-1-58571-448-3
ISBN-10: 1-58571-448-8
$6.99

December

Fractured
Wendy Byrne
ISBN-13: 978-1-58571-449-0
ISBN-10: 1-58571-449-6
$6.99

Everything in Between
Crystal Hubbard
ISBN-13: 978-1-58571-396-7
ISBN-10: 1-58571-396-1
$6.99

Other Genesis Press, Inc. Titles

Other Genesis Press, Inc. Titles (continued)

Other Genesis Press, Inc. Titles (continued)

Other Genesis Press, Inc. Titles (continued)

Other Genesis Press, Inc. Titles (continued)

384

Other Genesis Press, Inc. Titles (continued)

Path of Thorns	Annetta P. Lee	$9.95
Peace Be Still	Colette Haywood	$12.95
Picture Perfect	Reon Carter	$8.95
Playing for Keeps	Stephanie Salinas	$8.95
Pride & Joi	Gay G. Gunn	$8.95
Promises Made	Bernice Layton	$6.99
Promises of Forever	Celya Bowers	$6.99
Promises to Keep	Alicia Wiggins	$8.95
Quiet Storm	Donna Hill	$10.95
Reckless Surrender	Rochelle Alers	$6.95
Red Polka Dot in a World Full of Plaid	Varian Johnson	$12.95
Red Sky	Renee Alexis	$6.99
Reluctant Captive	Joyce Jackson	$8.95
Rendezvous With Fate	Jeanne Sumerix	$8.95
Revelations	Cheris F. Hodges	$8.95
Reye's Gold	Ruthie Robinson	$6.99
Rivers of the Soul	Leslie Esdaile	$8.95
Rocky Mountain Romance	Kathleen Suzanne	$8.95
Rooms of the Heart	Donna Hill	$8.95
Rough on Rats and Tough on Cats	Chris Parker	$12.95
Save Me	Africa Fine	$6.99
Secret Library Vol. 1	Nina Sheridan	$18.95
Secret Library Vol. 2	Cassandra Colt	$8.95
Secret Thunder	Annetta P. Lee	$9.95
Shades of Brown	Denise Becker	$8.95
Shades of Desire	Monica White	$8.95
Shadows in the Moonlight	Jeanne Sumerix	$8.95
Show Me the Sun	Miriam Shumba	$6.99
Sin	Crystal Rhodes	$8.95
Singing a Song...	Crystal Rhodes	$6.99
Six O'Clock	Katrina Spencer	$6.99
Small Sensations	Crystal V. Rhodes	$6.99
Small Whispers	Annetta P. Lee	$6.99
So Amazing	Sinclair LeBeau	$8.95
Somebody's Someone	Sinclair LeBeau	$8.95
Someone to Love	Alicia Wiggins	$8.95
Song in the Park	Martin Brant	$15.95
Soul Eyes	Wayne L. Wilson	$12.95

Other Genesis Press, Inc. Titles (continued)

Other Genesis Press, Inc. Titles (continued)

Title	Author	Price
Things Forbidden	Maryam Diaab	$6.99
This Life Isn't Perfect Holla	Sandra Foy	$6.99
Three Doors Down	Michele Sudler	$6.99
Three Wishes	Seressia Glass	$8.95
Ties That Bind	Kathleen Suzanne	$8.95
Tiger Woods	Libby Hughes	$5.95
Time Is of the Essence	Angie Daniels	$9.95
Timeless Devotion	Bella McFarland	$9.95
Tomorrow's Promise	Leslie Esdaile	$8.95
Truly Inseparable	Wanda Y. Thomas	$8.95
Two Sides to Every Story	Dyanne Davis	$9.95
Unbeweavable	Katrina Spencer	$6.99
Unbreak My Heart	Dar Tomlinson	$8.95
Unclear and Present Danger	Michele Cameron	$6.99
Uncommon Prayer	Kenneth Swanson	$9.95
Unconditional	A.C. Arthur	$9.95
Unconditional Love	Alicia Wiggins	$8.95
Undying Love	Renee Alexis	$6.99
Until Death Do Us Part	Susan Paul	$8.95
Vows of Passion	Bella McFarland	$9.95
Waiting for Mr. Darcy	Chamein Canton	$6.99
Waiting in the Shadows	Michele Sudler	$6.99
Wayward Dreams	Gail McFarland	$6.99
Wedding Gown	Dyanne Davis	$8.95
What's Under Benjamin's Bed	Sandra Schaffer	$8.95
When a Man Loves a Woman	LaConnie Taylor-Jones	$6.99
When Dreams Float	Dorothy Elizabeth Love	$8.95
When I'm With You	LaConnie Taylor-Jones	$6.99
When Lightning Strikes	Michele Cameron	$6.99
Where I Want to Be	Maryam Diaab	$6.99
Whispers in the Night	Dorothy Elizabeth Love	$8.95
Whispers in the Sand	LaFlorya Gauthier	$10.95
Who's That Lady?	Andrea Jackson	$9.95
Wild Ravens	AlTonya Washington	$9.95
Yesterday Is Gone	Beverly Clark	$10.95
Yesterday's Dreams, Tomorrow's Promises	Reon Laudat	$8.95
Your Precious Love	Sinclair LeBeau	$8.95

Order Form

Mail to: Genesis Press, Inc.
P.O. Box 101
Columbus, MS 39703

Name _____
Address _____
City/State _____ Zip _____
Telephone _____

Ship to (if different from above)
Name _____
Address _____
City/State _____ Zip _____
Telephone _____

Credit Card Information
Credit Card # _____ ☐ Visa   ☐ Mastercard
Expiration Date (mm/yy) _____ ☐ AmEx   ☐ Discover

Qty.	Author	Title	Price	Total

Use this order
 	
form, or call
 	
1-888-INDIGO-1
	Total for books _____
	Shipping and handling:
	  $5 first two books,
	  $1 each additional book _____
	Total S & H _____
	Total amount enclosed _____
	Mississippi residents add 7% sales tax

Visit www.genesis-press.com for latest releases and excerpts.